A Mersey Killing

A Mersey Killing

Brian L. Porter

Published 2015 by Creativia
Paperback design by Creativia (www.creativia.org)
ISBN: 978-1515046868
Cover art by http://www.thecovercollection.com/

Other Books by the Author

Thrillers by Brian L Porter

- All Saints, Murder on the Mersey

- A Mersey Maiden

- A Study in Red - The Secret Journal of Jack the Ripper

- Legacy of the Ripper

- Requiem for the Ripper

- Pestilence

- Purple Death

- Behind Closed Doors

- Avenue of the Dead

- The Nemesis Cell

- Kiss of Life

Short Story Collection

- After Armageddon

Remembrance Poetry

- Lest We Forget

Children's books as Harry Porter

- Wolf

- Alistair the Alligator, (Illustrated by Sharon Lewis)

Coming soon

- Tilly's Tale

- Dylan's Tale

- Charlie the Caterpillar, (Illustrated by Bonnie Pelton)

- Hazel the Honeybee, Saving the World, (Illustrated by Bonnie Pelton)

- Percy the Pigeon, (Illustrated by Sharon Lewis)

As Juan Pablo Jalisco

- Of Aztecs and Conquistadors

Acknowledgements

So many people were instrumental in various ways in helping to ensure *A Mersey Killing* came to final fruition, it would take too long to mention them all, but hopefully those whose names are not mentioned here will know who you are, and how grateful I am to each and every one of you. Some, however, I felt I must include by name, so here goes.

Thanks must go to my publisher, Miika Hannila at Creativia Publishing, who had such faith in the book that he issued a contract for it before the first chapter was completed, and likewise to Mario Domina, CEO of ThunderBall Films, who optioned the book for movie adaptation at around the same time. Such confidence in one's work is truly rewarding for an author.

On a more personal level, sincere and loving thanks go to all the members of my extended family in the great city of Liverpool. Mostly my father's cousins and their descendants, my thoughts and recollections of you all helped mould most of the characters in the following story. The wonderful, typical Liverpudlian personalities of 'Aunty Ada' and 'Aunty Alice' combined to become Connie Doyle, and cousin George appears as George Thompson. Ron and Iris, with whom we stayed often in my early teens, helped me to form some of the personalities that make up many of the background characters.

A word of gratitude goes to my cousin, Rachael Tiffen, who graciously allowed me to use the names of her children, Ethan and Clemency as characters, and to Ethan and Clemmy personally for giving me their personal approval for me to do so. I hope you enjoy reading the book. As an author, I find it so much easier to develop a character who is based on the reality of a personal acquaintance. It enables me to add substance to the character that might otherwise be difficult to incorporate effectively.

I owe a debt of thanks also to my fellow author and dog lover, Carole Gill, the successful author of a number of bestselling horror novels. Read her vampire books if you dare! During a period of technical difficulty towards the end of the book, when it looked as if the final completion of *A Mersey Killing* might be delayed by many weeks, her help and support proved invaluable. A million thanks, Carole.

Similar thanks go to the aforementioned Mario Domina, who also helped immensely during this period.

To all the people of the wonderful city of Liverpool, thank you for being there, and for providing me with the inspiration for *A Mersey Killing*.

As always, I save my final thanks for my dear wife, Juliet, my fiercest critic during the writing of all my books. If she doesn't like it, it doesn't go into the final manuscript. Her patience, (often worn thin), and unerring support have been as always, a tower of strength time during the entire writing process.

Contents

Introduction   1

Author's note   3

Chapter 1   4

Chapter 2   8

Chapter 3   17

Chapter 4   23

Chapter 5   28

Chapter 6   36

Chapter 7   42

Chapter 8   54

Chapter 9   62

Chapter 10   67

Chapter 11   75

Chapter 12   82

Chapter 13   87

Chapter 14   95

Chapter 15   102

Chapter 16   113

Chapter 17   117

Chapter 18   121

Chapter 19   129

Chapter 20   136

Chapter 21   146

Chapter 22   156

Chapter 23   163

Chapter 24   175

Chapter 25   184

Chapter 26   195

Chapter 27   204

Chapter 28   210

Chapter 29   214

Chapter 30   220

Chapter 31   224

Chapter 32   229

Chapter 33   246

Epilogue   262

About the Author   268

Introduction

The year is 1961, and the city of Liverpool is just beginning to rock to the sounds of the new wave of popular music finding its way to the UK from the United States. At the birth of what would become known as 'The Swinging Sixties' four young men come together with dreams of pop stardom in their eyes, and begin following that dream in Liverpool's various clubs, some with illustrious names such as The Cavern and The Iron Door, but mostly in those venues little known outside the great port city. Playing for minimum fees, here, in the environment that would spawn such names as The Beatles, Gerry and the Pacemakers and more, Brendan Kane and the Planets begin their journey towards eventual recognition.

In what will become a sweeping tale of almost epic proportions, we skip to the eve of the millennium. It is 1999, and as the city of Liverpool undergoes a transforming programme of modernization and redevelopment, workers on a project to reclaim an old disused wharf and dockside warehouse uncover the skeletal remains of a long dead murder victim. Both kneecaps of the victim appear to bear the marks of a classic IRA 'kneecapping' and before long, Detective Inspector Andy Ross and his assistant, Detective Sergeant Clarissa (Izzie) Drake, find themselves involved in an investigation that sends them back in time, back to those heady days of the sixties when the city rocked to the sound of the new brand of British popular music, but when passions greater than anything they at first envisage had led to the ultimate crime, cold-blooded murder! A chance clue leads to the eventual identification of the remains, and to a new mystery, involving a young woman, missing for over thirty years. When a new murder occurs, connected to the investigation, Ross realises the case is not quite as 'cold' as it first appeared, and begins a race against time to prevent further killings as the past and present collide and the case takes a new sinister turn.

Author's note

A Mersey Killing is a work of fiction, and as such, the main characters and many of the places mentioned with the work that follows are the creations of the author's mind and are not intended to be confused with any real persons, living or dead. It has been necessary, however, in order to create a work that is credible and believable to make certain references to actual people, places, and events in order to invoke the time and era of the book's setting, i.e. the city of Liverpool in the early nineteen-sixties. Where this has happened, it has been done with the greatest reverence and respect for those mentioned in passing, none of whom are actual participants in the fictional work, and that the reader will soon realise are there merely to help create the ambience of a very special time in the world of music, and in the wonderful vibrant city that gave birth to the phenomenon that came to be known as 'The Swinging Sixties.'

Spelling and Grammar

Please note that this book is written in British, (UK) English, and here in the UK, many spellings differ from those in the USA. Also, many of the characters in the book speak the local Liverpudlian dialect, which means I have amended the spellings and grammatical use of certain words to indicate the phonetic pronunciation of the words affected.

Chapter 1

OPENING BARS

The Cavern Club in the spring of 1961 was, to use the idiom of the day, 'really rocking'. A raucous crowd of teenagers was dancing, screaming and in some cases, eating a typical Cavern lunch of sandwiches, soft drinks, (the club had no liquor licence), or maybe tea or coffee. Rory Storm and the Hurricanes, a popular local group of the day, completed their set and the crowded club, built in a converted, disused warehouse, filled with the sound of the clapping and cheering of happy and almost delirious youth. The drummer of the band, one Ringo Starr, would later rise to worldwide fame as a member of The Beatles, but their days of taking the music world by storm still lay a little way in the future. For now, he grinned at the applause, as did the other members of the group, who reveled in the ovation they received from the appreciative young audience. Like the Beatles, Rory Storm and the Hurricanes would later be signed by the iconic musical entrepreneur, Brian Epstein, without, sadly, achieving the fame of Liverpool's most marketable asset of the sixties, but for now, they were content to be one of the most popular groups on the ever growing local music scene. At the time, 'beat' music and rock 'n roll was only allowed in The Cavern Club during their lunchtime sessions, the club being a 'Skiffle Club' where only a smattering of jazz would be allowed to deviate from the norm. That would all change very soon thanks to the burgeoning sound of the sixties that would emanate from the streets of the great seaport.

Holding both arms out to his sides and lowering his palms in a request for quiet from the gathered throng of teenagers, Rory Storm smiled and spoke in a voice loud enough to be heard over the general hubbub of the club.

"Thanks, everyone. It's great to be appreciated. It's time for us to take a break, but I know you're gonna love the next group who're about to step up here for you. It's their first time here at the Cavern, so let's all give a real big Cavern welcome to *Brendan Kane and the Planets!*"

The audience cheered and clapped and as the sound rose until it seemed to bounce back from the brick walls of the club, Rory turned to his left and beckoned to the waiting group, positioned off stage, waiting for the moment to make their debut.

"Come on, Brendan, fellas," Rory shouted and the debutantes virtually ran onto the stage to yet more cheers from the throng of eager youth, always happy to hear and appreciate the latest groups to hit the local music scene. Comprising Brendan himself, the group's lead vocalist and rhythm guitarist, he was followed onto the compact Cavern stage by lead guitarist Mickey Doyle, drummer Phil Oxley and Mickey's younger brother Ronnie on bass. Without preamble the group launched into the first of the two numbers they would perform that day, their own arrangement of Chuck Berry's classic hit, *Roll Over Beethoven.* Within seconds of them beginning the club was rocking to the sound of the new group on the scene and Brendan Kane's voice, powerful and resonant, had the audience enraptured.

"Wow, that boy can sing!" "Fab" and other superlatives were soon being exchanged by the young listeners whose discerning ears were fast becoming attuned to recognition of those groups or singers who had the right musical sound and most importantly, voices that could make them stand out from the crowd in a rapidly expanding local music scene. As the last strains of the music died away at the end of their performance, the watching audience spontaneously burst into a rousing chorus of applause, whistles, and cheers, and Brendan looked hopefully towards the side of the stage, where the club's resident D.J, knowing a good thing when he saw, (and heard) it, held one finger up, signaling that the group could perform one more song, that being double what they'd expected to play that day.

Brendan quickly mouthed "Coming home" to the group members and Mickey Doyle's fingers began to pick out the opening melody of a song he and Brendan had written together. With a resonating beat and a 'catchy' guitar melody running through the song, any risk the group had taken in performing their own composition rather than one of the standards of the day soon evaporated as the audience foot-tapped and jigged their way through the new song, which the group was performing in public for the first time.

"That was great," said the club's D.J as the group left the stage to yet more rapturous applause. "You lads have a really good sound. I want you to come back again, and soon."

"That'll be terrific," Brendan replied, a beaming smile on his face. "How soon?"

"How're you fixed for next week?"

"Well, we're at The Iron Door on Tuesday."

"What about Thursday lunchtime?"

Brendan quickly looked questioningly at the other members of the group. He knew they'd have to arrange time off work or simply absent themselves from their jobs if they were to fulfill the engagement, but each one unhesitatingly nodded their agreement.

"Okay, we'll be here," he replied.

After staying at the club long enough to smoke a couple of cigarettes each and drink a coffee or a Coca-Cola, Brendan and the Planets made their way through the smoke-laden atmosphere and the happy crowd, towards the exit, accompanied by much back slapping and complementary comments from a number of the youngsters who'd obviously enjoyed their performance. *Perhaps*, thought Brendan as the group loaded their gear into the old Bedford van they regularly borrowed from Phil Oxley's father, *we might just have a decent shot of making something of the music business.* Phil drove carefully, not wanting to damage his precious drum kit or the others' guitars and equipment and one by one, dropped the group members off at their homes, or, in Brendan's case, outside the bookshop where he worked. Mr. Mason, the shop owner, didn't mind giving Brendan time off to attend his gigs, as, being forward-thinking, he realized that many of the younger crowd who knew Brendan were already visiting his shop regularly and he'd cleverly begun to stock a wide range of products, magazines and American comics that ensured a steady turnover from the new branch of his clientele. *Maybe,* he thought, *I ought to start stocking a few records, just in case.*

Mr. Mason cheerfully welcomed Brendan back to work, where the young man soon managed to lose himself in daydreams of future stardom as he went about the rest of his day's work.

Chapter 2

Clarissa Drake stood looking down, maybe thirty feet or so, towards the bottom of the old, dried up dock. Turning to the young man beside her, she spoke quietly, as she shivered in the early morning mist that drifted across the landscape from the nearby River Mersey.

"You know, Derek, if I didn't know better, I'd say he looks pleased to see us."

Before the young man could reply, a deep voice from behind them made them both jump slightly.

"Now then, Izzie, how many times have I told you about that sense of humour of yours?

Turning to face the man behind the voice, Detective Sergeant Clarissa, (Izzie) Drake, found herself staring into the eyes of her boss, Detective Inspector Andy Ross. Detective Constable Derek McLennan stood beside her, trying to make himself look small and insignificant in an effort to avoid the wrath of his boss. D.I. Ross in fact, despite his words, had an almost imperceptible grin on his face as he looked sternly at his sergeant.

"I'm sorry sir, but you know how it always affects me, seeing something like this. I'm just trying to lighten the moment a bit if you know what I mean."

The tall, swarthy-skinned Inspector took a step forward and looked down at the sight that had brought them here in the first place, the grinning rictus of the skull certainly looking to all intents and purposes appearing, as Izzie intimated, pleased to be revealed from its long incarceration in the clinging mud that had only now decided to reveal its macabre secret. Ross knew it had to have been there a long time, as the small wharf and dockside had been abandoned for many years and only now, in the course of urban renovation and improvement, had the collective mass of mud and detritus of years of neglect been slowly cleared away until the discovery of the remains brought all work to a halt. He turned to face the sergeant and the young detective constable who remained rooted to the spot beside her.

"Right then, let's get on with it. Izzie, try not to assign or assume gender until the doc has examined the remains, as well, OK?"

Izzie nodded her understanding.

"And Constable?" Ross looked into the eyes of the young detective.

"Sir?"

"I'm not going to chew your head off for standing next to the sergeant while she makes frivolous comments, so no need to look like you're about to be sent back to uniform, or fed to the Chief Superintendent for supper, okay?"

"Yes, sir, okay sir, I mean thank you, sir."

"How long you been in the detective division, lad?"

"Six months, sir."

"Lots to learn my boy, lots to learn. Now, let's get on with the job."

"Right sir, McLennan replied, following Izzie as she began the descent of the iron-runged ladder that led down to the muddy and rank smelling river bed below.

Ross quickly followed the two until all three officers stood quietly looking at the recently revealed skeletal remains that lay half in and half out of the mostly hard-packed surface of the ground that would once have been the bed of a busy and thriving riverside wharf.

The detectives took care not to approach too close to the remains, not wanting to disturb the scene before the medical examiner had had the opportunity to inspect the scene.

"Anyone know who the duty M.E. is?" Ross asked of no-one in particular.

Izzie Blake provided him with the answer.

"One of the paramedics up there said it's Fat Willy, sir."

Ross groaned. The nickname Blake used referred to Doctor William Nugent, a brilliant but terribly overweight police surgeon, an expert in forensic pathology, whose unfortunate weight problems had provided the members of Merseyside Constabulary with the excuse to make jokes at his expense, always behind his back of course. A rather dour Scot, the doctor's accent contrasted with the predominantly local Liverpool accent possessed by most of the local constabulary, some of whom found it difficult to keep up with the doctor's words at times, though he seemed to have no difficulty with the Liverpudlian accent, having lived in the city for as many years as anyone could remember. Nugent was also something of a stickler for the rules and Ross knew he'd better be on his toes and not cause any disturbance to the scene before him, lest he incur the wrath of the good doctor. Ross held both arms out to his sides, as though indicating an invisible barrier.

"Right, people, no-one gets any closer than this until the doctor arrives. Now, tell me what you see. You first, Sergeant."

Izzie Drake peered down at the skeletal remains and paused, as she gathered her thoughts. The skull and upper body were for the most part, fully exposed with the abdominal area still covered by a thick layer of mud and silt, and the lower legs and feet also exposed to the chill morning air.

"Well, sir looks to me as though the body has laid there for some time. If you look at the wall of the dock above us, we can see that the mud and silt must have reached up at least ten feet before the workmen started on the reclamation job."

Ross looked up, nodding his agreement with his sergeant, also taking time to notice the faded lettering on the side of the disused brick built warehouse, which read 'Cole and Sons, Importers,' many of the letters now indistinct and barely readable. He made a mental note to check how long the warehouse had lain empty and whether Cole and Sons had been the last company to have used the facility. Izzie continued.

"Whoever the victim is, or was, must have lain buried beneath the mud and silt for years, to have ended up so deep."

"Agreed," said Ross. "Go on, what else?"

"I'd lay odds on the fact this is a suspicious death. I just don't see anyone dying of natural causes and not being reported missing or nobody having the faintest clue where he or she was last seen, that kind of thing."

McLennan butted in.

"Unless the victim had a heart attack, or slipped and fell in the water all those years ago, no witnesses, and was just never found."

"Well done, Constable McLennan," said Ross. "That's good thinking. We may have to do a massive trawl of the missing person records once the doc gives us an idea of how long the remains have been down here. Anything else, Izzie?"

"Not yet, sir. I think we need to get the doctor's opinion before we begin formulating our own theories."

As if on cue, first of all a wide shadow, and then a large figure appeared on the dockside above, followed by the booming voice of Doctor Nugent.

"Well now, Inspector Ross. I see you've got something interesting for me this morning?" The Scottish accent was easily discernible to those around the pathologist.

"Morning, Doctor. Yes. Been here a while, I'd say, but I'd appreciate your professional opinion before we jump to conclusions."

"Aye, well, it's good to hear you're learning a thing or two. I take it no-one's disturbed the remains?"

"No, we've stayed well back to give you an undisturbed area around the victim."

"Aye well, I'd better be comin' doon then, eh? Francis, come on man, and bring your camera."

As if by magic the diminutive figure of Francis Lees, the pathologist's assistant appeared at his side, looking down at the death scene. "What the hell are you waiting for man? Get doon the ladder there and wait for me at the bottom. And make sure to catch me if I slip on those old rusty rungs."

The detectives looked at each other and smiled. The thought of Nugent's bulk falling from the ladder on to the hapless Lees gave them a moment of humour in the midst of their other wise grim task. The thought that Nugent's weight would probably force poor Lees's body into the mud and silt, suffocating the poor man, made him think they may end up with two bodies to remove from the dock before the day was out.

Lees quickly made his way down the ladder and dutifully stood almost to attention, his camera slung over his shoulder, as Nugent ponderously made his way down the rusting ladder, thankfully arriving safely at the bottom less than a minute after his assistant. Ross couldn't help but admire the way the pathologist, despite his bulk, managed to make his way down the ladder almost gracefully, and without any apparent difficulty.

"Now, let's see what we've got, eh?" said Nugent as he and Lees began their own examination of the scene. Lees's camera flashed incessantly as he photographed the partially revealed skeletal remains from every possible angle. Nugent knelt in the mud beside the skeleton and began a close examination. Ross, knowing the doctor's routine all too well, couldn't resist a quick question.

"See anything yet that might help us, Doctor?"

"Sshhh," Nugent urged.

"Does he think the corpse is going to talk to him?" McLennan whispered quietly to Izzie.

"Ah heard that, young man," Nugent snapped at the young detective. "Ah like tae work in peace if you don't have any objections."

"Of course, Doctor, sorry," said McLennan, blushing visibly.

"Aye, well, anyway, in response to your question, Inspector Ross, I do believe I have something for you."

"Already, Doctor?"

"Aye, already, but it doesn't take a genius in this case to ascertain that, in my humble opinion, you'll be looking for a murderer I think." Ross and Izzie Drake looked at each other, exchanging knowing glances. Both knew instinctively this was going to be a potentially long and difficult case to crack.

"How can you be sure so quickly?" he asked the pathologist.

"Aye, well, I dinna think this hole in the skull got here by accident." Nugent beckoned the inspector closer and pointed to the rear of the skull, which he'd raised carefully just clear of the mud. There, the two men looked closely at the gaping hole in the back of the skull, larger than would have been left by a bullet but still conversant with some form of blunt force trauma.

"Couldn't that have been caused by an accident, Doc?"

"Under certain circumstances, it may have been, Inspector Ross, but not in this case, I think."

"Why so certain?" asked the policeman.

Nugent pointed to a point about twelve inches to the right of the skull. Ross could see that the doctor, in the course of his close examination had uncovered the unmistakable form of a hammer.

"I'll wager a month's salary that yon hammer is your murder weapon, Inspector," said Nugent. "There's some staining on the hammer head that may be blood, and the shape and size of the hammer head would appear to match the shape of the wound in this poor unfortunate soul's head. I'll be able to confirm it when we get the remains back to the lab, but for now, I'm satisfied you have a murder on your hands. No chance of fingerprints after so long I'm afraid which leads me to the bad news that I believe the remains have possibly lain here for a long time, years in fact."

"Any idea of gender?" asked Izzie Drake.

"Not yet, Sergeant, but looking at the size of the feet, I'd hazard a guess at male," Nugent replied. "Inspector, I dinna want to disturb the remains too much where they lie at present. Can you arrange for a team to dig out the entire area surrounding the skeleton and transport the lot back to my lab? I can carry out a thorough examination there and give you as much information as the deceased is willing to reveal to me."

Ross groaned inwardly. It would be a massive task to remove the remains from their resting place, mud and all, without disturbing or destroying the skeleton, but at least once it was out of the way he and his team could carry out an intensive search of the surrounding area for clues to the identity of the victim or to the full nature of the crime. At least the possibility that this was indeed the murder site might make his task a little simpler, no need to go searching the length of the river bank for miles in both directions.

"I'll make the arrangements, Doc. Please, once you get the remains to your lab…"

"I know, Inspector. You'd like my findings as soon as possible."

"Thanks, yes, Doc. I know it's not as if I can see a quick solution to this one, but anything we can do to find out who this was, and when the murder occurred, might just help us bring a killer to justice."

"I wish you luck, Inspector, I really do," Nugent said as he rose from his position and beckoned Lees to follow him, and the pair began the ascent up the ladder back up to the dockside.

"Anything to add, Constable?" Ross directed the question at McLennan.

"Just a question really, sir."

"OK, ask away."

"Well sir, this dock or wharf or whatever the correct term is, was once connected to the Mersey by that channel, right?" McLennan pointed along the narrow channel along which the ships would have approached the dock from the river, unloaded at the dockside and then turned round in the basin they now stood in before heading back out to the Mersey.

"Right," said Ross, "so what's the question?"

"It's just that I don't see how they could block off the whole River Mersey so they could drain the dock and the channel, sir. How the heck did they manage it?"

"Good question, McLennan and I'm glad to see you're thinking about this. I'm no engineer but I think you'll find they drive large metal pilings into the river bed, erect some sort of temporary dam, then use massive pumps of some sort to drain the water from this side. When it's dry, they can then build the new reinforced river bank you now see at the end of the channel, thus re-directing the flow of the Mersey. They must have done this many times during all the redevelopment of the dock area, because I know there are a hell of a lot of these old inlets and channels that had to be closed off to the river before the developers could start work on their so-called urban redevelopment and improvement of the old dock area."

"Right, sir, I see. I was just trying to work out if the clearing of the channel might have any bearing on the timing of the death of the victim."

"Good thought, Constable, but of course, it could have happened any time when the dock was still operational or after closure as far as my thinking goes. But listen, you keep thinking lad, okay? That's what a good detective does, all the time, lots of thinking, mainly small points but then one day you just might hit on something important. The other thing we need to consider is whether the body was carried here by the tide and simply washed up here. The actual murder site and original dump site could be almost anywhere."

McLennan smiled, pleased the inspector had listened to his points and didn't think he was wasting his time, but wished he'd thought of the inspector's last point.

Ross next took out his mobile phone, and spent the next few minutes making arrangements for a specialist recovery team to attend the scene and remove the remains and the surrounding mud and silt in one large excavation, for transportation to the forensic lab, in order for Doctor Nugent to carry out what Ross knew would be a painstaking examination. There wasn't much they could do for the present, not until the remains had been removed and they had the opportunity to carry out a detailed examination of the surrounding area. Ross knew he'd have to call in a few uniformed officers as well as the members of his own team of detectives, and his own boss, Detective Chief Inspector Harry Porteous wouldn't be best pleased at the overtime bill that would probably ensue from a case that on the surface, at least, appeared to offer little hope of a quick and easy solution.

"Well," said Izzie as she and Ross stood staring at the remains, McLennan having been dispatched by Ross to begin the arrangements to have the remains carefully removed and taken to the lab.

"Well indeed, Sergeant," Ross replied, thoughtfully. "Well, indeed."

Chapter 3

Brendan Kane and his fellow musicians sat around the kitchen table in Brendan's parents home, a small two up, two down red-brick terraced house, much like thousands of others in the city. The young men sat around Brendan's Mum's kitchen table, with drummer Phil, unable to keep his hands still, constantly fiddling with a bottle of Camp Coffee in one hand and another of Heinz Tomato Ketchup in the other. To one side of the room, a small coal fire burned in the hearth, adding warmth and a feeling of cozy security to the room. Near the fire, a load of washing stood draped over a wooden clothes horse, the smell of damp washing adding to the homely feel of the room. Despite the domestic warmth and atmosphere of his parents' home, like many others of his own age, Brendan nurtured dreams of being able to move up in the world, to leave behind the rather grim and humdrum workaday existence endured by his Mum and Dad and others of their generation. His father, Dennis, had spent his entire working life as a docker, a hard life, with much physical toil required on a daily basis. The years had taken their toll on Dennis Kane, and Brendan, despite having the greatest of respect for his father, wanted more from life, a house with a garden instead of a front door that opened straight onto the street, a few of the modern conveniences perhaps, like a dishwashing machine similar to those he'd seen in the shops in the city centre, and one of the new fangled automatic washing machines. Brendan knew his Mum was luckier than most, in owning her twin tub machine with the spin-dryer that took the worst of the water out of the clothes. Still, the washing draped on the clothes-horse was a reminder that his mother still did a great deal of washing by hand and dried it the best she could in front of the fire.

Like the rest of the group, he felt his best chance of achieving his dreams just might be through their music. He'd received his guitar, a second-hand but good condition twin pick-up Hofner, as a Christmas present one year from his parents, who were well aware of their son's love of music, and who'd scrimped and saved for months in order to buy their son the instrument and a second-hand amplifier to go with it. Second-hand or not, to young Brendan, the guitar had been, and still was, the greatest gift his parents could every have given him, and he was determined to pay them back for their financial sacrifice, just as soon as he could.

"Listen up lads," said Brendan, as he pointed to a stack of papers laid out on the table in front of him. "Here's the receipts for every gig we've done so far. We're doing okay locally, but I think we need to try and branch out, you know, like, maybe get a recording contract."

"Christ, Brendan," Mickey replied, flicking back a permanently an-noying lock of hair that always fell across right eye, "We'd all love to do that, man, but getting a recording contract isn't as easy as that, and you know it."

The others all nodded their agreement with Mickey's statement.

"Yeah, look, I know that, but that guy Brian Epstein, you know, his Dad owns a furniture shop in town? Brian's the manager of the mu-sic department and he's started out managing some of the local beat groups. He's signed The Beatles, and we've played the same stage as them, right? Someone told me they've got a recording contract already with a record coming out next month. They wrote it themselves, it's called *Love me Do*. I heard last week he's also got Gerry and the Pace-makers on his books and a couple of others, and they're all local and doing okay under his guidance."

Phil Oxley joined in the conversation.

"Yeah, I've seen him around in some of the clubs, like The Cavern, The Iron Door, places like that."

"But has he ever seen us and heard us play?" asked young Ronnie.

"Exactly," said Brendan. "We need to make sure he's there in one of those clubs when we're on stage, make sure he hears and likes us. Then maybe we'll get picked up by him, too."

"Yeah, but he's not the only manager in the business, is he?" said, Ronnie. "I know for a fact that a couple of groups have had demo recordings made at Pete Kemp's studio in the city centre. Maybe we could do that and send copies of the demo off to Mr. Epstein and some of the big recording companies, you know, like Decca, E.M.I. and Polydor?"

"Sure, Ronnie," said Brendan. "We could do that, spend a load of dosh we haven't got on getting a demo made, and then buy enough copies to send around the industry, only for some producer's assistant to listen to a few bars if we're lucky and then throw the disc in the bin. We only get three pounds a gig man, and we have to pay Phil's dad a bit towards the petrol we use when he lends us his van, so we ain't got a whole lot of spare cash to throw away on a demo that hardly anyone will hear."

"But how do other groups manage then?" asked Ronnie. "Surely lots of record companies do have people who listen to new talent when they get the demos in the post?"

Mickey chimed in.

"Ronnie, I think what Brendan's getting at is that most of the groups whose demos get heard are probably sent in by their managers, who already know the producers and such like at Decca and places like that."

"Yeah, exactly," said Brendan. "That's why we need someone like Brian Epstein to notice us. It doesn't have to be him of course, but he's local, and we've probably got more chance of being heard and spotted by him than by anyone else, and we don't exactly know many managers of pop groups personally, do we?"

"Okay," said Ronnie. "What do you think we should do then, Brendan? How do we get him to see and hear us? We can't exactly go begging to him, can we? You know, *'Please Mr. Epstein, we're real good. Come and listen to us and sign us up.'*

"We use our brains, Ronnie. That's what we do. Look here," Brendan said. "These receipts show we make a small profit on every gig, not a lot, sure, but enough to maybe get a few leaflets printed. My idea is to get them printed with a few of our 'coming soon' dates, you know, when we've maybe got three or four bookings lined up and we make sure copies of the leaflet are delivered to his dad's shop, to the music department and to his office. I've found out he's got one in town, where he runs his management stuff from. Then we get that gorgeous sister of yours, Mickey, to help us out."

"And what do we want Marie to do, exactly?" asked Mickey.

"Well, she's a real looker, right, and she and her mates go out to the clubs regular to listen to the music, right?" They all nodded in agreement, apart from Mickey, who appeared unsure of just what Brendan was about to suggest.

"What we do is, we ask her to go to a few of the clubs where we know he hangs out and see if she can get to talk to him, just drop him a few hints about this really great group she's heard, that's us of course, and that he ought to go to The Iron Door, or wherever we're booked that week, and listen to us. She can tell him lots of kids are following us and that we've got a great sound. What bloke can resist a really good looking bird like your sis, Mickey?"

"Sounds good," Mickey replied, "but how do we know which clubs he's going to be at so Marie can try and talk to him?"

"Yes, I know, that's the one big problem with my plan. Maybe she could spend a week or two doing her best to corner him and then we get the leaflets posted, sharpish like, and distribute them so he gets copies just after talking to Marie, and we might get lucky."

"Bloody hell, Brendan, there's a load of ifs, buts, and maybes in there, don't you think?" asked Ronnie.

"I know Ronnie, but come on fellas, don't you think it's worth a try?"

After another five minutes of discussion, with no-one having come up with a better idea to try to gain the recognition of the man they saw as a way into the recording industry, they reached an agreement, and Mickey promised he'd speak to his sister Marie, who he agreed would probably be pleased to enlist her friends in helping them to put Brendan's grand plan into operation.

After another half hour of discussion and agreeing to meet at Brendan's house at seven p.m on Friday night before going on to a gig at the newly-opened Pelican Club, the group went their separate ways, leaving Brendan to clear away the receipts and the mugs that had held their frequent cups of tea, leaving his Mum's kitchen as clean as possible when she came home after her shift at the launderette.

The front door opened soon afterwards, and Brendan's Dad walked into the house, having spent an hour at the pub, enjoying a pint or two with his friends. He made his way straight to the kitchen, where Brendan was sitting at the table, deep in thought.

"Hey, son, how you doing?" Dennis asked.

"Alright, Dad, Just thinking stuff, you know."

"Aye lad, you do a lot of that there thinking, don't you? I hope you're going to stick at that new job of yours and not turn into too much of a dreamer over all that music stuff you and your mates are so keen on. There's no future in that life, you should know that."

Brendan sighed. He and his father had had this conversation many times in recent months.

"You're wrong, Dad, really. There's a real future out there if you're good enough, and I know me and the lads have a real chance if we can just get spotted. That's what we've been talking about before you came home."

"Oh aye? And just what does Mr. Mason think of all this 'beat music' lark, eh? He's got some patience, I'll say that for him, letting you have time off to go and play that so-called music of yours during the day."

"It's only the odd hour here and there, Dad, when we get a lunchtime gig, and then I'm only actually away from the shop for a couple of hours, and one of them's me lunch hour anyway, and Mr. Mason says he thinks I should follow me dreams, we all should."

Dennis Kane waved a dismissive hand in his son's direction. No way would the hardened old dock worker ever understand the modern generation.

"Aye well, if you say so, son, if you say so. Now be a good lad and put the kettle on and make your old Dad a nice cup of tea, eh?"

Brendan nodded at his father, rose from the table and picked up the kettle from the cooker hob next to the sink unit, quickly filling it and putting it on to boil on the gas ring, all dreams of being a future pop star, for the moment, like the slowly boiling kettle, placed on the back burner.

One day, Dad, I'll prove you wrong, and make you proud of me, he thought, without actually saying the words. He knew he'd never convince his Dad until maybe he and the group actually made it big, and perhaps even then his Dad wouldn't think being a musician and singer was what he'd deem a 'proper job.

The kettle whistled as it came to the boil and Brendan dutifully made the tea, and Dennis took his with a quick "Thanks, son," and made his way into the small parlour at the front of the house, and turned on the small black and white television in the corner, the one Brendan hoped to one day turn into one with a glorious colour screen, like the ones in that big shop in the city.

Brendan took his own cup of steaming hot tea upstairs with him to his bedroom, where he turned on his small portable transistor radio which he kept permanently tuned to Radio Luxemburg, lay down on his bed and allowed himself to drift into his daydream of music stardom as the latest sounds of the pop charts assailed his brain, the tea soon growing cold as he became lost in the early sounds of the sixties.

Chapter 4

MERSEYSIDE POLICE HEADQUARTERS, 1999

On the sixth day after the discovery of the remains, Ross sat alone at his desk in his small but functional office at police headquarters. The painstaking task of removing the remains from the abandoned dock had taken almost two days to achieve, and the inspector now awaited the results of the post-mortem on the unfortunate soul whose last resting place had gone unmarked and unrecognized for God knows how many years. After six years as a Detective Inspector, Ross had to admit to himself that this could turn out to be his most baffling case to date. As a rule, most murders tended to follow a similar pattern. Either through love, jealousy, hatred or for financial reasons, one individual would one day snap and instigate the death of another. In the majority of cases, the body would be found sooner rather than later, and certainly not years later, as in the current case. Of course, identifying the victim helped, and again was usually achieved fairly quickly even when no identification was present on the body. Only in rare cases did it take a length of time for the police with all their modern resources to identify a murder victim. This time, however, things were very different. In the case of the skeletal remains which even now, Dr. Nugent and his assistant, Lees were carrying out an autopsy of sorts on, there was no hope of fingerprint identification and the few items of trace evidence found in the vicinity after the removal of the body had provided little if any hints that would put a name to the victim, and without a name for the deceased, any hope of finding the killer would prove minimal.

Ross picked up the report that lay on his desk, a single sheet of paper that contained the list of items recovered from the mud and silt that had accumulated around the decomposing body over the years. The remains of one boot, obviously a man's had survived in enough detail to be estimated at a size ten. Nugent, of course, had been correct in his assumption the remains were those of a man. Perhaps the other boot had degraded and been washed away with the tidal flow from the dock while it was still operational, Ross hypothesized. Next, a few coins, totalling six shillings and tenpence in pre-decimilisation currency, that had probably been in the deceased's pockets had been found, cleaned and from the date of the most recently minted coin discovered it was possible to assume with some degree of certainty that the murder had taken place no later than nineteen sixty six.

"Bloody hell," Ross spoke aloud, "that's over thirty years ago. How the hell am I supposed to find this poor sod's killer if I can't even find out who he was?"

"Talking to yourself, now, are we, sir?" came the voice of Izzie Drake from the doorway. Ross had been so engrossed in his personal thoughts he hadn't heard her knock gently before entering his office.

"Well, there wasn't anyone else here to listen, was there, Sergeant?" he replied, quickly regaining his composure after initially appearing surprised at Drake's sudden appearance.

"I'm here now, though, sir. You managed to come up with anything new from looking at that list?"

Ross quickly scanned the short list of items once again, for probably the tenth time since the forensic team had compiled it, and sighed before replying. The actual items found were currently in the evidence locker down in the basement of the headquarters building, and the two detectives had spent a few hours trying to glean something, anything, from staring at the assortment on the day they'd been brought in, under Izzie's supervision after she'd led the team in a painstaking search of the dock.

"I'm no miracle worker, that's for sure, Izzie. I mean, what have we got? A bit of an old boot, a few coins, a few pieces of cloth that may or may not have been part of the victim's clothing, a metal comb, a few drinks cans, various makes of beer and soft drinks apparently identifiable, a few glass bottles, whole and in pieces and that strange piece of plastic one of your searchers picked up. Any or all of this stuff could just as easily have been thrown into the water by someone not connected to the murder. We just don't know, and I can't see how we're ever going to know, if you want the truth."

"I know sir. It seems like an impossible and pretty thankless task if you ask me. Doesn't the chief superintendent realize we're on a hiding to nothing with this one?"

"He probably does, Izzie, but he puts a bit of pressure on D.C.I Porteous to get a result and he puts the pressure on me and we just have to do our best."

Izzie Drake walked across to the window of Ross's office, and appeared to stare into space for a few seconds. Ross recognized this as one of Izzie's regular ways of gathering her thoughts and waited patiently for her to speak. She turned back from the window, and as Ross looked at her expectantly, she voiced her thoughts.

"Look, sir, I know this a wild thought, but what about the guys in the cold case squad? Our skeleton might just refer back to one of their cases."

Merseyside Police did in fact have one of the best cold case units in the North of England, as the inspector knew only too well, and Ross deliberated for a few seconds before replying to his sergeant.

"Under normal circumstances I'd probably agree with you, but, and it's a big but, I know for a fact that the Cold Case Squad have to work under very specific terms of reference. The most important prerequisite for them to become involved in a case is that, quite simply, there has to be a case for them to become *involved* in. In other words, it has to be a case that already exists on the unsolved books, and sadly for us, in this case, as we have no identity for our victim, we have nothing to cross reference it against, to see if they have our victim listed in any past crime statistics."

"Damn it," said Drake. "I really thought I might be on to something there."

Ross smiled.

"You still might be, Izzie. If we can find out who our victim is, and he's listed in an unsolved case file somewhere then Cold Case might be interested in taking the case over, if the boss agrees."

"And why wouldn't he, sir?"

"Simple, Izzie. Because if he thinks there's any mileage for positive publicity to be gained from his own murder squad solving an old case, he's unlikely to want to hand it to the wrinkly squad."

Drake sighed.

"Internal politics at work again, eh, sir?"

"'Fraid so, Izzie."

Before they could continue their discussion, the phone on Ross's desk rang. Drake moved to leave the office, but he held up a hand to tell her to stay where she was. The call might be important to their case, and indeed, after a minute of what Drake took to be serious listening by her boss, he spoke into the mouthpiece.

"Okay, thanks, Doc. Sergeant Drake and I will be with you shortly."

Izzie looked intently at Ross as he hung up on Doctor Nugent.

"Results of the autopsy, or should I say examination of the bones, I assume, sir?"

Ross nodded his head and spoke as he quickly tidied the papers on his desk into a neat pile and then placed them in the top left drawer of his desk, locking it with a key which hung on the key ring that also contained his car keys.

"Such as it was, yes. Our dour but brilliant pathologist says he's come up with one or two things, but he'd rather explain to us in person rather then over the phone. Of course, that's his usual stance, always wanting to over-dramatise any little bit of trivia he might have discovered, and present it like he's bloody Sherlock Holmes or something, so let's not get too excited until we see and hear what he has to say."

"Understood, sir, but, from what you just said, I'm assuming he's found something of interest?"

"According to the good doctor, yes he has. So, let's get on over to the mortuary, and see what he has for us."

"Right, sir. Should we tell D.C.I. Porteous we're going over there?"

"No point, Izzie, not unless or until we have something to report to him. If he needs me he can always reach me through my mobile, and I'd rather talk to him with something positive to report rather than just give him my travel itinerary for the morning. Just tell D.C. McLennan where we're going just in case the boss does ask where we are while we're gone. Go on, and give D.C. Ferris a heads-up too. He might need to get in touch if he comes up with anything."

Drake returned to the squad room where she quickly brought the two Detective Constables up to date. McLennan was busy going through missing persons files going back for a number of years, though how he hoped to cross reference a name with an as yet unidentified skeleton was anybody's guess, and the older and more experienced D.C. was studying the photographs taken by the crime scene techs, of all the various items of detritus and rubbish, or potential evidence, however you looked at it, discovered around the victim's remains.

Ten minutes later, she was behind the wheel of the Mondeo pool car assigned to Ross, as they made the short drive to the city mortuary. Hopefully, they would find something of interest in the results of Doctor Nugent's examination of the mystery skeleton.

Chapter 5

THE MORTUARY, 1999

Drake and Ross stepped into the sunlight as they alighted from the Mondeo in the car park outside the mortuary building. As Ross stretched to his full height, relieving the stiffness in his neck and back, Izzie Drake couldn't help but admire the man who she worked closely with.

Detective Inspector Andy Ross might be the wrong side of forty, but his full head of dark brown hair and his healthy skin tone gave him the look of a man almost ten years younger. Drake had noticed a framed photo of his parents in his office soon after she'd started working under Ross, and had commented on the handsome couple in the picture. Ross explained that his father, a military policeman at the time, had met his mother during a posting to the Far East in the fifties, and fell in love with the beautiful dark-skinned daughter of a wealthy shipping merchant. Apparently Ross's mother came from an old Anglo-Indian family, with a strong hint of Spanish blood in the mix, hence her mother's maiden name of Martinez. It was therefore easy for Izzie to see where her boss got his good looks from.

Izzie often envied Ross's wife, Maria, a doctor in general practice not far from where they now stood, looking at the entrance to the mortuary building. She wished she could meet a man with the looks, integrity and self-assurance of Andy Ross, but her luck with men never seemed to follow a straight or true course. Maybe one day, but for now, work took priority over everything else.

"Ready, Sergeant?" Ross asked as Izzie pressed the button on the remote and the car answered with a beep as the door locks engaged.

"Ready as I'll ever be, sir. God, I do hate these places."

"Don't we all? I doubt this place is anyone's favourite place to be on a warm, sunny day, except of course, someone like our friendly neighborhood pathologist, the good Doctor Nugent."

"Not forgetting his faithful hound, Lees, of course," Izzie chuckled as she spoke.

Ross joined in Izzie's lighthearted banter for a few seconds.

"God, yes. I must say, Lees is almost more cadaverous than some of the poor sods in this place, looks like a good meal might kill him."

"He's good at his job though, eh, sir? Doctor Nugent won't have anyone else assisting him, so I've heard."

"True. Well, here goes."

The two detectives stood at the entrance to the building where an intercom system was in place, beside a small keyboard which only staff had the code to, in order to effect immediate entry. A notice adjacent to a small silver button read 'Press here for entry' and Ross duly pressed where indicated. Almost immediately, a tinny disembodied voice squeaked from the small speaker above the button.

"Hello. Please state your name and business."

"Detective Inspector Ross and Sergeant Drake, Merseyside Police, for Doctor Nugent. We're expected."

"Ah yes, I have your names here. Please push the door when the buzzer sounds, Inspector."

Ross and Drake entered the building as instructed and walked a short distance along the corridor immediately inside the door, quickly arriving at another door beside which a small window looked into an equally small cubicle. Within, a young man sat at a small desk with a computer screen and keyboard in front of him, obviously the disembodied voice from moments earlier, Ross surmised. The man wore a lapel badge that gave his name as Peter Foster, the title Mortuary

Reception below the name. Foster spoke to the detectives through a grill in the glass partition that separated him from mortuary visitors.

"Good morning, may I see your identification please, Inspector Ross, Sergeant Drake?"

Both officers produced their warrant cards and passed them through the small gap at the bottom of the glass. Foster checked them carefully. Ross couldn't remember seeing him here on previous visits to the building.

"You new here?" he inquired of Foster.

"Been here a month, Inspector," he replied as he passed the warrant cards back to the detectives. "Sorry if I seem over careful, but we've been instructed to be very fastidious and only allow authorized personnel into the actual examination suites."

"No need to apologise for doing your job the right way, Mr. Foster," Ross replied. "It's a rare thing to find nowadays."

Foster smiled, grateful to the inspector for putting him at ease. Ross assumed not everyone was as understanding as he was about being held up in their attempts to enter the 'business end' of the mortuary, as he thought of it.

"Thank you, Inspector," Foster smiled again. "I presume you know your way to the autopsy rooms?"

Ross noted the change in terminology; Foster acknowledging his professional status rather than using the terms presumably used with grieving relatives and so on.

"We do indeed."

"Doctor Nugent is in Autopsy Room Two," said Foster, as he handed over two 'visitor' badges which Ross and Drake proceeded to pin on their jackets.

"Thanks for your help, Mr. Foster," Ross smiled at the young man, who beamed an equally expansive smile back at the detectives.

"You're welcome, Inspector. Please remember to hand the badges back to me before you leave the building."

Ross nodded and the two walked through the door that opened magically as Foster pressed a switch, out of sight to those outside his small but functional cubicle, which, Ross thought, he probably thought of as his office.

As soon as they entered the next corridor the two officers became instantly aware that they were now in what could best be described as the 'mortuary, proper' as their olfactory senses were assailed by the smell familiar to such establishments the world over, that heady mix of formaldehyde and disinfectant. Their nostrils twitched involuntarily as they followed the wide corridor, its walls a pallid 'hospital green' in colour, until it suddenly opened up into a large circular room with large double doors spaced evenly around it, each bearing a small plaque carrying the room, or 'autopsy suite' number.

"At least we don't have to watch any bodies being sliced and diced this time," Izzie Drake said with a tinge of relief in her voice.

"Something to be grateful for, I suppose, Izzie," Ross replied, himself relieved that he wouldn't need to avail himself of the 'Vick's Vaporub' he and most other police officers usually smeared under their nose to help combat the smell of decomposition and putrefaction. No need either, to dress themselves in the surgical scrubs usually worn when attending autopsies either, as Nugent had advised earlier on the phone. No matter how many autopsies he'd attended over the years, Andy Ross had never been able to get used to the odours associated with the process of post-mortem examinations. With nothing but a set of skeletal remains on the table today, both detectives would be spared the gruesome sights and smells of a regular autopsy.

They paused for second or two outside the doors to autopsy room two, then Ross slowly eased one of the double doors open enough for himself and Drake to pass through. The detectives walked in to the room, which contained all the usual paraphernalia associated with the process in hand, steel autopsy table with channels at the sides for the blood to drain along into waiting receptacles at the end of the table, a set of large cold-boxes set into the far wall, where the bodies would be stored and further tables and counter tops, all in gleaming steel, holding saws, drills, cutting tools and everything a proficient pathologist could ask for in order to determine his or her findings.

As the door slowly closed silently and automatically behind them, both Ross and Drake found themselves staring in surprise at the sight before their eyes. In the centre of the room the skeletal remains lay, displayed in the middle of the autopsy table, with Doctor Nugent standing on the opposite side of the table to the detectives, facing them as they entered the room. With his back to them, Francis Lees was busily dictating something into a small hand-held recorder, probably on Nugent's instructions, his voice low and inaudible from where they stood.

What took Ross and Drake by surprise however was that, for the fist time in either officer's memory, there was a third person in the room with the pathologist and his assistant. Ross in particular was quite amazed as he took in the sight of an extremely beautiful blonde-haired woman, dressed not in surgical scrubs as Nugent and Lees always were, despite Nugent's instructions to the opposite to Ross, but in an extremely expensive looking light blue skirt suit, the hem of the skirt ending just above the knee, revealing just enough for Ross to appreciate a terrific pair of legs. Topped off with a short white lab coat, the newcomer looked more like a consulting psychiatrist then a pathologist and Ross knew immediately that something was definitely different about this examination of Nugent's, that much was for sure. Ross led the way as he and Drake approached the trio at the table.

* * *

"Ah, Inspector Ross, and the good Sergeant Drake, come in, come in," Nugent urged, "I have someone here I'd like you to meet."

Avoiding the urge to reply that such news was rather obvious, Ross instead replied, "I see, Doctor, and just who is this lady that we are to have the pleasure of meeting?"

"Well," Nugent went on, "As you know, I'm pretty much acknowledged as one of the leading pathologists in the country, and there's not much that leaves me floundering, but this time, I did feel the need to consult another expert in order to give you a true picture of what these remains might mean to your investigation."

Ross ignored Nugent's blatant statement of his own self-importance and waited as the pathologist continued. "Allow me to introduce you to Doctor Hannah Lewin. Hannah's an old friend of mine, and she's a professor of forensic anthropology, at Cambridge."

"Forensic anthropology?" Ross queried.

"Aye, Inspector Ross. My speciality is in working with something a little, er, fresher than our friend on the table, and knowing Hannah was in town for a lecture at the University, I took the opportunity to ask her opinion of our remains."

"I see," said Ross, reaching out to shake hands with Hannah Lewin. The woman however, held her hands up, and stepped back, Ross able to see she was wearing rubber autopsy gloves. "Oops, sorry, Doctor, or should I say professor?"

"Hannah is fine, Inspector," she smiled at him. "I never like all these grandiose titles, do you?"

"Well, no, I suppose not, then you must call me Andy, and this is Izzie," Ross replied, as he nodded in the Drake's direction.

A flicker of recognition passed across Ross's face as he went on, "I think I've heard of you, Hannah. Didn't you assist the police down south with the identification of the bones found in the old factory building in Herefordshire a couple of years ago?"

"You're quite right, Andy," Hannah replied. "It was in Leominster to be precise, an old shoe factory that Samuel Metcalfe used as a burial site for his victims, nine of them to be precise. I was able to determine cause of death and also individual identifications for the majority of the remains."

"Ha, got you," Izzie suddenly exclaimed. "I've seen you on the telly too. You were on that show that told the history of the Viking bones at the settlement in Hillingdale last year, weren't you?"

Hannah Lewin smiled at Izzie's remark.

"I was indeed, Sergeant, er, sorry, Izzie. Are you interested in such things?"

"A real history buff, that's me," Izzie replied. "I love to learn from the past, and the history of our country is really what shapes its future, don't you think?"

"Certainly," said the anthropologist, impressed with Izzie's enthusiasm.

Ross gave an exaggerated cough, eager to bring the conversation back to their reason for being in the autopsy suite. Hannah returned to her professional persona as she spoke again.

"I'm really pleased to meet you both. Doctor Nugent has told me you're very good at your jobs. He speaks highly of you, don't you, William?"

Nugent grunted, obviously feeling a little uncomfortable at Hannah Lewin's bluntness.

"Aye, well, no need to go making them big-headed now, is there lass?"

"Oh, don't be so gruff, William. Now, shall we get on with what we're here for?"

"Aye. Let's do that," Nugent went on, relieved to be back on familiar territory. He looked at Ross and Drake as he now spoke in his usual, professional tones. "As you know, there was really nothing but bones when we finally extracted the remains from the dockside river bed. The lack of hair or any tissue after so many years of immersion, first in the water and then in the mud and silt that had built up in the disused dock area had ruined any chances we may have had of obtaining a good DNA sample and of course, even then, we wouldn't have known what the hell to compare any such sample with. Facial recognition was definitely out of the question, and that's when I thought Hannah's expertise might be of assistance to us."

"You're sure it's been there since before the dock was drained, then?" Drake asked the pathologist.

"Aye lass, I'm pretty sure of it. You see, we know the dock was drained about ten years ago, as part of the urban regeneration plan for the whole docks area. If the body had been tossed in there after draining, it would, I'm sure have been discovered sooner and would not have sunk into the river bed and been buried in the mud as it was when we found him. Hannah has conducted a pretty extensive initial examination in the time she's had available and has some findings to report to you, I'm pleased to say."

"Anything you can add to the investigation will help, I'm sure," Ross replied. "We have very little to go on so far."

"Well, I can't actually tell you too much, but I do have one or two points of interest to give you," Hannah Lewin replied.

As Ross and Drake waited, she picked up a clipboard from the side of the autopsy table and began her report to the detectives.

Chapter 6

The crowd had gone home, and Brendan and the group sat quietly around a table at The Iron Door Club, sipping Coca-Cola through straws as they waited for Marie to bring Mr. Oxley's van round to the front, Mickey's sister having taken on the role of driver for the group whenever she had a free evening. The group's drum kit and instruments were waiting at the rear entrance ready to be loaded into the van as the boys relaxed after another night in the smoky atmosphere of the club.

"Still no sign of our big break then, Brendan," said Mickey. "Even your great master plan didn't work did it? Marie and her mates did all they could to get that Epstein fella in the right place at the right time and we know he's been in a couple of clubs when we've been playing so he must have heard us."

"If he has, that means he doesn't rate us," said Phil Oxley, a hint of sadness in his voice. "Why don't we just admit we're not as good as we think we are? The Beatles are number two in the charts with *Please Please Me*, it's great, and they write all their own stuff, while we turn up everywhere and play cover versions of other people's music. We're just not original enough Brendan. You've got a great voice, lad, but we don't have what it takes to write enough of our own songs, and maybe that's what's holding us back."

Brendan Kane nodded sadly at his friend, knowing in his heart of hearts that Phil was probably correct in his summing up. Yet, something in his heart refused to allow him to give up on his dreams, at least not yet.

Before he could reply to Phil's depressing statement, Marie bounced into the club and called out to the group.

"OK, you lot, who's for home then? Come on, get loaded up, we haven't got all night, you know. I've got work in the morning and need some sleep, even if you lot don't."

The little group began to rise from their seats but, as they did so, Phil Oxley raised a hand to signal them to stay put.

"Listen everyone, before we go, I've got some more bad news."

"Oh God, Phil, what is it now?" asked Brendan, as tiredness suddenly washed over him like a tidal wave. He wanted nothing more than to get home and sleep. He too didn't want to be late for work the next day. Mr. Mason was a great boss, but wouldn't tolerate a lame excuse like sleeping in because he'd been out late at a gig.

Phil's face took on a serious look as the others slumped back into their seats, Marie standing just behind Mickey, anxious to leave and get them all home. She'd keep the van parked outside her home overnight as usual and return it to Mr. Oxley's home the next day as always, on her way to work.

"It's about the van, actually," said Phil. "Dad says he's still okay with us using it at night, but, well, things are a bit tight at present. He's had to let his mate Mick go, and he used his own van to make deliveries during the day, and there just isn't enough work to keep them both 'gainfully employed' as Dad puts it."

Phil's father had been a ship's carpenter, a highly qualified tradesman, until the shipyard where he worked suffered a downturn in new ship-building contracts. Along with others, he'd suffered the ignominy of redundancy, but had used his redundancy payout wisely and started a small, but initially profitable business, creating hand-made furniture. His friend, Mick Donnelly had joined him as a part-time employee, working with Dave Oxley on the manufacturing side of the business and then using his own small van to make deliveries to the homes of customers. With Mick gone, Dave would need his own van to be available every day, and the group would have to manage without his generous loan of the vehicle.

"Maybe you could use the drum kits most of the clubs have in place, Phil," said Mickey, knowing that Phil's drum kit was the largest piece of equipment they had to move from place to place. Most clubs possessed amplifiers they could use for their electric guitars, though he knew it would still be a problem for everyone carrying their instruments, including the acoustic guitars they often used through the streets of Liverpool, on foot or on buses.

"Are you kidding me?" Phil said, a hint of anger in his voice. "I saved every penny I earned from me paper round for three years, and me Mam and Dad paid the rest of the cash for them drums. I know they're second-hand, but they give me the right sound I want, and I'm not about to start using some heap of old crap that everyone and his uncle has probably used for years, and don't forget, I paid three quid to get our name stenciled on the front."

Bassist, Ronnie, always the quiet member of the group now spoke up.

"So, what do we do now, then? Do we give up, pack in the group, like?"

"Not if I can help it," Brendan replied, firmly. "There has to be a way we can carry on. We just need to think it through."

"We can tell the clubs we can only do evening gigs from now on." Ronnie suggested.

"Yeah, then they'll think we're being uncooperative," said Mickey.

Brendan thought for a few seconds, and then said, "Look, for now, nights it is, no daytime gigs, okay? Phil, tell your Dad thanks from all of us. We really appreciate him letting us use the van all this time, and tell him we understand how things stand for him, and we hope business'll get better for him, real soon."

Phil breathed a small sigh of relief. He'd expected a row of some sort after making such an announcement. All in all, he thought, Brendan and the others had taken things pretty well, so far, though he still had another bit of bad news to share with his mates.

"Thanks, Brendan, I'll tell him what you said, but, well, there is one more thing."

Seeing hesitation in Phil's expression, Brendan pressed him further.

"Oh Christ, Phil, for fuck's sake, spit it out, man. How much worse can things get?" Suddenly remembering that Marie was standing behind Mickey, he added, quickly, "Sorry about the language, Marie, love." Marie just nodded at him, knowing he was more than a little worked up.

"It's the petrol," Phil went on. "Dad hasn't minded us using his fuel, up to now, I mean, he knows they're only short trip to most of the clubs and round our houses like, and we pay a bit towards the fuel, but with money short and everything..."

"Is that all?" Brendan sighed. "Tell your Dad we'll put an extra gallon a week in the tank, Phil. That should cover the few miles we clock up when we use it. If we don't have any gigs some weeks, we'll give it a miss, but if we all chip in a bit from our take from each gig, we'll hardly notice a couple of shillings a month."

The club manager was gesticulating to Brendan from the club exit. He needed to lock up and wanted Brendan and the group to leave him in peace to get on with it and allow him to go home. Brendan acknowledged him with a wave, and within a couple of minutes the group was in the van, Marie at the wheel, heading for their various drop-offs.

That night, sitting at the kitchen table, his parents fast asleep upstairs, a sleepless Brendan Kane held his head in his hands, as a wave of depression swept over him. Despite his outward display of positivity in front of the other members of the group, he had a sinking feeling in his gut that was telling him the days of Brendan Kane and the Planets might be numbered. If they were, he needed to formulate a new plan if he was ever going to achieve his dream of pop stardom. Later, in bed, with just the sound of his old Westclox Big Ben alarm clock ticking away on his bedside cabinet, and the occasional creaking sound as the house seemed to settle itself down for the night, the germ of an idea began to grow in the recesses of his mind. The others might not be too keen, he thought, but there was a way forward, and Brendan became determined to explore the avenue that had just revealed itself to him in his most private of thoughts. He suddenly heard the sound of his Dad experiencing a coughing fit in the next bedroom. The thin walls of their house meant that little was private between rooms, particularly in the dead of night, and Brendan was quite used to the occasional sounds of his parents indulging in passionate love-making, though how they still managed it at their age he really couldn't comprehend. *For Christ's sake*, he always thought as the sound of his father's heavy breathing and his mother's gasping, combined with the banging of the headboard against the adjoining wall had kept Brendan awake many a night, *they're in their bloody forties!* Brendan just couldn't imagine being that old, and now he listened as the coughing gradually died away and all fell silent once again.

Brendan's Dad smoked around twenty cigarettes a day, and despite the advent of filter tipped cigarettes which were supposed to reduce the recently announced health risks associated with smoking, Dennis Kane happily continued to smoke the same Capstan Full Strength unfiltered cigarettes he'd always enjoyed. In his mind, filter tips were meant for women and 'pansies', not for 'real' men. He didn't know of one single man down at the docks who smoked filter tipped cigarettes. Brendan's Mum smoked the new brand, Cadets, and even if he'd occasionally smoke one of his wife's cigarettes if he'd run out of Capstan, Dennis would invariably break off the tip and smoke it 'neat' as he put it.

Brendan would occasionally smoke one of his Dad's cigarettes, surreptitiously 'nicked' from his father's packet, as Dennis would never dream of keeping count of his smokes, though he'd happily give one to Brendan if he asked. Trouble was, they made Brendan cough a lot and the last thing he wanted was to break into a coughing fit in the middle of a performance, so he was determined not to become a regular smoker and limited his indulgence to the odd one when he felt in need of a quick 'lift' such as was provided by the nicotine in the little white sticks, and never of course, on the day of a gig. Brendan had noticed his father had been coughing a lot more recently, just a 'smoker's cough' his Dad called it, but Brendan worried his Dad might be suffering from some kind of chest disease as a result of a lifetime's inhaling of the smoke. For now though, such thoughts died away in tune to the gathering silence from the next room and, still thinking of his new master plan for his own future, Brendan Kane drifted into a dreamless, peaceful sleep.

Chapter 7

"Before I tell you what I've ascertained so far, I need to ask you something,"

"Go ahead, ask me anything," Ross replied, wondering just what was in the mind of Hannah Lewin.

"When you searched the area around the site where the remains were found, I presume you found various items?"

"We did, but we have to consider the fact this was a wharf, a dock for loading and unloading of ships, and all sorts of rubbish will have been thrown into the water over the years, and a fair amount since it closed down."

"I know that, Inspector,"

"Andy, please," he interrupted.

"Yes, sorry, Andy. Anyway you found this hammer, right?"

Hannah held up the hammer that had found in close proximity to the skeleton.

"Well, actually, it was Doctor Nugent who found it, as he carried out his initial examination of the remains at the scene. It was quite close by and had obviously also been disturbed by the digger when they were clearing the dock."

"No other tools? Any specific metallic fragments, drinks cans excluded?"

"No, just the hammer. Doctor Nugent thought it may have been the murder weapon."

William Nugent gave a sort of nervous cough, untypical of the man, as he waited for Hannah to continue. Before she did, she beckoned with her hand to draw the two detectives closer to the remains on the table.

"Well, for once, my friend William is in error."

Nugent coughed again, and began to speak.

"Yes, but…"

"Oh, do shut up, please, William. Nobody says you were negligent. You weren't in a position to make a full examination in situ so you couldn't have been expected to see the rest."

Nugent appeared mollified by Hannah's words and stood back a little to allow her to go on.

"Look here," she said, as the detectives moved closer to the table. She held the hammer closer to the skull until it was lined up with the hole that was previously thought to be the cause of death.

"What are we looking at?" asked Izzie Drake.

"Here," said Lewin. "The small perforation in the skull was almost certainly made by the hammer but from the small indentation present, I can almost certainly say this blow, though it would have certainly incapacitated the victim and possibly caused a loss of consciousness, really did not pierce the skull sufficiently far to cause any damage within the brain cavity. And, once the skeleton had been fully cleared of the thick sludge and mud that covered the midsection, we saw these."

Hannah pointed towards the skeletal legs, and Ross and Drake's eyes followed her finger until it came to a stop, and both detectives immediately knew exactly what she was indicating to them.

"Bloody hell," said Ross.

"Oh shit," added Drake.

"Exactly," said Hannah Lewin.

"Not quite what you expected us to find, eh, Inspector?" came the voice of William Nugent, over Ross's shoulder.

"That's why you wanted to know if we found any metallic fragments?"

"Yes, it would have helped of course, but it doesn't change the fact that your victim was shot in both kneecaps before he ended up in the river. I hoped you might have found the remains of the bullets or shell casings from the shooting. They would have helped me to identify the type of ammunition used and therefore give you a possible identification of the type of murder weapon. As it is, I can still hazard a guess, but you need facts, not guesses really."

Both Ross and Drake continued to appear a little shell-shocked at this new revelation. Ross's thought immediately went back in time to his teens, when the TV news and the newspapers were full of stories about 'The Troubles' in Northern Ireland, and the IRA's use of kneecapping as a means of spreading fear among the community, and often used as a deterrent when applied to those they believed had betrayed their cause, perhaps by talking to the police or the troops deployed in that benighted province during that sad time. He decided not to mention those thoughts right now; that being something he would save for discussion between himself and Drake back at the station. The inspector let up a silent prayer that if and when they identified the victim, he wouldn't find himself embroiled in a case involving the terrible and bloody events that had taken place back in sixties Belfast. With the Northern Irish capital lying just across the Irish Sea from Liverpool he knew the chances were high that any number of IRA members and members of their opposition in the loyalist community factions had at any given time used the port of Liverpool as an entry and exit point for their forays to mainland Britain, and the ramifications of having to investigate an IRA killing on his home turf were enough to make Ross shiver involuntarily. For now, though, he eventually asked,

"So, you don't think the blow to the head was fatal, and we now know the victim was kneecapped as well, before being killed, as there'd be little point doing such a thing post-mortem, so I have to ask you, what do you think killed the poor bugger?"

Hannah Lewin stood looking down at the pitiful-looking assembly of bones that lay before them on the cold steel of the autopsy table for a full twenty seconds before finally replying to Ross's question.

"Well, I'd agree with your assumption regarding the bullet wounds to the knees, absolutely no point in taking such measures against a corpse. They certainly would have been excruciatingly painful, but, like the blow to the head, not fatal in themselves, and therefore the only assumption I can make, and it is only an assumption, based on the lack of confirming evidence, is that your victim was probably shot first, and then, while on the ground he was struck on the head and then thrown alive into the water."

Izzie Drake, her face a mask of a mixture of anger and horror now asked,

"Are you saying they, whoever they were, just tossed him in the river like a piece of rubbish and left him to drown?"

"That's my best guess, Sergeant," Hannah Lewin replied. "There doesn't appear to be any other answer to the question of how your victim found his way into the water, does there?"

"That's just horrible," said Drake, who then went on, "What makes you sure the body was thrown into the water, and not into the dried up dock after it had been closed off from the river?"

"That's where we come to the rest of the results of my examination," said Hannah Lewin.

"Please go on, Hannah," Ross encouraged her.

"Well, from the state of the bones I can tell you there is enough evidence to suggest they were immersed in water for a long period of time. Also, there was sufficient detritus found in the immediate vicinity of the remains after cleaning to be able to date some of it, the drink cans for example, and under the remains we found these coins, none of which bears a date later than 1963, not conclusive I know, but they were probably in the victim's pockets and fell through the bones as the clothes gradually deteriorated in the water, hence them being found in the mud immediately below the remains. There were four old cans in the mud we cleared away, two Coca- Cola cans, one Sprite and one

Tizer, and each still bore the date stamps on the base that helped me identify when those cans went on sale."

"You can determine such things after all this time?" asked the sergeant, becoming engrossed with Lewin's findings.

"Oh yes, that's not difficult at all. I've done work around the world on burial sites and communal graves and you'd be amazed at the huge databases that are being built up to assist in the identification of all sorts of artifacts found on and around corpses and skeletal remains."

"Amazing," said Drake, as Ross then also intervened with a question of his own.

"Okay," he said, "but, can you give me anything else at this point that will help us to identify just who the victim was?"

"I think I can," Lewin smiled at the inspector. "I can tell you that the victim was male, which Doctor Nugent of course had already ascertained, I know, and, from the shape of the skull I can tell you the victim was almost ninety nine percent of Caucasoid extraction."

"A white male then?" Ross asked, then added, "but, you said only ninety-nine percent, Hannah. Explain the one percent, please."

"This is Liverpool, after all, Inspector," she replied. "You must remember that over the years there has been a great deal of inter-marriage between people of various races, typical in most large ports around the world. Your victim may have been of mixed race origin, one British parent, the other of any other race exhibiting similar Caucasoid characteristics, but if I had to testify on the spot, I'd say yes, this poor soul was a white male of between fifteen and thirty years of age."

"Okay, I accept that," Ross said, thinking for a moment of his own, mixed-race background, and then, "The bullet-holes, Hannah? Small calibre I presume?"

"Definitely," she replied. "A shotgun would have done far more damage, particularly from close-range."

"Close-range?" asked Izzie.

"Of course. You're not going to shoot someone in the knees from long distance, Sergeant. Whoever did this had to be standing in close proximity to the victim and obviously had to be within close firing range so as to be on target with both shots, so to speak."

"You're right of course. I should have known that," Izzie said, feeling slightly foolish in front of the forensic specialist.

"Don't worry about it," Ross interjected, refusing to criticize his assistant. He knew all this new information was a lot to take in and he'd seen Izzie's face when she'd realised just how the victim had probably been eliminated. It wasn't a particularly good way to go, if there ever was such a thing. "I do have a question, though."

"Of course, please ask anything you want," Lewin replied.

"Leaving the shooting aside for a moment, why didn't the body rise to the surface? I thought dead bodies always floated after a period of time."

You're correct, of course, and under normal circumstances, a body sinks as the lungs fill with water, and stays there until bacteria in the gut and chest cavity produce enough lighter than air gasses, methane, hydrogen sulphide and good old carbon dioxide, at which point the cadaver will float to the surface like a balloon. In the case of this poor young man, something obviously prevented that, which probably means he was weighted down before being allowed to sink into the water. There would probably have been enough heavy items on a dockside for your killer, or killers to utilize as a weight. Or they may have used a number of smaller items and placed them in his pockets, or he may simply have got trapped in some underwater detritus, which held the body down and kept it from floating to the surface. I can take a look at the scene if you like. There may be something that gives me a clue as to what kept the body under water, instead of returning to the surface."

"Thank you, yes that might be a good idea. I'll arrange it and get back to you, give you an escort to accompany you. Perhaps Doctor Nugent would like to go along too?"

Nugent replied enthusiastically to Ross's suggestion.

"Aye, well, that might be a good idea, Hannah. Two sets of eyes and two minds would be better than one, don't you think? Lees can assist us on site, take photographs and record anything we find."

"A very good idea, William," Hannah Lewin responded. "If you make the arrangements, we can make our detailed study of the site whenever it's convenient for you, Andy," she said to Ross.

"Sure, Izzie, can you arrange for D.C. McLennan to pick the doctors up tomorrow morning and take them to the wharf and give them whatever assistance they need?"

"Yes, sir, I'll make sure I see to it when we return to the station," Drake replied.

That one point dealt with, Ross now moved the conversation back to the subject of just who their victim could have been. He directed another question at Hannah Lewin.

"You said you had more information that might help with identification, Hannah?"

"Yes, as a matter of fact, I do. If you look here," and she pointed to what appeared to be a small, but noticeable line across one of the lower bones of the leg. Both detectives leaned in closer to get a better look at what she was indicating. "This is the tibia, and this," she pointed again at the paler looking groove-like line in the bone, "well, this is a sign of a break at some time, long healed by the time of death, possibly occurring some time in the victim's youth, maybe a sporting injury, or an accident of some kind. Oh yes, as I've previously speculated, your victim was definitely young, certainly under thirty five, and most likely around twenty years old at the time of death, give or take a year."

"I see, and you can be reasonably sure of that?" Ross asked, already knowing the answer likely to be forthcoming. Hannah Lewin struck him as not being the sort of person to make such statements without being sure of her facts.

"Of course, Andy. First of all, we have enough teeth to give us a pretty good estimate of age and then there are other contributing factors, most of which are highly scientific and probably wouldn't interest you, though they will be in my final written analysis of the remains."

"Oh, please, go ahead and humour me. Tell me just a little bit about how you determined the age of our victim."

Hannah sighed, thinking the detective was perhaps testing her skills prior to fully accepting her findings. Then again, he had a job to do.

"You really want the text book version? She asked, and as Ross smiled and nodded she simply smiled back and with the words, "Very well," she began. "There are multiple ways that we can estimate how old the person was at the time of death, it's kind of like a puzzle and as forensic scientists, we have to join the dots in order to achieve a result. So, first of all, we can estimate the age of skeletal remains by dentition. You probably know from your experience of similar cases that there are certain teeth that erupt at certain times, etc."

Both Ross and Drake nodded, both understanding Lewin so far, and the scientist carried on, sounding to Ross almost as if she was quoting directly from a text book, so sound was her knowledge, it seemed to him.

"Now, apart from the teeth, we can also determine age from the cranial suture fusion sites, long bone length, though not an exact science, and changes to the pubic symphysis surface. A young adult displays a rugged surface transversed by horizontal ridges and intervening grooves, and the surface eventually loses relief with age and is bounded around the age of 35. Additionally, we can estimate the age of a murder victim by obtaining a radiograph of specific bones in the victim's body, mainly the hand and wrist. By comparing these to an atlas of bone growth, the victim's age can usually be detected."

Hannah Lewin fell silent and looked directly into the eyes of Andy Ross. When he said nothing for a few seconds, she spoke once again.

"I did try to make it as clear and helpful as possible. I hope it made some sense to you both."

Ross smiled and looked first at Drake and then at the pathologist, before finally responding.

"Hannah, you are an undoubted expert in your field and you know damn well we were hardly able to follow any of that accurately but thank you. I believe we got the gist of what you're saying and wholeheartedly accept your findings of our victim's age, don't you agree, Sergeant?" He looked to Izzie for her response.

"If you say we agree, sir, then yes, without a doubt, we agree, most assuredly, we agree."

Izzie couldn't help but grin as she replied to the inspector, and before they knew it, the two detectives, Hanna Lewin and even the usually stiff and gruff William Nugent were laughing together. The laughter served to act as a release of the tension that had built up as Hannah Lewin had delivered her in-depth technical 'lecture' on determining the age of a human being's bones, and as they each returned to their normal, professional demeanors, the pathologist added:

"Oh yes, there was one other thing too. I think you'll find it very interesting,"

"Do go on, please," said Ross.

Lewin walked to the back of the room where a long, counter-top style table ran the length of the wall across the width of the room. Ross immediately recognized the three boxes of possible evidence his team had recovered in the vicinity of the skeleton, in a radius of ten yards from the last resting place of the remains.

"We received these earlier this morning, sent across from your own crime scene people."

William Nugent joined in the conversation again. In fact, Andy Ross was quite surprised to have witnessed the long silence from the big Scotsman, quite out of character from his own experiences with the man. Ross wondered if perhaps Nugent was a little overawed by the skill and expertise of the younger, and certainly much better looking expert who now held the attention of everyone in the room.

"Aye," he said, "And I must say your people turned up a considerably varied collection of items, most of which are probably nothing more than the detritus of many years, having been thrown into the water as nothing more than rubbish."

"Hey," Ross replied, leaping immediately to the defence of his crime scene analysts. "You need to remember, Doctor, that my people had no idea what they were looking for or what might or might not be significant to the case. That body may have lain in place for years or may have floated into its final resting place some time after death so yes; they collected anything and everything that may have a bearing on the case. They had a job to do, and they did it, whilst thanklessly crawling around in the filth and the mud beside that old wharf."

"Och, dinna get yer knickers in a twist, Inspector. I'm no criticizing your people at all. Just mentioning that there was quite a bit of stuff in there for us to wade through in order to locate anything of significance. Perhaps in future, ye'll kindly allow me to finish ma sentence afore ye begin berating me. A'hm just doing ma job you know, same as you and the good sergeant here."

When irate or disturbed, Ross had noticed that Nugent had a habit of slipping into the broadest of Scottish dialects, clearly betraying his Glaswegian roots.

Okay, okay, truce," Ross said, smiling broadly at Nugent. "We're all tired and have been working long hours, so I apologise if I was a little quick off the mark there."

Nugent 'harumphed' and added, "Aye, well, I accept your apology, Inspector, and I apologise too if ye thought I was having a go at your people. Hannah, please go on and tell our friends here what we found."

With his rant over, Nugent's accent had moderated to his usual slight Scottish lilt, a fact Ross noticed and found instantly amusing, though he fought hard to keep himself from grinning at the humour he felt at the realisation. Izzie Drake, however, found herself thinking the same as her boss and covered her mouth with one hand, effecting a louder than necessary cough as she did her best to cover the smile that had appeared on her face.

"Are you alright?" Lewin asked, as Izzie finally brought her smile muscles under control and retuned her hand to its place at her side.

"Yes. Thank you. I'm fine, just a tickle in my throat. I'm sorry to have interrupted you, Doctor…er…sorry, I mean Hannah. Please show us what you've found. Sorry boss," she said as she turned to Ross, who knew quite well what she'd been doing.

A Mersey Killing

"No problem, Sergeant Drake. Happens to us all. Please, Hannah, carry on."

Lewin lifted the lid off one of the stiff cardboard evidence boxes and lifted out a small, see-through cellophane packet and walked back to the small group gathered around the autopsy table. As she placed the packet on the table she also took another, similar packet from the right hand pocket of her white doctor's coat, which she preceded to place next to the first packet.

"When the skeletal remains had been completely cleaned this little item was found under the pelvic area, obviously having at one time been in the victim's trouser or jacket pocket. As you can see, not only is it the same material as the piece your people discovered, but when placed together, they make a rather nice fit, making them, in my opinion, two parts of the same whole."

"The piece of plastic!" Izzie exclaimed.

"Well no, not plastic actually," Lewin corrected the sergeant.

"Really?" Drake asked.

"Go on, please Hannah," Ross urged. "If it's not plastic, then just what exactly is it?"

Before replying, Hannah Lewin opened the two packets, and removed the two small pieces of material, then brought them together to show the detectives how they fitted together to form an almost perfect heart-shaped item.

"Does it remind you of anything, now?" she asked.

"Well, now you mention it, no, not really," Ross replied.

"It does resemble something I've seen before," Drake answered, "though I'm not sure what, or where."

"First of all, it's not just a piece of plastic," Lewin went on. "It's what's known as tortoiseshell and this," she held up the two pieces of material so they could all see clearly, "if I'm not very much mistaken, is a guitar pick, or plectrum, an item commonly made from the material. If I'm right, and I think you'll find I am, then it's quite probable your victim was a musician, Inspector."

52

"Well, blow me down," said Ross, "and it's Andy, remember. A guitar plectrum, of all things."

"Yes," Drake now added. "I knew I'd seen something like it before, way back at school, when some of the kids took guitar lessons, though I'm sure they were more of the shape of a small shield."

"They come in quite a few shapes and thicknesses," Lewin said. "I believe it depends on whether the musician was a lead or rhythm guitarist, playing a steel stringed instrument or an acoustic model or something like that, though, not being a musical person, I'm not certain on that."

Ross hesitated for a second, almost tempted to inject the light-hearted comment that he was surprised to find there was something Hannah Lewin didn't know, but diplomacy won out and instead he replied, "Hannah, thank you. If you hadn't identified it, we'd have probably ended up discounting it as just a piece of useless plastic, with no relevance to the case. Now we know we're probably looking for a possible young guitarist, dating back to the sixties, young, having suffered a broken leg at some time in his youth."

Hannah smiled. "I know it's not a lot to go on and certainly far from a positive identification, but..."

"Hey, it's a damn sight more than we had to go on before we walked in here this morning, right, Izzie?"

"Right, sir," Drake replied, as she wondered to herself just how the hell they were going to find anyone from thirty something years ago matching such a brief and sketchy description, but, as Ross had just said, it was a step forward, albeit a small one.

Chapter 8

LIVERPOOL, THE SUMMER OF '63

"You've got to be kiddin' us, man," Mickey Doyle shouted at Brendan's latest pronouncement.

The four group members, Brendan, Mickey, Ronnie, and Phil, together with Marie were sitting on the grass in what they all knew simply as 'The Park.' The Park was in fact a small grassed area just a couple of streets away from Brendan's home, identified, as it's grand name suggested by the council's generous provision, in one corner of the fenced-in area, by a number of items of play equipment designed to amuse the younger children of the area. As well as four traditional swings the play area possessed a slide, a small roundabout, powered of course by the eager little hands that would propel it in a whirl, and a 'Bobby's Helmet', the odd, conical structure that served as a kind of rocking roundabout-cum climbing frame, and the source of many resulting accidents involving cut and bleeding knees, elbows and fingers and the occasional broken arm from the numerous accidents that seemed to proliferate during the warm sunny, summer days such as today. Brendan's favourite, in his younger days, had always been the little hand-push roundabout, which he and his pals from the local junior school would spin round and round until they couldn't go any faster, then grab a hold of one of the metal hand rails, jump on, and then bend over the small domed centre of the apparatus, peering through the small gap between the dome and the wooden slats of the seating area, and then suddenly jumping up and feeling the eerie sensation of accompanying dizziness that inevitably followed. It took quite some doing to remain in control of one's faculties in such a dizzy state and more than once, Brendan and his mates had lost their hand-hold and fallen from the roundabout, propelled by centrifugal force onto the hard concrete surface into which the structure was mounted, and of course, more cuts and bruises would be sustained, but, what the heck, it was fun, and that was what being a kid was all about, after all.

The summer holidays being in full-swing, the play area was currently busily occupied by a number of young children all enjoying the same activities Brendan and the other members of the group had indulged in some years earlier. It was from one particularly nasty fall from the Bobby's Helmet that the twelve-year old Brendan Kane had broken his left leg and subsequently spent many weeks in a plaster cast, steadily gathering the signatures of friends and relatives on the plaster-of-Paris cast, until the day it was removed, and Brendan almost reluctantly said goodbye to the crutches that had made him feel just a little important and had drawn much sympathy on his behalf from his school mates. It was a strange coincidence that lead guitarist, Mickey Doyle, had suffered a similar fracture at the age of thirteen, not from the same source, but during a school football match, an accident which in Mickey's case had left him with a barely noticeable limp, and ended his own boyhood dream of becoming a professional footballer. Mickey found himself watching as a group of young boys enjoyed an impromptu game of football, using jumpers for goal posts, just as he and his mates had done.

Now, however, the raucous laughter of the boys and the happy squeals and screams of the girls in the play area seemed to disappear into the ether as all eyes and ears among the group sitting on the grass, some hundred feet or so from the swings, turned their attention to Brendan and Mickey as a potentially explosive argument gathered strength. Marie's transistor radio was blasting out Elvis Presley's *Devil in Disguise,* the current number one in the UK Top Twenty, but Marie turned the volume down as the argument gathered momentum.

"I mean it, Brendan. How the fuck can you even think of doing this to us?" Mickey asked, his voice growing louder with almost each word that spilled angrily from his lips.

"Look, Mickey, everyone," Brendan said, defensively, "I just said the word *might,* not *definitely,* at least not yet."

"Fuck you, Brendan," Mickey went on. "You're talking about splitting the group up so you can go off and try to make it on your own. Just where the fuck would that leave the rest of us, eh? Three piggin' years we've stuck together through thick and thin, trying to make it, man. Now, just because things are a bit tough, you want to fuck us off and go and do your own thing. It stinks, man, that's what I think."

"Yeah," Phil Oxley now joined in, "You just wanna dump us, ain't that right, Brendan? Christ, man, I know we've not done so many gigs since we lost the use of the van in the daytime and the night jobs have dropped off a bit, but that's no reason to split up. We're still popular and getting bookings, even if they're a bit fewer."

"Look," said Brendan, realising his new plans weren't exactly being received well, "I said we ought to try one last time to make a breakthrough, and if things don't work out then it might be time to think about splitting up. We wouldn't be the first group to give up you know. Not every group in the city or in the country, come to that, makes the big break, I just think that if that happens, I might stand a chance of a solo career as a singer, that's all."

"Oh yeah, and just how do you propose we go about tryin' to make this last attempt at making the breakthrough? I'm thinkin' maybe you've got some plan up your sleeve, right? Ronnie asked in a less threatening voice than the others, trying to be the voice of reason as the argument became more heated.

"Well, yeah, I have as a matter of fact, if any of you are prepared to hear me out without wanting to knock me block off."

"Go on then, mister bloody big-shot Brendan Kane," said Mickey, his voice laced with a heavy dose of sarcasm. "Let's hear your latest master plan."

Silence fell for a few seconds as Brendan gathered himself for a moment, and almost prophetically the sound of *Do You Want to Know a Secret?* from the local group, Billy J Kramer and the Dakotas, came from Marie's radio.

"Okay, then. Here's what I'm proposing," Brendan began, "I've been doing some adding up and such like and the group's bank account is pretty healthy, considering the fewer gigs we've been doing."

"It shouldn't take a fucking Einstein to work that out," Mickey interrupted. "We haven't exactly spent much of it apart from money for travel to gigs and replacement strings and things."

"Are you going to listen to me, or not?" Brendan bit back at his friend.

Mickey held both arms out to the side in a gesture of supplication.

"Sorry, do go on, mastermind." Mickey's voice was heavy on cynicism as they waited for Brendan to continue.

"Right, what we do is use the majority of what we have in the bank to produce a demo disc. We record a couple of covers that demonstrate our talents to their best effects, that's vocals, guitars, and drums. We show how well we harmonise together, and use two tracks that will show how diverse we can be in style and performance. Then, we send them to every major record company, and every independent producer we can think of. It won't cost the earth for the stamps, and then, we wait a reasonable time to see if we get any replies. If we do, great, but, if we go past an agreed cut-off date and we haven't heard anything positive, then we seriously consider the fact that we're just not going to make it, guys, and the time will have come to try something new."

"With the 'something new' being you going off on your own to seek your fame and fortune," Phil Oxley said, scornfully. Brendan knew he was on the verge of losing not only the support but the friendship of these three young men with whom he'd put in so many hours over the years in their attempt to break into the music business. He tried to remain calm as he went on,

"Look, fellas, it might be the best thing for all of us. You guys can keep the name of The Planets if you want to, or change it if you want. Maybe with a new lead singer, you might still have a chance of getting somewhere."

"And just maybe we'll sink like a stone being thrown into the Mersey," said Ronnie. "We'd have no chance without you fronting us, Brendan, and you know it."

Suddenly, as the sound of The Searchers' *Sweets for my Sweet* faded away on the radio, Marie Doyle unexpectedly entered the boys' argument.

"Here, you lot, listen to me a minute would you? You might not like it, but I think Brendan's right. You've all tried really hard to make it, but just how many years are youse goin' to keep floggin' away at this? I think if you were going to make it big, someone would have spotted you by now and offered you a contract. I'm not saying youse guys are crap, 'cos you're not, you're good, dead good, but so are a lot of groups out there, okay? Brendan isn't saying he wants the group to split up just like that, is he? He wants to give it one more go and if it works, you'll all be happy. If it doesn't, you can't say you never tried, and if Brendan wants to try and make a go of things on his own, then youse lot should just accept it and wish him luck. That's what I think, anyway."

A shocked silence fell over the group. Marie's defence of Brendan's idea had truly taken the others by surprise.

"Are you serious, sis?" Mickey Doyle spoke, incredulous at his sister's apparent betrayal of the group.

"Course I'm serious," she replied. "Look, listen to me. I've driven you lot all over Liverpool, Birkenhead, even as far as St.Helens, Wigan, and even bloody Southport to gigs over the years. I might not get up on stage with you and play the guitar or drums, but I feel just as much a part of this group as the rest of you, so I think I've got some say in this, don't you?"

A general murmur of agreement gave Marie the impetus to continue.

"You know as well as I do that loads of groups have started out and then folded in a lot less time than we've been together. Want me to name a few? There was The Trojans, you know, Dave Morris and his mates, The First Sound, The Lee Gibson Band, and lots more. They all gave it their best shot but had the sense to know when to quit. You lot have got to be realistic too. No one wants you to succeed more than me after all the time I've given to the group, but sometimes we can't always have what we want. All of you have been dead lucky to be able to get time off work from your bosses when we had daytime gigs, and God knows how many sickies you've all pulled from time to time, when we've got back from a late night gig and you've been too knackered to get up and go to work the next day, but that's not really professional is it?"

A kind of pall appeared to gather over the little group as Marie fell silent. The children carried on playing on the swings and roundabout, the sound of Peter, Paul and Mary's *Blowing in the Wind* issued forth from Marie's transistor radio, but all these peripheral sounds simply dimmed in the minds of the members of the Planets as Marie's words sank home and for a few seconds, no one seemed prepared to break the silence.

Eventually after what felt like an age to everyone but in fact was only the space of about ten seconds, her brother Mickey sighed heavily, and in a softer voice than the one he'd previously displayed during the voicing of his anger at Brendan, said,

"Wow, sis, you've really given this some thought haven't you?"

"Yes, Mickey, I have."

"I know you're usually the sensible one in the family, but I'm still not sure about this."

"Me neither," said Phil, while young Ronnie Doyle stayed silent, not sure how to react to his elder sister's words.

"And you think I am?" Marie said to her brother. "Come to that, do you think Brendan's sure? None of us is sure, Mickey, but nothing is certain in life is it? Brendan is being realistic, that's all, and I think we should listen to him and give things one more try, a big push to try and get you noticed and if it fails, then, well, let's do what he suggests, and at least give one of us a chance to make something of their talent. Brendan might just have a chance as a solo performer, and you never know, if he makes it, he might just need a backing group one day in the future, right Brendan?"

"Well, there's always a possibility," Brendan replied, caught on the hop by Marie's comment. The truth of the matter was that he hadn't thought things through that far ahead.

Within minutes, thanks to Marie's intervention, tacit agreement was reached to go along with Brendan's idea. It had become clear to the others that Brendan had basically made his mind up and if they were going to split up, better to do so after having a last attempt at achieving recognition in the business. At least, they all agreed, if nothing else, they'd each have a copy or two of their demo disc to play to their children or grandchildren in the future, some proof that they had at one time nearly made it as recording artists.

As they left the park on that warm, sunny, summer's afternoon, they would also have been surprised to learn that Marie had not only stood up for Brendan's idea from any altruistic sense, but that for nearly three months, she and the lead singer had been indulging in a much closer relationship than any of them could have possibly dreamed about, one that would have also caused consternation in other ways if their relationship became public knowledge. There were other factors involved in the couple keeping their liaison secret, though for now, love's young dream made them both oblivious to the possible consequences of their current course of action.

A slight breeze rustled the bushes that lined the park boundary and a small gust caught the hem of Marie's new, floral summer dress, revealing a little more of her legs than she'd like, and she quickly smoothed her dress down, but not before attracting a wolf-whistle from a young man walking past on the other side of the street from the park. Mickey quickly shouted, "Fuck off, pervert," and the group couldn't help but laugh, as Marie blushed with embarrassment. As a bank of thick cloud rolled in to blank out the sun, Marie walked behind the others, lost in thought, and then turned off the radio. Somehow, the gesture seemed appropriate.

Chapter 9

Izzie Drake stood before the mirror on the rear wall of the ladies wash-room a few minutes after she and Ross returned from the mortuary. Unlike the smaller mirrors over the wash basins on the other side of the room, this one was a full-length version, thoughtfully provided by someone who'd had the foresight to realise that ladies, in particular, might want to check their overall appearance before venturing onto the streets to continue the fight against crime. In practice, it allowed uniformed officers to ensure nothing looked out of place and that their appearance was of the standard required of their position as represen-tatives of Merseyside Police. Whatever the reason, Izzie was grateful for the chance to quickly take stock of herself after the day's earlier activity.

For some reason, despite the mortuary being one of the most anti-septically clean places she'd even known, Drake always felt as if she needed a bath or at the very least a shower, after visiting the place. It just had that effect on her, as if being surrounded by the presence of death and decomposition somehow tainted her hair, her clothes, her entire being, and as much as she tried to talk herself into ignor-ing such irrational feelings, the damn place still affected her like this, every time.

Peering at herself in the mirror, she saw a moderately (she thought), pretty woman, still with a youthful look about her at the age of twenty nine, her shoulder-length hair a dark brunette with a lustrous sheen that needed no special shampoos or treatments to maintain its good looks. A quick wash in the morning and she was good to go, ready to face the day and whatever it may bring, even a visit to the morgue. Izzie considered herself lucky in that respect, and her trim figure was accentuated by the well-cut navy skirt suit she'd chosen for the day's work. With the warmer weather she felt more comfortable in a skirt, though she'd be the first to admit there were times when trousers definitely proved a rather more practical option.

Satisfied with her appearance, and relieved to be back on the familiar grounds of the headquarters building, she made her way back to the C.I.D. section and in particular, the office of Andy Ross.

As she knocked and entered the D.I's office, Izzie found Ross sitting behind his desk, a cup of coffee in one hand and a copy of Hannah Lewin's preliminary report in the other. Lewin had worked fast in getting it typed up and faxed through to Ross in double-quick time.

The look on Ross's face was one she'd seen before and knew only too well.

"You've got your worried look on your face, sir."

"Very observant of you, Izzie. You're right of course. Tell me, what did you make of Doctor Lewin and her conclusions?"

"Oh, she of the very beautiful face and shapely body, and..."

"Okay, Izzie, that's enough," Ross grinned. "Any chance you can be serious here, bearing in mind my worried look, you know, the one you seem so concerned about?"

Izzie grinned back at her boss; pleased she'd been able to levitate the moment into something a little less morose.

"Well yes, right you are, sir. I know she appears to be on the ball and a complete expert in her field, so I've no reason to doubt a word she said. But, that's not what's really on your mind is it, sir? It's the bullet wounds to the kneecaps; the possible IRA connection isn't it?"

Ross smiled an ironic smile. He knew his sergeant was familiar enough with his moods and expressions to be able to read him very well indeed, one of the traits that helped them work so well together. "I can't hide anything from you, can I, Izzie? And yes, you're quite correct in your assumption. I remember the sixties only too well, growing up with the non-stop news of gradually escalating troubles over the water in Northern Ireland. I just hope we're not walking into a potential minefield here, with political implications if we find evidence of an IRA or Provo killing having taken place here in the city. With the peace process well underway nowadays, the last thing the politicians will want is something like this. Then again we may find the murder has nothing at all to do with the Irish, and that would at least be a weight off my mind."

"So, a nice domestic would do the trick, eh, sir?"

"No murder at all would be preferable, Sergeant, but, if we have to solve one, then yes, I'd rather it didn't have connections with either political or terrorist activity."

"So, what's our next move?"

"We need to speak to the contractors who were working on the reclamation for a start. I know Hannah and Fat Willy Nugent are going to check the site out tomorrow, but there's a chance the workmen who made the original discovery have knowledge or information they don't even realise they're in possession of."

"Such as, sir?"

"If I knew that, we wouldn't be wanting to speak to them, now would we, Izzie?"

"Very true. Anything else?

"You know as well as I do that identifying the victim has to be our first priority. We don't have a lot to be going on with but at least Hannah Lewin has given us a couple of scraps that might help."

"You mean like the broken leg, for example?"

"Exactly. Assuming our victim is local, it might help if we can start by getting local hospitals to check their records for all youngsters between, let's say ten and fifteen to begin with, let's say twenty five to thirty five years ago. Heck of a list probably I know, but we have to begin somewhere. Local kids would obviously be treated locally so let's check all Liverpool and Birkenhead medical facilities first. It's possible our lad came to school from Birkenhead through the tunnel. I know quite a few secondary pupils made that journey, even in my day."

"You want me to take charge of that sir, or hand it to one of the team?"

"You do it, Izzie. I don't want one of the junior officers taking it on and then not being as thorough as I know you will be. It is a pretty thankless task I know, but…"

"Say no more, sir. I know what you mean. I'll get on it soon as we've finished here."

"Good, thanks Izzie. While you're doing that, I'm going to disappear for a while. I'm going to have a word with the boss, see if he has any contacts with anyone involved in the anti-terrorist people from back then. I want to know if there was any significant IRA or Loyalist activity going on in the early sixties that might have had any connection with the city. If anyone knows, the anti-terrorist squad will, I'm sure."

"We still don't know if the body was dumped in the water before or after the warehouse facility and the wharf ceased operating, do we, sir? Who do you think should check that out?"

"Let's give that to D.C. Ferris. He's got great local knowledge. God knows why that man has never managed to pass his sergeant's exams, he's a first class officer but seems a bit devoid of ambition."

"Maybe it's got something to do with his son, sir? You know, not wanting to commit to the extra hours he'd have to put in if he got his stripes."

Ross silently berated himself for forgetting an important part of one of his junior officer's backgrounds.

"I'd forgotten he has a disabled child. You're probably right, Izzie. Thanks for reminding me."

"That's okay, sir, and don't go beating yourself up just because you can't recall every aspect of every officer on the team's home lives. How he manages sometimes, I don't know. It must be awful trying to juggle his shifts with the need to make sure he or his wife can take the lad for his regular dialysis sessions and check-ups and everything."

"Very true, Izzie. So, yes, Okay, put Ferris on checking up on the old warehouse. I want to know everything possible about the place. Exactly who owned it, when it closed, who worked there, the whole kit and caboodle."

"I'll put him on it before I start checking the hospitals, sir. Anything else for now?"

"No, I think that's enough to get things moving in the right direction. So you go and do what you have to do while I go and have a word with D.C.I. Porteous."

As Izzie Drake left the office and closed the door behind her, Ross rose from behind his desk, picked up the as yet quite thin case file, and quickly followed his sergeant out of the door, and made his way to the office of the Detective Chief Inspector. Things were starting to move, albeit slowly, but any progress was better than none at all, he mused as he walked, deep in thought, to instigate his next line of inquiry.

Chapter 10

COLE & SONS

Detective Constable Paul Ferris was in a hurry. Dashing from the kitchen of his neat, two-bedroom semi-detached home, still chewing on a piece of toast, he grabbed his jacket from the coat hook at the bottom of the stairs, throwing it on whilst running upstairs as fast as he could. His wife, Kareen, turned and smiled at her husband as he scurried into the bedroom of their son, Aaron.

"Running late again, darling?" she grinned, as she helped five-year old Aaron on with his shirt.

"Hi, Dad," the youngster said, cheerfully.

"I have to go, Kareen," Ferris gasped, out of breath. "It's a murder inquiry and the boss has given me an important slice of the investigation to work on. I need to get to the station and go through some files before I head off to the docks."

"The docks? Who got killed? You hardly said two words last night when you came in."

"We had other things on our minds last night, remember?" said Ferris, happily remembering a very intimate evening with his wife the night before. They had always made a point of trying to avoid work talk in the evenings, and Paul hadn't mentioned his current assignment yet. He'd normally have told her about the new case over breakfast, but today was different as Kareen had to take Aaron for dialysis for his failing kidneys very early, and had been forced to forego their usual breakfast chat. Paul Ferris replied to his wife, looking at his watch as he did so.

"Well, that's it, babe, we don't know who got killed."

"What? Someone's dead and you don't know who it is? When did this happen?"

"Er, about thirty years ago."

"Thirty *years*. Are you kidding me?"

"It's a skeleton, not a body."

"Paul, make sense will you?"

"Kareen, babe, I've really got to go. Tell you later, okay?"

Quickly kissing his wife on the lips, Ferris dashed from the room, almost tripping over one of Aaron's toy cars which had been left strategically right behind where he stood.

"Be careful, Paul," Kareen shouted, but Ferris was already halfway down the stairs, and in seconds he was out the door and pressing the unlock button on his car's remote. Another twenty seconds and the Ford Escort disappeared round the corner at the end of the street and Paul Ferris began his first full day on the investigation.

* * *

Once at his desk, Ferris lost no time in booting up his computer. One of the reasons Ross loved having Ferris on his team was the D.C's aptitude and skill in all computer-related tasks. Put simply, Paul Ferris and computer technology appeared made for each other. While Ross struggled to master the art of creating and sending an email, Ferris had the talent to use a computer to produce results Ross could only dream about. The current task assigned to Ferris was, by his own standards pretty mundane and not too challenging, but that did nothing to reduce the level of importance attached to the information he'd been asked to find. Having been fully briefed the previous day by Izzie Drake, Ferris had already sent inquiries to various organizations that would hopefully provide him with what he sought.

Most important of all had been a request for information on the company of Cole and Sons, sent the previous afternoon to Companies House in London, where details of the company registration should be available. Having checked his email and seeing nothing from his contact in the capital, Ferris picked up the phone on his desk and in a couple of minutes was engaged in conversation with Jane Hill at Companies House, a useful contact he'd cultivated during a previous investigation.

"Paul Ferris, here Jane, Merseyside Police. You helped me out last year with the Briggs investigation. Hope you remember me."

"Of course, Paul. Good to hear from you. How are you? And that little boy of yours?"

"I'm fine, Jane, thanks. And Aaron's doing okay, still needs regular dialysis though. He's on the waiting list for a transplant, but, well, you know…"

"Sorry, Paul, yes, I know it's hard and very much a waiting game, but I'm sure things will work out for him. But, you didn't call me to talk about Aaron, did you? It's about the request you sent yesterday, Cole and Sons, right?"

"That's right," Ferris replied. "I know it's early, but wondered if you might have anything for me yet. This time, it's not just a fraud case we're investigating. We're looking into a murder that took place some years ago, on the wharf where Cole's warehouse is, or was, seeing as it's been closed for a long time, as far as we know."

"Hold on a minute, please Paul." He heard the sound of Jane's fingers tapping on her keyboard, followed by the sound of rustling paper, and then her voice came back on the line.

"Sorry about that. I'd done some of the checking before I went home yesterday and just wanted to confirm something before ringing you myself."

"You have something for me then, Jane?"

"Yes, I'll send you this in an email in a few minutes but for now, I'm sure you'd like to hear the gist of things, yes?"

"Yes, please Jane. Give me what you've got so far."

"Right, seems Cole and Sons of Liverpool was an old family firm, and the 'Cole' of Cole and Sons was Josiah Cole, who incorporated the business back in 1898."

"That long ago?" Ferris asked, a little surprised the warehouse had been around over a century.

"That's what it says here," Jane Hill went on, "and Josiah eventually handed over the company title to his sons, Walter and Frederick Cole, who held joint ownership of the business until the company ceased to exist, as far as our records show, in 1955."

"Right," Ferris said, thoughtfully. If what Jane said was true, and it would be of course, the warehouse either changed hands or stood empty for a long time prior to the redevelopment of the docks area. He knew he still had work to do.

"Jane, what exactly was Cole and Sons business? You know, what kind of a warehouse was it?"

"It was a bonded warehouse, Paul."

"Hmm, interesting," Ferris replied. A bonded warehouse would have held dutiable goods, wines, spirits, tobacco and so on prior to it being exported, or until duty had been paid to allow it into the UK. Definitely enough to provide a motive for nefarious goings on, he surmised, but then realised the place had probably been closed for years before the murder. *Think again, Ferris*, he thought to himself. "Don't suppose your records show what happened after the Cole's closed the place down?"

"Sorry, Paul. There's only so much we can do for you. Our records can only tell you if a business was registered at that address and as far as those records are concerned, no company has ever registered as operating from that address. Maybe the Cole brothers are still alive, and may be able to help you, or perhaps your local Chamber of Commerce will have more local knowledge of what use the place was put to, if any, after it closed down."

"Understood, Jane, and thank you. The Chamber of Commerce is the next stop on my list. Would be odd if a place like that just stood empty for so many years without being utilized in some way. Anyway, it's been good talking to you again, and thanks for all your help."

"My pleasure, Paul. Sorry, it wasn't much. Hope you find your killer before too long though. You take care of yourself, and that family of yours."

"I will, and you look after yourself too. Thanks again."

After hanging up on Jane Hill, Ferris turned his attention to the local Chamber of Commerce. The secretary of the Chamber informed the detective that the old Cole & Sons warehouse had in fact been used on a number of occasions over the years, having been rented out to various small companies or individuals on short-term leases. A mail order business, a small local company specializing in the manufacture of bespoke toilet seats, and a parcel delivery company were among those who'd rented the warehouse for varying lengths of time, anything from three months to a year, but as far as the secretary was concerned, the place had then fallen into disrepair, with a leaking roof among its drawbacks, some time around nineteen sixty five, ten years after the Coles had closed their business down. When asked by Ferris if he knew whether either of the Cole brothers was still alive, the question drew a blank reply. He was advised to have a word with the chairman of the chamber, who, he was reliably informed, had been around for as long as anyone could remember and if anyone knew anything about the Cole brothers he'd be the man. So, armed with the telephone number of George Irons, Ferris took a quick coffee break and ten minutes later picked up his phone once again.

* * *

"Well, well, Walter and Frederick Cole, now there's a blast from the past," said George Irons, after Ferris had explained the reason for his call.

"You knew them, then, Mr. Irons?"

"Oh, yes, Detective Constable, I knew them both well. They were very active in the affairs of the Chamber at one time. I was a much younger man back then and ran my own private coach business of course. Did great business with workers outings to the seaside and so on. Thirty something years ago, seems like a lifetime ago, but anyway, that's not what you want to know is it? As for the brothers, they took over the bonded warehouse when their father died, and carried on a successful business until poor Walter succumbed to a heart attack quite early in life. He'd never married so the business passed completely to his brother. Freddie carried on for a year or two but quite frankly, I don't think his heart was in the business any longer and he eventually decided to pull out. I remember he put the business up for sale as a going concern, but there were no takers. Anyway, one day he announced he'd closed the place down, just like that. The workers were all laid off, all the fixtures and fittings were sold, fork lift trucks, the lot."

"How many people worked for, er, Freddie, Mr. Irons?"

"Ten, maybe twelve, if I'm not mistaken."

Ferris refrained from asking if the chairman knew any of the workers. That would be too much to ask for after so many years, and of course, he wouldn't have had anything to do with the day to day business of the warehouse.

"Well, thanks for the information, Mr. Irons. Just one more question, and I'll leave you in peace."

"It's a pleasure, Constable. Please, ask away."

"Well, the place had lain idle for years before the docklands redevelopment began. Do you know if it's been used for any other purpose over the years, and who actually owns the place?"

"Can't help with the first part of that question, I'm afraid, but as for who owns it, well, as far as I'm aware, Freddie Cole still owns the property. I'm sure he'll be able to tell you if he's rented it out at any time over the years. If he has, it would probably have been through a letting agent, and they'd be the ones to tell you what it's been used for and who rented it."

Ferris thanked George Irons, there being nothing else he felt he could learn of any relevance from the man. Next on his list had now become Frederick, 'Freddie' Cole. A quick check of the electoral register gave Ferris the address he needed and he decided that it was time to get some fresh air. A personal visit would give him the chance to get out from behind his desk and he was becoming deeply interested in the case. What, if anything did the Cole's warehouse have to do with the skeleton found deep underneath the waters, or in this case, the mud of their former dockside wharf?

Ferris left a message on the desk of Sergeant Drake, who he knew was out doing the rounds of local hospitals, before heading out of the building and was soon on the road, to the district of Wavertree, where Frederick Cole was registered as residing.

* * *

Izzie Drake, meanwhile, was enduring something of a frustrating morning. She'd been amazed at how many hospitals in the area simply didn't retain records as far back as she needed to go. Of those that did, she'd faced the usual 'patient confidentiality' argument, until she'd explained this was a murder inquiry and she wasn't looking to obtain personal medical histories of any particular patient, just that in order to identify a victim, the police needed to ascertain certain information which thankfully the various hospitals finally provided.

In the period she was looking at there had been a total of two hundred and sixty six cases of youngsters in the target age range with broken right legs in the period. She felt relieved she wasn't looking for a left leg victim, of whom there'd been over a hundred more in that time. Thankfully, she'd been able to cut that list down by deleting any who hadn't suffered the break to the femur. Next, looking at the area of the break from the photos provided by Hannah Lewin she was able to eliminate a further thirty five as the fractures had occurred too low down on the bone. She'd finally whittled the list down to forty two possibilities. As Lizzie sat at her desk, feeling a headache coming on, she wondered how she could reduce the list further before presenting it to Andy Ross. She rose from her desk, walked across to the coffee machine at the far side of the C.I.D office, and poured herself a mug of very strong, black coffee, returning to her desk with her mind ticking over, still working on her next step. As Izzie opened the top drawer of her desk and took two Advil tablets from a bottle she kept there, ready to swallow when the coffee cooled a little, Paul Ferris walked into the room, fresh from his sojourn to Wavertree.

He raised a hand in greeting as he caught sight of his sergeant, and after a long and fairly hit and miss morning for both officers, it was time to compare notes.

Chapter 11

NEW BRIGHTON, MERSEYSIDE, 1964

The seaside resort of New Brighton, part of the town of Wallasey, sits at the northeastern tip of the Wirral peninsula, across the Mersey from its much larger neighbour, Liverpool. The resort received its name from its founder, Liverpool merchant James Atherton who, in 1830, purchased most of the land at Rock Point, and began to develop it as a genteel and fashionable resort for the gentry of the day much like other fashionable resorts of the day, and in a similar way to the better known South Coast resort of Brighton, hence 'New Brighton.' The New Brighton Tower, modelled on the famous Eiffel Tower, and the tallest in the country was opened in 1900 but closed in 1919 and was dismantled by 1921. Below the tower stood the Tower Ballroom, which remained after the tower closed and retained its use as a venue for entertainment, and hosted numerous concerts in the 1950s and 60s, including performances by The Beatles, and other international stars. Brendan Kane and the Planets made two appearances at the ballroom which would eventually be destroyed by fire in 1969.

For now, however, the resort played host to a young couple seeking something of a getaway from their usual habitat and surroundings. Brendan Kane and Marie Doyle had found themselves growing ever closer together over the preceding months, and it was now evident to both of them that their feelings were deep and of a highly romantic nature. In short, Brendan and Marie were in love.

Marie was dressed in a new cream and silver striped blouse and her new knee-length half-lined navy skirt that fitted her perfectly and accentuated the femininity of her figure. Her stockings were new, too, and she'd borrowed a pair of black shoes with two inch heels from her best friend, Clemmy. She'd bought the skirt especially for this day with Brendan, who wore a crisp blue shirt and a pair of new jeans he'd ordered from his Mother's mail-order catalogue, together with his black 'winkle-picker' shoes, highly polished as always. Marie thought he looked incredibly handsome.

Having crossed the Mersey on the early morning New Brighton Ferry and then spending an idyllic two hours listening to music on Marie's transistor radio, whilst kissing and canoodling on New Brighton Beach, Brendan and Marie now sat holding hands in a small caravan, rented by Brendan for one week on one of the popular caravan sites that had sprung up to cater for holidaymakers in the area. Though he knew he and Marie would probably only have one or two opportunities to slip away to the caravan during the week, he felt it was worth the financial outlay in order to give them these precious hours together. Living in such a close environment as they did with the group, privacy was something that didn't come easily, and the couple had no wish to make their feelings for each other public knowledge, at least not yet. Marie had stood by him when he'd made the suggestion about trying the demo disc and possibly breaking up the group if things didn't go their way, and the others might feel aggrieved if they thought she'd only supported Brendan because of her feelings for him.

Having spent months making their plans for the disc, Brendan Kane and The Planets had finally recorded their demo disc the previous week and now awaited the delivery of the consignment of their 'last chance' recording to arrive, after which they'd circulate copies of the disc as previously arranged. After that, their fate would be in the lap of the Gods, and the various record producers and recording companies.

"You're sure nobody knows we're here, Brendan?" Marie asked, nervously.

"I told you, we're totally safe here," he replied. I booked this place weeks ago, paid cash and used the name Davis, so please stop worrying."

"You do know I have to be back home by tea-time or me Mam and Dad'll wonder where I am?"

"They think you're out with the girls, right?" Brendan asked.

"Yeah, they do. They don't mind me doing stuff with the group, Brendan, but this, well, it's different isn't it?"

Brendan slowly slipped an arm round Marie's shoulder, pulling her closer to him.

"Everything's okay, Marie, honestly. You trust me, don't you?"

"Course I do, you silly bugger. I wouldn't be here with you now if I didn't trust you, would I, you dozy mare?"

Brendan laughed, a laugh Marie had always found infectious, and in seconds the couple were both giggling and then, suddenly, Brendan leaned in close and kissed her, passionately, on the lips. The kiss seemed to last for ages, and Marie finally pulled away gasping.

"Wow," she exclaimed.

"You're so beautiful, you know that don't you?" said Brendan, not really expecting a reply.

"If you say so, Brendan," Marie managed, before he kissed her again, a long, slow kiss that made her knees go weak and made her feel a dampness between her legs. Brendan didn't say anything else, but his hand slowly began to make its way under the hem of Marie's skirt, gradually feeling its way upwards along the length of her leg, stopping for a moment as his fingers reached the top of her stocking. Marie felt her breath coming in small gasps as the thrill of the moment began to overtake her.

"Don't stop, Brendan, please," she gasped, her voice husky as Brendan's hand moved higher and Marie opened her legs a little to allow him access to her private places, where no man, before today had been granted access. His fingers gently slipped into her panties and found their way in between her legs, where Brendan found her wet and ready for him to take things even further.

"Wait," she whispered in Brendan's ear, and she gently removed his hand from its place under her skirt. Marie stood up and slowly raised the hem of her skirt, allowing Brendan a view of her shapely legs and then slowly she reached behind her, unzipped the skirt and allowed it to fall to the floor. Her panties followed, and as she stepped out of the tiny white lace-trimmed knickers, Brendan gazed almost in awe at the sight before him. Marie knelt in front of him and reached up to unfasten the buttons of his shirt, which soon fell open to reveal his chest, covered in dark brown hairs, and she ran her hand through the hairs for a few seconds, bringing a tingle to his skin and Brendan felt himself growing harder in anticipation of the next few minutes. Marie moved to try to remove his jeans, but, making her wait to prolong the moment, Brendan kissed her once again before leading her by the hand into the dormer area of the caravan, where he quickly closed the curtains and pushed Marie, very gently, on to her back on the bed, which he'd made up the previous day, hoping for just such an eventuality. Marie lay on the bed, looking up at him as he slowly reached down, took her face in his hands and kissed her again. His hands reached behind her and after a little fumbling, he managed to unfasten Marie's bra, and as he pulled it from her, he was able to marvel at the sight of her perfectly formed breasts, the nipples dark and engorged and standing erect, perhaps as erect as he was at that moment. He reached out and gently took each one in turn between his fingers, manipulating them gently as Marie closed her eyes and reveled in the new and exciting feelings his attentions were setting off in her body. When he stopped using his fingers and moved closer, taking her left nipple in his mouth, Marie shuddered with the pure thrill of what was happening to her, and a small groan escaped from her lips.

"Oh, God, Brendan. What are you doing to me? I've never felt like this before. I think you should know, though, that I've never, well, you know, I've never actually done this or anything like it before."

Brendan shushed her gently, placing a finger on her lips and whispering back to her, "Neither have I."

"But, you must have," Marie exclaimed in surprise. All those gigs, the girls flocking round you, surely you..."

"Never, Marie. I've fancied you since the day we met, and I've waited all this time in case I saw some sign from you that you felt the same."

"I never knew."

"Well, you know now,"

"Mmm, "she gasped as Brendan fell silent once more and moved his mouth to take her other nipple between his lips. This time, he allowed his teeth to gently nip at her breast, and Marie could barely contain the wave of arousal that swept through her body. Brendan took hold of Marie's hand and guided it to the growing bulge in his jeans. She didn't need telling what to do as she lowered the zip and moved to unfasten his belt. As she pushed his underpants down, his erect penis sprang from within, and Marie gasped again at the sheer size and weight of the throbbing thing that she held in her hand.

Neither of them could wait any longer, and as Brendan's fingers probed inside her wet opening, she spoke in that husky, expectant voice once more, "Please Brendan, make love to me, now."

Brendan Kane didn't need any further encouragement and he pushed Marie onto her back on the bed and pushed her legs apart. Marie helped by spreading her legs wide, and as Brendan moved on top of her, she took hold of him and guided him into herself, giving out a small cry as he penetrated her for the first time.

"Are you alright?" Brendan asked as she cried out.

"Don't stop, please, don't stop," she replied.

Brendan soon settled into a slow, rhythmic movement in and out of her virgin vagina, and Marie urged him to move faster until he could no longer hold back and he felt a massive release as he ejaculated into the girl of his dreams. Marie suddenly felt a welling up of emotions coming from deep within and she cried out again as her body was overtaken by a series of spasms that seemed to go on and on, until they finally subsided, leaving her breathless and amazed at their intensity.

"Oh, my God, Brendan," she exclaimed. "That was amazing. I wonder if it's like that for everyone the first time."

His breathing returning to normal, Brendan looked down at Marie and smiled. "I don't know and don't care. All I know is it was great for us, and that's all I care about. I love you, Marie."

"I love you too, Brendan," she replied, as he slowly pulled out of her, and rolled off to lie beside her. Marie just lay there with her legs wide apart for a minute, and then, pulling herself together, she rose from the bed and reached for a box of tissues that she saw on the small shelf in the room. She self-consciously wiped herself and leaned over to pick her underwear up from the floor, and was soon dressed once again, standing beside the bed, smoothing her skirt down as Brendan finally rose, pulled up his jeans and fastened his belt and zip. They sat gazing into each other's eyes for what seemed an age, as Marie's radio played quietly in the background. Marie had discovered the pleasure of listening to the new pirate radio station, Radio Caroline, broadcasting from somewhere in the North Sea, and like many teenagers, derived an almost guilty pleasure from tuning in to the illegal broadcaster. When Kathy Kirby's *Secret Love* came bursting forth from the tiny radio's speaker, the couple stared harder at each other and almost simultaneously spoke the same words, "That's our song!"

It was impossible to say whether either one of them had thought about using any form of contraception, as neither of them mentioned it to the other. The time of general knowledge on the use of contraception and family planning was years away in the early sixties, so it was quite possible that neither one of the couple possessed much awareness or understanding on the subject. For now, both Brendan Kane and Marie Doyle were filled with the first flush of love and sated from the resulting consummation of their newly-declared feelings for one another.

A short time later, after locking up the caravan and making their way back to the beach, where they enjoyed a half hour lying on the sand together, holding hands, saying little, but occasionally staring longingly into one another's eyes, the time came for them to make their way back to the ferry terminal, where, all too soon, they were crossing the Mersey, back to Liverpool and the reality of their everyday lives. They would get the chance to return to New Brighton later in the week, but for now, home beckoned for them both. Marie would soon be sitting down to tea with her family, while Brendan would have a bite to eat and then wander down the road to the pub to enjoy a pint or two with his Dad, who, Brendan thought, hadn't been himself recently, appearing to have lost weight and coughing a lot.

As they kissed each other goodbye after the ferry docked, Brendan felt a deep longing for Marie as he watched her walk away towards her bus stop, her hips seeming to sway with additional sensuality as her flared skirt added to the sway of her hips, and later that night, both of them would dream of their time together earlier that day, and look forward with intense anticipation to their next planned visit to the caravan, their own secret place.

Chapter 12

"Well, Paul, any progress?" Izzie Drake asked D.C. Ferris as he took a seat in the chair at the end of her desk.

"Of a sort, Sarge," he replied, "though I'm not sure it'll get us very far with the case."

"Okay, just tell me what you discovered in deepest, darkest Wavertree."

""Strange place, Sarge. Lots of nice houses and yet there's loads of students from the university living out there, too. Did you know lots of well-known people lived there at one time, and some still do?"

"Go on then, I know you're dying to tell me who."

"For a start, John Lennon and George Harrison lived there at one time, and Kim Cattrall, you know, the actress?"

"Yes, I do happen to know who Kim Cattrall is, Paul, thank you."

"Leonard Rossiter, and lots more."

"Thanks for the celebrity guidebook tour," Drake grinned. "I take it you looked all that up on your trusty computer before you even left the building this morning?"

Ferris smiled back at her and replied, sheepishly, "Well, yesterday afternoon actually. Just wanted to check out the territory before hitting the streets, like, you know?"

"Bloody hell, Paul. You sound like something out of 'Hill Street Blues'. Come on now, what did you discover from the surviving brother?"

Ferris pulled his notebook from his pocket, opened it up to check his notes as he spoke, and began:

"Frederick, he made me call him Freddie by the way, Cole, is the last surviving member of his family. Seems he and his brother Walter, who he referred to as Wally, were always close and worked well together after the death of their father, Josiah. Freddie became sole proprietor of the business after Wally's death from a heart attack, and he carried on running the business successfully, according to him, until his wife, Mary died in a road traffic accident five years after Wally's death."

"Any suspicious circumstances surrounding the wife's death, d'you think?"

"I seriously doubt it, Sarge. He was in the car with her at the time. Poor bloke was left blind in one eye and with one leg shorter than the other as a result of the crash. Still has a limp and walks with a stick. Didn't stop him running the warehouse though, until Mary died and he told me his heart just went out of it, and he tried selling up but there were no takers."

"So, what did he do with the place?"

"He handed redundancy notices to his ten staff, paid them off more than generously, sold off the fixtures and fittings and placed the warehouse in the hands of a commercial letting agent. Over the years a few small companies and individuals rented it on short term leases but the cost of continually maintaining the fabric of the building itself made the whole thing a financial liability. When the redevelopment of the docklands area began and the council approached him with a view to him selling the warehouse and land for future redevelopment, he jumped at the chance to offload the place. He sold up, over a year ago, and as far as he's concerned, the council will probably be selling it on to some property developer who'll build luxury apartments on the site."

"And that's all you found out?"

"Well, yes, and a couple of names of the companies who leased the place, but they all seem to have come along well outside the time frame we're looking at for the murder."

Izzie Drake leaned back in her chair for a few seconds, lost in thought. Finally, she spoke again.

"It may not seem much, but you've managed to eliminate certain people and organisations from the investigation."

"I have?"

"Yes, it's now that obvious none of those who used the warehouse after Frederick Cole closed the place could have been involved if they came into the picture years after the death of the victim. If what Cole told you is true and we don't seem to have any reason to doubt his word at this point, the warehouse was closed, standing empty and mothballed at the time of the murder so the chances of the murder having anything to do with the goods that would have been stored in a bonded warehouse are also zero. Whatever happened on the wharf outside Cole and Sons' warehouse took place long after the closure and had no connection to the business previously carried out there. That may not seem much, but it is progress of a kind, Paul."

"Glad you see it that way, Sarge. How did your hospital visiting go?"

"Pretty much inconclusive, I'm afraid. I've managed to narrow the list of potential victims down to about forty five, but don't see how we can possibly trace every former kid who broke his leg back in the sixties. Some will have left town, others may have died, and some will just have dropped off the radar. I don't want to sound negative, but I'm just not sure if this case is going anywhere. If we can't identify the victim, what chance do we have? It happened over thirty years ago according to forensics, and I don't see the Chief Superintendent letting us spend too many hours on it, what with all the current crimes on the books that need resolving."

Drake knew their chances of success in the case were virtually non-existent without that vital piece of evidence that might give their victim a name. Until they had that, the remains in the old dock were just that, a set of bones, remains of a nameless victim of violence who would probably never be identified, a crime forever unsolved.

* * *

Detective Chief Inspector Harry Porteous looked across his desk at Andy Ross. He'd been unable to give his D.I. much to go on with regards to the subject of terrorist activity in the city in the nineteen-sixties. He knew Ross was fighting what appeared to be a losing battle with the skeleton case, as he thought of it, and wasn't sure just how long he should let his murder squad spend time on the problem of the bones in the dock.

"Like I said, Andy, when you first called me I spoke with my contacts at the Anti-Terrorist Squad, and as far as they're concerned, there was nothing going on in the city around that time. Of course, it's possible the IRA and the Loyalist groups used us a point of entry or exit to the mainland, but no evidence exists to suggest any terror cells were actually active here at the time."

"Right, sir, so my question is, just how far do you want us to take this inquiry?"

"I can't afford to let you spend much longer on the case, Andy. We need our people working on active cases, rather than a murder that took place thirty-odd years ago. I know every victim is entitled to justice, but if we can't I.D. the victim, we can't possible catch the killer. You say Dr. Lewin is going over the site of the discovery once again, so let's see if her search uncovers anything else. If not, and if your people haven't found anything during the inquiries you've got them conducting at present, I think we need to gradually wind this inquiry down."

Ross fully understood his boss's point, and for the most part, agreed with him, though it rankled with him that a murderer would appear to have got away with a violent killing and had managed to escape the retribution of the law for over thirty years.

"Just give me a couple of weeks, sir, please. I don't want to give up without giving this a really good try. Someone killed that young man, and I want to find the bastard who kneecapped and bludgeoned a young man and probably threw him alive into the Mersey to drown in agony."

Porteous swivelled his high-backed executive chair round until he was facing the large plate glass window that gave his office a great view over the city he and his men and women did their best to protect. He stared off into space for a few seconds, as Ross patiently sat waiting for a decision. His mind made up, the D.C.I turned his chair back to face Ross.

"One week, Andy, that's the best I can do. If you can't make any progress in that time, we close the case, and mark it unsolved, Okay?"

Ross nodded, pleased to have been given some time, at least, to pursue the case. The nameless victim still had a chance to find justice. Leaving Porteous's office, he made his way back to his office, suddenly feeling an urgent need for a strong cup of coffee, and a crisis meeting with his team of detectives.

Chapter 13

The phone call Andy Ross received the following morning came as a pleasant surprise. The feelings of negativity and impending failure began hanging like the Sword of Damocles over the Inspector and his team since the previous afternoon. As much as none of them felt good about the possibility of allowing a murderer to go free, even after such a length of time, the prospect of being pulled off the case loomed large and such a result was abhorrent to every member of Ross's small team. Even young Detective Constable McLennan appeared to have lost some of his normally infectious enthusiasm.

"We're not going to just give up though, sir, are we?" the young D.C had asked. "I mean, it's still a body, isn't it, that is, I mean, I know it's a skeleton, but it's a victim, murdered, right? Our duty must be…"

"Please do not try to tell me what our duty is McLennan. As much as I sympathise with your youthful exuberance and sense of justice, we have a duty to follow the orders of our superior officers, and if D.C.I Porteous says we close the case in a week, we close it. If we want to keep the investigation alive, we have to identify the victim, got it?"

"Got it sir. Sorry, sir," McLennan had replied, looking rather sheepish and shamefaced at having voiced his opinions so strongly. In truth, Ross had every sympathy with young Derek McLennan. He too hated the thought that they'd quite literally unearthed a murder victim from many years earlier and due to lack of clues and identity, they could be forced to close the case almost before it had got off the ground, thus allowing the murderer to continue living in the belief that he or she had got away with their crime, scot-free.

"Ross here," he spoke as he lifted the receiver and held it to his ear.

"Andy, it's Hannah Lewin."

"Oh, hello, Doctor Lewin."

"It's Hannah, remember? And listen, you know you said William and I could go and have another ferret around the skeleton recovery site?"

"Uh huh," said Ross, suddenly feeling a sense of anticipation at the way the forensic scientist was speaking.

"Well we did, go for another dig that is, and we've just returned to the lab. I really think you should come down here and see what we found."

Now Ross was as alert as he could possibly be.

"You've got something?" he asked

"We've got something," she replied. "How long will it take you to get here?"

"I'll go find Sergeant Drake and we'll be there within the hour, and Hannah?"

"Yes?"

"Well done, and thanks."

"You don't know what we've found yet. Isn't it a bit premature to be thanking me?"

"Just let me be the judge of that, okay?"

"Okay," she replied as she replaced the phone on its cradle.

"Izzie," Ross shouted at the top of his voice. "Get in here, now, and bring McLennan with you."

Soon afterwards, Ross, Drake and young Derek McLennan were in the car heading for the mortuary. Ross had made the decision to include the young detective constable in the visit in order to give the man added experience, and in view of McLennan's earlier statement about the case, he wanted to show him that they were, in fact, doing all they possibly could. Perhaps a visit to the morgue would give McLennan something of a reality check. It might just make him aware of the difficulties the case presented, and anyway, it was time he saw how the youngest detective on his team handled such a visit.

Peter Foster was once again on duty in reception and this time smiled warmly in recognition as Ross and Drake walked up to this cubicle cum office, closely followed by D.C. McLennan,

"Back again so soon, Detective Inspector?" asked Foster. "You must like it here."

"Needs must I'm afraid, Mr. Foster. You seem a lot happier today than when we called last time."

"Ah, a good win at the weekend, Inspector, always cheers me up for the week."

"I see," said Ross, "an Everton supporter eh?"

"Correct," Foster replied,

"Me too," said Ross, and Foster beamed at him as he identified himself as a fellow fan of Everton Football Club. A wry smile on the face of McLennan gave him away as a fan of the red half of the city, in the form of Liverpool F.C. The young constable maintained a diplomatic silence in the presence of his boss.

Foster buzzed the three officers through and they were soon back in the presence of Doctors William Nugent and Hannah Lewin, Lees the assistant lurking in the background, and on this occasion, another man stood beside Hannah Lewin.

"Ah, come in, please, Inspector," William Nugent urged. "Sergeant Drake, good to see you again, and who might we having the pleasure of entertaining here?" he said indicating young Derek McLennan.

"Good morning Doctor," Ross replied. "This is Detective Constable McLennan, the newest member of my team. Thought he'd maybe learn a thing or two from joining us this morning."

"Aye, a good idea, I'm sure. Pleased tae meet ye, laddie," Nugent reached out a hand to McLennan, who shook hands firmly with the pathologist. "A fine handshake ye have, laddie. You'll go far, I'm sure."

McLennan blushed and Ross came to the rescue of his embarrassed young officer.

"And who have we here, may I ask, Doctor?" his eyes turning to indicate the newcomer. The answer came from the man himself, dressed in a plain navy blue suit, white shirt and red bow-tie which, to Andy Ross immediately screamed 'academic' who quickly walked round from the other side of the autopsy table, his hand outstretched in greeting. The man's black shoes were polished to an almost mirror finish. As Ross politely shook hands with the newcomer, the man swiftly identified himself.

"Alan Slade, Inspector. Please to meet you."

"That's *Professor* Alan Slade," Hannah Lewin interjected. "Alan's a forensic orthodontist."

"Ah, I see, I think," said Ross.

"Hannah asked me to give her a second opinion on the teeth in your mystery skull, Inspector. Hope you don't mind," Slade said.

"Not at all," Ross replied.

Hannah Lewin quickly added,

"Alan is a freelance expert in his field, Andy. I know how frustrating this case is proving to be for you and thought Alan might see something I haven't that might help identify our victim."

Ross nodded, "And have you found anything new, Professor?"

Slade glanced at Hannah before continuing.

"I can't exactly say what I've found is new compared to Hannah's previous analysis, but I can confirm that the amalgam used in the fillings in the victims mouth are a silver amalgam typically in use during the late fifties, early sixties. What we call composite amalgams came into regular use during the sixties but this amalgam pre-dates them so we can certainly say that victim received the fillings in his younger days. I've taken a full set of dental x-rays which we can normally use to generate positive identity, but we would need the patient's dental records against which we can compare the x-rays."

As a look of disappointment appeared on Ross's face, Izzie Drake spoke the very thoughts in his mind.

"So we're really nowhere nearer to a positive I.D. are we?"

"That really depends how you look at it," Slade replied. "It's probably true that a lot of dental surgeons who were actively practicing in the fifties and sixties are now either retired or deceased, but we still have a chance of making a positive identification, if your victim was treated at a practice that is still in existence. What you need to do is send copies of the x-rays to each practice in the city and ask if they match any young male patients, probably of junior school age, from your timeframe. The other thing I can confirm is that your victim was certainly no older than twenty one or maybe twenty two at the time of his death. I presume you'd like the exact details of how we determined the age, Inspector?"

"I'll take your word on that for now, Professor, but would like a written copy of your findings as soon as possible, please," Ross replied, a hint of optimism creeping into his voice. It wasn't much, but it was a tiny glimmer of hope provided by the joint efforts of the pathologists. "McLennan, as soon as we get back to the station, I'd like you to compile a list of dentists in the city, and as soon as the dental x-rays arrive you can circulate a request to all dental practices in the area in the hope that one of them might have the records of the deceased. It's a long shot after all this time, but well worth the effort."

"Will do, sir," said D.C. McLennan, as he wrote his orders up in his notebook.

"There's something else," Slade said.

"Go ahead, Professor," Ross spoke with expectation in his voice. He was beginning to warm to this dapper little man.

"Well, back in the nineteen fifties and early sixties, I do believe there was a system in operation where what were known as 'school dentists' would visit schools in the area, mostly infant and junior level I think, and carry out routine dental checks. It's possible the education department might be of some help in that area of investigation?"

"Hmm, a little more complicated to check out with the all the changes in the education system over the years, but yes, thank you,

Professor, it's an avenue worth pursuing if we come up empty-handed with the dentists. Anything else?"

"Just that your victim was well-fed, the teeth showing no signs of poor diet or undue decay for their age."

"Right, well, thank you for that, and thank you to you too, Hannah for having the Professor here take a look at the teeth."

"I'm glad it may have helped," said Hannah Lewin. I know I told you that teeth can play a big part in identifying the dead, but even we forensic pathologists need a point of reference in order to come up with a definite identification. But all this leads me on to the real reason William and I asked you here today."

"There's more?" Ross asked.

"Oh yes, isn't there, William?"

"Aye, that there is, lass," Nugent replied. "Go ahead, Hannah, you tell them. After all, you were the one who had the brainwave in the first place."

Lewin now asked the small group to follow her to the counter top that stood against the far wall of the room. Standing there was a battered and faded boot, still easily recognisable as being of the western, or cowboy style of footwear. In addition, propped up against the wall itself where the counter top ended was the rusted, misshaped carcass of an old bedstead, little more than a few springs and a partial frame, with one remnant of a leg barely attached at one corner.

Hannah first of all indicated the rusted old bedstead.

"One thing we discovered when I was working abroad, with mass graves or any old burial sites where water was involved, was that heavier items can often find their way down through muddy river bottoms and so on into the next layer of strata, mud, or whatever. William and I, together with Mr. Lees, spent a morning getting down 'n dirty in the old dock until we came up with this old thing, and the boot, possibly the pair to the remnants your people found. I think you might just find that this is the reason the body never floated back to the surface when it should have done."

"Of course," said Drake. "The body could have sunk and got caught in the old springs of the bedstead. The boots would have got trapped by the springs and prevented it from floating."

"That's precisely what I believe happened, Sergeant," said Lewin. "I think you might even be able to date the boot as well. It's degraded a bit but should still be identifiable. It certainly appears to have been an expensive item, not some cheap imitation leather or synthetic. Whoever owned it and its partner would have treasured such a pair of boots, I'm sure."

Feeling they'd learned all they could from the current visit, Ross thanked the three scientists and he, Drake and McLennan headed back to Merseyside Police H.Q. where McLennan eagerly separated from the two senior officers, eager to 'get his teeth' into his new role in the investigation. He knew it wouldn't be easy but was determined to do all he could to effect an identification through the dental records check. Until the x-rays arrived from Professor Slade later that day, he'd prepare the ground by compiling a list of all those dental practitioners he'd need to contact. Andy Ross and Izzie Drake had just returned to Drake's office and were reviewing the information they had to date when the phone on Ross's desk began to ring. "Does someone have eyes in my walls, Izzie? Two minutes back in the office and the damn thing rings."

Izzie Drake smiled as she watched Ross reach out and pick up the phone.

"D.I. Ross," he snapped into the offending instrument.

After a few seconds, he spoke again.

"You have got to be joking." A pause as he listened again and then, "Well for Heaven's sake, get someone to show them to my office, right away, Miller."

Replacing the phone on its cradle, he looked at Izzie Drake and said, sounding much calmer than he felt, "That was Sergeant Miller on the reception desk downstairs. He says there are two men standing in front of him who claim to have information relating to the identity of the skeletal remains found, at the wharf near Cole and Sons warehouse. Apparently, they'll only speak to the detective in charge of the investigation. They'll be here in a minute, soon as Miller can get someone to escort them up here."

"That's amazing, sir. Let's hope they have genuine intel. Do you want me to leave you to speak to them in private?"

"No, Izzie. Stay here. Whatever these guys have to say, I want you to hear it too. Make sure you take notes of everything they have to say."

Ross quickly re-arranged the papers on his desk in an effort to make it look a little more business-like in front of his visitors, but within a minute a knock on the door signalled their arrival. *Maybe it's time our luck changed,* thought Ross as he motioned to Drake who moved to the door, to usher their potential informants into the office.

Chapter 14

MEMORIES

Izzie Drake thanked the female uniformed constable who'd escorted the two men up to Ross's office and led them in and repeated the names given to her by Constable Greening at the door.

"Michael and Ronald Doyle are here to see you, sir."

Ross looked at the two men, both probably in their fifties, who'd walked into the room, and, even without being told their names, he'd have had no problem in discerning them to be brothers. Although the elder of the two was rotund and showed evidence of a beer drinking habit, evidenced by his overhanging belly, and the leaner of the two appeared fit and more meticulous in his dress and demeanour, their facial characteristics were such that the familial resemblance was inescapable.

"Come in, gentlemen, please. Have a seat." Ross gestured to the two chairs Izzie had recently placed in front of his desk in preparation for the interview. The two men sat, and the elder brother spoke.

"We'd prefer Mickey and Ronnie if you don't mind."

"Sure," Ross replied. "I'm Detective Inspector Ross, and this is Detective Sergeant Drake," he went on, as he indicated Izzie, who'd taken up a standing position near the door. "The desk sergeant tells me you may have some important information for us relating to recent events?"

"Yes, we do," said Mickey. "First of all, we saw this," and he took a folded up newspaper from the inside pocket of his brown leather jacket and passed it across the desk to Ross. It was a copy of the Liverpool Echo, opened at the page where the Force's Press Liaison Officer's release to the press had been printed. It had been a short piece, merely stating that skeletal remains had been discovered in the vicinity of a former warehouse in the city's docklands area and that the police were pursuing inquiries in an attempt to identify the victim, the remains appearing to be between thirty and forty years old.

"I see, please go on."

"Well, I saw it first, and then when he came round to my house, I showed it to Ronnie and we both thought the same thing."

"And just what was this, 'same thing' you both thought of?" Ross asked.

Mickey looked as if he was on the verge of tears, and looked at his brother, who now spoke for the first time.

"We didn't just jump to conclusions, Inspector. You have to understand that this has hung over us for a long time, and we might be wrong in our assumption, but, well, we think you might have found our sister, Marie."

Ross's heart sank. Of course, the press release hadn't given any indicator of the gender of the victim, and he wondered how to let the brothers down gently. First, however, he thought it prudent to probe a little deeper.

"I'm sorry to tell you that the remains that were unearthed were those of a male, not a female, and therefore can't be the remains of your sister."

Ronnie and Mickey looked at each other, and it was plain to Ross that a certain amount of confusion existed in their minds. Perhaps a little relief that it wasn't their sister, but at the same time a continuation of some long-held stress that held both men in its thrall.

"Oh," said Mickey, and "We seem to have wasted your time, Inspector," Ronnie added.

Ross looked up at his sergeant, standing by the door, and she nodded back at him, instinctively knowing where he was about to direct the interview.

"Mickey, Ronnie, please, it might be important and helpful if you can tell us why you thought the remains could have been those of your sister. When did she go missing, and what exactly led up to her disappearance, because I'm presuming you're telling us she'd been gone for a long time?"

Mickey still appeared quite upset, and he gestured with his hands for Ronnie to tell their story. After taking a few seconds to gather his thoughts, the younger of the Doyle bothers began his tale by first passing a photograph across the desk, which Ross picked up and smiled as he saw the subject of the old black and white image.

"This was you?" he asked.

"Yes," said Ronnie. "We were both in a pop group back in the early sixties, Brendan Kane and The Planets. I know you won't have heard of us, but we did okay for a while, even played at The Cavern and The Iron Door, and all the major clubs in the area. We really thought we had a chance to follow in the footsteps of The Beatles, Gerry and The Pacemakers and their ilk. Sadly we never quite made it. Mickey was our lead guitarist, and I was the bass player. A chap called Phil Oxley was our drummer and Brendan Kane himself was lead singer and rhythm guitar."

"And Marie?" This question came from Izzie Drake, who'd moved from her place by the door to take a seat in the corner, off to the side of Ross's desk.

"Marie was our sister, of course, but not a part of the group, as such. But, back in the early days she often drove the van for us, ferrying us to and from gigs. At first, we used our Dad's van, but when his business began to fail he laid off his mate who had a van too, and we were restricted to only using it at night. Anyway, Marie was kind of like an honorary member of the group, always with us, and we'd not have got as far as we did without her."

Ross felt there was something more here, and wanted to hear the rest of the Doyle's story.

"So, what happened, Ronnie? You said you didn't make it, so what happened to the group?"

"Well, we gradually got fewer gigs when we had to stop playing at lunchtimes, and one day Brendan dropped a bombshell, saying he thought we should cut a demo disc and if it didn't get us a recording contract, he wanted us to split up, end the group, you know?"

"And you weren't too happy with that?"

"No, none of us were. We'd been together for about five years as a group by then. We probably knew he was right, deep down but we felt as if he'd betrayed us all, wanting to just give up and then he said if we did, he'd be going on to try and launch a solo career. You can imagine, that went down like a flippin' lead balloon. We were in the little park near where Brendan lived and I can remember it was a really warm summer's day. We'd been arguing about the future for a while and the thing was, when he'd first announced his plan, Marie had actually agreed with him, which kind of took the rest of us by surprise. Anyway, to cut it short, we made the demo disc at a studio in town, long closed now, by the way and Marie went and helped Brendan to mail copies to just about every recording studio and management agency in the country. As you've probably guessed it never got us anywhere and a few months later the group spilt up as we'd reluctantly agreed and Brendan went off to start what he believed would be a new, solo career."

"But that didn't work out for him either, did it, little brother?" Mickey joined the conversation, his words tinged with a bitterness he found hard to disguise.

"No, it didn't." Ronnie continued. "He tried and failed to make the breakthrough on his own. After a couple of years, his solo career had died and the last we heard, Brendan was planning on going to America. He thought he'd have a better opportunity over there, more potential exposure, as he thought the States might prove a better market for a solo singer."

At this point, Mickey Doyle felt the need to interject.

"Yeah, but there was worse to come, Inspector Ross. None of us knew that Brendan and Marie had been secretly 'carrying on' together for years, sneaking off to make love whenever they could. Marie knew our parents wouldn't approve of her having sex outside marriage. They were dead straight, you know, real old-fashioned about those things. It wasn't all as free and easy as everyone thinks back in the sixties you know."

Ronnie took over once again.

"Anyway, one day, everything came to a head. There was a massive row between us all, and well, we never saw Brendan after that day, and soon after that, Marie disappeared too, but because she was an adult, and because we had no proof whatsoever that foul play was suspected, the police at the time either couldn't or wouldn't do much when we reported her disappearance to them. To be honest, we, and Mickey here, especially, have been doing all we can to trace her over the years. When we saw that report about the skeleton in the Echo we thought…well…you know what I'm saying, right?"

Ross thought carefully as he hesitated before answering Ronnie Doyle. A theory was forming in his mind, and he needed to ask just one question to confirm whether the wild idea that had formed as he'd listened to Ronnie's story might be possible. Eventually, he decided to test his theory.

"This is all very interesting, Ronnie, but of course, my priority is identifying the remains we found at the old wharf. I sympathise with your loss in regards to your sister's disappearance, and from what you've told me I have the very strange feeling that Marie may be connected to our current case. You coming here today may just have been the 'wild card' we've been waiting for, the chance to begin putting this case together at last."

"In what way, Inspector? You said the skeleton was male, so it can't be Marie," said Ronnie, looking a little confused.

"Let me just ask you one question, please, well, maybe two."

"Okay, go ahead."

"You'd both known Brendan since you'd been boys growing up together, yes?"

Both men nodded yes.

"Can either of you tell me whether, at some time during his school life, Brendan Kane suffered a broken right leg, and whether, round about the time of him supposedly leaving you all behind to go off to America, he owned a very expensive pair of brown cowboy style boots?"

The Doyle brothers gaped open-mouthed at Ross's words. The detective might have been a mind reader as far as they were concerned.

"How the fu... er, sorry. How the heck do you know that, Inspector?" said Mickey.

"The answer's yes to both questions," added Ronnie. "He broke his leg in a playground accident and those boots were Brendan's pride and joy. He'd ordered them especially from America. How do you...?"

Ronnie fell silent in mid-sentence as he caught on to Ross's train of thought. He spoke again.

"You think those bones belong to Brendan, don't you, Inspector? You think he never went to the States; that he died all those years ago and no-one knew about it."

Andy Ross chose his next words very carefully. If the bones were indeed the mortal remains of Brendan Kane, the Doyle brothers just might be considered potential suspects, although them coming forward like this made him seriously doubt the possibility. They'd hardly come in here after all these years if they'd been responsible for putting the body in the water in the first place.

"I think there's a strong possibility, yes. I need to know a lot more before we can confirm it. For now," he turned to Izzie, "Sergeant Drake here will go and get us some coffee, and, if you're not in any great hurry, I'd like you to tell me more, and especially about the last time you saw Brendan Kane and your sister, in as much detail as possible."

Izzie Drake nodded and left the office to return soon afterwards with coffee for all four of them. Ross had allowed the men a five minute break to gather their thoughts while she'd been absent and now he turned to Ronnie once more.

"Ronnie, please, think hard, and take me back to the nineteen sixties. Tell me exactly what happened."

Ronnie Doyle closed his eyes, and as he allowed his thoughts to wander back in time, the memories came flooding back...

Chapter 15

1966 AND ALL THAT

Nineteen sixty-six had been a good year so far for the people of Liverpool. The blue half of Merseyside had celebrated an F.A. Cup triumph for Everton, while the reds of Liverpool had claimed the league title. All this was followed by England's memorable World Cup victory in a thrilling final at Wembley against West Germany. Musically, The Beatles continued to dominate the pop charts, with *Paperback Writer* hitting the number one position in June. Liverpool's own darling of the pop charts, Cilla Black released the beautiful *Don't Answer Me* in the summer after earlier recording the title track to the Michael Caine film, *Alfie*, with Burt Bacharach.

For the music industry in general, there had been a few trials and tribulations, with Radio Caroline South's pirate radio ship *MV Mi Amigo* running aground in January on the beach at Frinton, and in other news the country had been horrified by the terrible case of the Moors Murders which finally saw Ian Brady and Myra Hindley go on trial for the brutal torture and slayings of three children.

A wind of change swept the fashion industry. Almost overnight, Mary Quant's mini-skirt was suddenly 'in' and for the first time, the amount of leg shown by the young women of Britain showed teenage boys and men alike that women really did have legs that extended up and beyond their knees.

For the younger generation then, all seemed well, but for the former members of Brendan Kane and the Planets, life had taken an unfortunate downturn. Following the inevitable break up of the group after the failure of their demo disc two years earlier, Brendan, still full of belief and ambition had launched himself on a grueling tour of the clubs in Liverpool and its surrounding area. He'd saved hard after the initial split with The Planets and had first taken driving lessons, and after passing his driving test had bought himself a second-hand Hillman Minx, picked up for thirty pounds at a local motor auction. He'd carried on working at the bookshop by day and would drive himself to gigs at night, usually ending up tired beyond belief by the end of each week, and having to start all over again as Monday dawned once more. At least he had his own place, having rented a small flat above a shop in the city centre. Sadly, he'd as yet failed to attract that elusive recording contract, though his dreams of stardom kept him going through the tiredness.

He and Marie continued to see each other, usually at the flat, and the couple had somehow managed to keep their relationship a secret until a few months earlier, when a friend of Mickey's had seen them kissing and romantically entangled, quite by chance in a pub in Wigan. Mickey, who, with the others had long suspected a romance between the couple, and who was now working as a bricklayer had tried to be sensible and had sat down with his sister and tried to talk her out of the relationship with Brendan, telling her it could lead to nothing. Marie however, informed her elder brother about the long-standing nature of their love affair and even though Mickey attempted to change her mind by bringing accounts clerk Ronnie in on the secret, Marie would hear none of it. Mickey and Ronnie then confronted Brendan, who refused to listen to their entreaties to end the affair.

A kind of lull ensued, as the former group members saw less and less of each other, though Brendan maintained a closer relationship with Phil Oxley than he did with the brothers, who, for the sake of their sister, maintained a civilized silence about the affair with Brendan. Phil had at least managed to remain in the music business, now playing drums regularly for a local dance band, not quite pop stardom, but it was regular work and paid well.

* * *

Brendan held Marie close as they lay together in bed in the small city centre flat. Marie's head rested on his shoulder as they relaxed in the aftermath of a particularly passionate love-making session.

"It's just not happening for me here, Marie. In England, I mean. Look how long I've been trying, first with The Planets, and now on my own. I know I can do better, I just know it."

"But Brendan, darling, just what else can you do that you haven't already tried?"

Lying naked beside him, the warmth and intense satisfaction of their recent lovemaking still coursing through her body, the truth was, Marie wasn't really too concerned about Brendan's career at that particular moment. All that changed with his next words, however.

"I can go to America. That's what else I can do, Marie."

The look of shock on Marie's face was palpable as his words struck home like an arrow to her heart.

"America? You've got to be joking, Brendan, surely."

"No joke, Babe. The States could be just the place to start and build up a whole new career."

"But nobody in America has ever heard of you. What makes you think you'll have a better chance of success over there than you've had here?"

"I've got to try something, anything or I'll go through my life wondering what might have been if I hadn't tried. I thought you'd understand that."

"Understanding is one thing, but, what about us, Brendan? Sounds as if your mind's made up and you're prepared to just bugger off to America and leave me here. I thought you loved me. I thought we had a future together, that we'd be together forever. Not much chance of

that Brendan, is there, with you on the other side of the world and me stuck here in an office in Liverpool for the rest of my life?"

Brendan leaned over and tried to kiss her, but Marie turned her face away at the last minute, leaving him with a mouthful of blonde hair. Taking her head in his hands, he gently turned her face until they were facing each other once again, and with a smile on his face he said,

"Do you really think I'd just leave you here all alone?"

Marie looked questioningly at him.

"Well, I…"

"Look, you silly girl, you know I love you, always have and always will. I was going to explain things a bit better. Didn't mean for it to come out like it has, but anyway, I want to go over there and maybe try a change of name, get an agent or a manager or whatever it takes to get started in America, and I want you to come with me, you daft bugger."

"Me? Go to America with you? Are you crazy?"

"No, Marie, I'm not. Why shouldn't you come with me? We want to be together, don't we?

"I know, but me Mam and Dad'll never allow it, especially me Dad. You know how strict he is on religious things."

"Oh, come on, Marie. This is the nineteen sixties for God's sake. All that Papist and Proddie stuff is way out of date now, except for that lot over in Ireland."

"God, don't let me Dad ever hear you saying, that word, you know, Papists. He'd go ballistic."

"Give over, Marie. I bet he calls Protestants proddies, though and that's okay is it?"

"Look, I know he's a bit of an old dinosaur, but he's still me Dad. He'd never agree to me living with you over here, never mind in bloody America."

"Who said anything about living together? I meant I want you to go with me as my wife. I want you to marry me, Marie. Say you will, please."

A look of pure shock showed on Marie's face as she took in Brendan's words. She felt her hands beginning to tremble as she pulled herself up into a sitting position in the bed.

"Brendan, of course I want to marry you. You know I do, but, Mam and Dad won't allow it, you know they won't."

"Then we don't ask them. We go over to America and get married there. I've read about places where you can go, wedding chapels they call them. All you need's your birth certificate and a couple of witnesses, and you have to have some kind of blood test I think."

"What for?"

"Oh, I dunno. Probably to make sure you're not carrying any diseases or something. Anyway, if we plan it carefully and quietly we can probably be there in a couple of months."

"Two months? Oh God, Brendan, I so want to say yes, but it's all so sudden and well, a bit scary, more like a lot scary really. I mean, I couldn't just up sticks and leave without a word to anyone."

"We can wait until nearer the time and then maybe just tell Mickey, or maybe Ronnie. They love you too, even though they might be pissed off with me, and if we can show them it's what you want and it's going to make you happy, I'll bet you they won't say anything to your Mam and Dad, at least until after we've left."

Marie's head was awhirl with all Brendan had said in the last few minutes. She needed time to think. Sliding her legs out of the bed and on to the floor, she reached across and quickly slipped Brendan's blue denim shirt over her shoulders.

"Where're you going? Brendan asked, admiring her legs as she paced out of the bedroom.

"Kitchen," Marie replied. "I need a drink. Want one?"

"Sure, just a Coke, please."

Marie quickly lifted two bottles of Coca-Cola from the small fridge in the kitchen, pausing for a moment to listen to the song playing on Radio Luxembourg, Cilla Black's *Don't Answer Me*. She stood admiring Brendan's new Grundig radio as she found the bottle opener and removed the tops from two bottles of Coke, then returned to the bedroom, holding one bottle out towards Brendan, who took it from her gratefully, and took a long slug from the bottle.

"Well?" he asked.

"Let me think, Brendan. I want to say yes, you know I do, but it's a massive step."

"Okay, I understand. Let's not say anything else tonight. Just promise me you'll think about it."

"Of course I will, silly. I just need for it all to sink in, work out how to sort everything out, you know?

In truth, Brendan had blurted out his American idea pretty much on the hoof and hadn't really thought it through. He'd no real idea about how to go about emigrating to the USA and knew he'd have to do some fast, serious fact-finding now that he'd revealed his plans to Marie. Could he really plan and execute his ideas in the space of two months. Would Marie say yes?

After he and Marie made love once more, the couple dressed, and an awkward silence descended upon them as neither appeared to know quite what to say to each other in light of the evening's turn of events. Brendan drove her home and dropped her on the corner of her street, watching her as she walked to her door, then he drove home, fell into bed, and spent a sleepless night as his mind raced, alive with thoughts of a future with Marie in a brave new world, as man and wife, with a new career and a whole new life ahead of them. He knew he had two major hurdles to overcome if he were to turn his latest dream into reality. First, he needed Marie's commitment to join him if he did manage to arrange to leave Liverpool and head for the USA, and secondly, and perhaps most important, there remained the problems that might ensue from her family when they found about their plans.

* * *

The Red River Café was hardly the most salubrious establishment in the area. Standing at the end of a row of pre-war terraced houses, close to an area bombed extensively during the war and still bearing its scars as a bombsite, the café was, nevertheless a popular meeting place for the younger generation and it was here that Brendan had arranged to meet former group member, Phil Oxley. One of the reasons for the Red River's popularity was the beautiful Wurlitzer Juke Box that stood in one corner of the establishment and Sam Beckett, owner of the café, always made sure it was filled with the latest chart hits, making his place a major attraction for the local youths and young adults, eager to sit and feed the machine with money in order to hear their latest favourites.

Arriving two minutes before the pre-arranged time, Phil walked though the café door to find Brendan waiting for him, seated at a table near the window. Phil took a seat at the Formica-topped table, and reached across to shake hands with his old friend.

"Hiya, Phil. How's things?" Brendan asked.

"I'm doing good, Brendan, thanks. How about yourself?"

"That's what I wanted to talk to you about, Phil, but hey, let's get a drink first. What'll you have?"

"Espresso for me, please," Phil replied and Brendan pushed his chair back, rose and walked to the counter. In a minute or so the satisfying hiss of the espresso machine signalled the coffee was ready and he returned to the table with two cups of espresso on a plastic tray, which he placed on the table before regaining his seat and smiling at Phil.

"So, how's it going with the dance band, Phil? Bit different from The Planets, eh?"

"It is, but they're a good crowd, the fellas in the band. Mostly a lot older than me, of course, but hey, some of that dance band music is really cool, you know? The swing sound and the big band sounds like those bands in the war played really get people up and dancing, and Bob, the bandleader says I'm one of the best drummers they've had for years, and you know, a lot of the band music was like the roots of a lot of our rock 'n roll. The Jive, the Lindy Hop and lots more all came out of the big band music during the war."

"That's good mate, it really is. But listen, I've something important to tell you, and to be honest, I could do with your advice."

"Well, there's a first. Not often you've ever been unsure enough to want my advice, mate."

Brendan smiled as he replied, "Well, there's always a first time, Phil and this is really important, and I'm just not sure what to do."

Phil realised his friend was deadly serious and he could see worry etched on Brendan's face, and so he dropped the air of flippancy he'd at first adopted and prepared to listen carefully to his friend.

* * *

Half an hour later, Brendan finally came to the end of his story, Phil having listened to his friend with only sporadic interruptions for the occasional question, and to replenish their espressos at the counter.

"So, Phil, what d'you think?" Brendan looked at Oxley hopefully after finishing presenting his ideas for the future to his friend.

"What do I think? I think you're bloody mad, Brendan Kane, that's what I think. Bloody hell, man, you've always been a bit of a dreamer, you know you have, but this is taking it to the limit, man. You've told me in your own words you don't really know much about moving to the States, so, if you're serious about this hare-brained scheme of yours, you'd better contact the US Embassy or whoever you need to get in touch with to find out if your idea even has a chance of working. You might not fit the, what do they call it...? Oh yeah, the criteria, that's the word. You might not fit the criteria they set for people wanting to go and live over there. No, be quiet and friggin' listen to me," he said quickly as he could see Brendan was about to interject and interrupt his reply. "You've asked for my help and my advice, so let me tell you what I think, then you can have another go, okay?"

Brendan nodded and Phil continued.

"As I see it, that's the first part of your problem, and probably the easiest bit to get sorted. The hard part is Marie, and I don't mean the bit about marrying her, or persuading her to go to America with you. She'd go with you like a shot, man. You'd have had to be blind, deaf and dumb not to see how much she's been love with you these last few years. Oh yes, Brendan bloody big man Kane. We all knew, even though you'd both worked hard at keeping it a secret for a long time. Eventually you couldn't disguise the looks that passed between you and we all thought you'd tell us when you wanted to and we just kept quiet and let you play your little game of secrets."

"How long had you known?" Brendan had to ask, unable to keep silent any longer.

"Oh, from soon after we cut the demo disc, not long before we packed in the group. But anyway, like I said, that's not the big problem. It's her family, Brendan. They're staunch Catholics, you know that. They're not going to take too kindly to their only daughter running off with some proddie kid to get married and then moving halfway around the bloody world to live in another bloody country. You might just win Mickey and Ronnie round in the end but it's their parents that's your problem. They'll kick up such a stink, Brendan lad, they really will."

"But they can't stop us, can they, Phil, if we really want to go?"

"You're not thinking straight, man. Look, Marie is twenty, right?"

Brendan nodded in the affirmative.

"Well then, until she's twenty-one, she can't get married without her parent's permission. That's the law, Brendan, and that's all there is to it."

"Shit," said Brendan, his face a mask of frustration. You mean we've got to wait another six months until her birthday?"

Phil thought for a few second before replying, a sudden thought giving him and idea that might just help his friend.

"There's one way you might be able to get round it, I've just re-membered something"

"What? Come on, Phil, don't muck about, what is it?" Brendan asked; eager to hear of anything that might help him out of what he saw as a serious setback to his plans.

"Elope to Scotland," Phil spoke with a broad grin on his face.

"Scotland? Why the bloody hell should we go to friggin' Scotland?"

"Because, you numpty, the law's different up there, that's why. Have you never heard of people running away and eloping to Gretna Green?"

"I've heard of the place, sure, but I've never really thought about getting married before so can't say I've really thought much about those stories."

"Brendan, man, they're not stories, it's a fact. In Scotland, it's legal to get married at sixteen. All I think you have to do is qualify by living there, just for a week or two, I'm not sure, you'd have to find out. It's just over the border in Scotland. The two of you could bugger off up there, stay in a B & B or something and then get married, all nice and legal, and her parents couldn't do a thing about it when you come back as Mr. and Mrs. Brendan Kane."

The smile that appeared on Brendan's face stretched from ear to ear as he listened to Phil's potential solution to one of the major hurdles standing between him and Marie becoming a legally married couple.

"You're a bloody genius, Phil," he exclaimed. "If I can get Marie to agree to come away with me, it might just work."

"Yeah, but remember you need to find out about going to the States first, and if I were you I'd try and get Mickey and Ronnie on your side too. You're gonna need some back-up eventually when their parents do find out. They're going to want to cut your bloody legs off, and maybe other more sensitive body parts too when they find out what you've been doing with their precious Marie."

"I've hardly had much to do with them since the group split up, Phil. I know they were pissed off at me when we folded, and I've only seen them now and then since, so I doubt they'll be too happy about helping me out here."

"You're a real prat sometimes, Brendan, you know that? Sure they were mad at you. We all were, but like I said they've known about you and Marie for a while and if they weren't your friends, don't you think they'd have tried to split you up before now? Just because they were angry back then doesn't mean they're going to do anything that might hurt Marie or interfere with her happiness. Give 'em a chance, man."

"But, how? What do I say to them?"

"Tell them the truth, man, you might be surprised."

"Will you help me Phil? To set up a meeting with them, I mean? I'd feel better with you there to back me up, you know?"

"What, just in case they want to give you a good battering?" Phil laughed.

Brendan tried to return the smile but it wouldn't form on his face.

"You really don't think they'd want to...?"

"Give over, you great pillock. With Marie there with you? They're not morons you know. Anyway, yes, for old time's sake and because I happen to think you and Marie are good for each other, I'll help you."

Brendan jumped up from his seat at the table and almost ran round to the other side where he wrapped his arms round Phil's shoulders and hugged his friend.

"Thanks, Phil, I don't know how to thank you."

"Hey, be careful, you'll give people the wrong idea," Phil laughed.

Brendan drew back, smiling like a Cheshire cat and grabbed Phil's hand and shook it briskly.

"That's more like it, mate," Phil chuckled. "Well, let's have another coffee and try and work out how we're going to sort your bloody mess of a life out, eh?"

Chapter 16

A TIME TO TELL

"And you know all about this meeting because?" Ross asked, as Ronnie Doyle sighed, and took a couple of deep breaths as he paused in his narrative. Both the inspector and Sergeant Izzie Drake had found themselves being drawn inescapably into the past as they'd sat listening to Ronnie's story. The man could certainly weave a good tale and had the knack of being able to communicate his thoughts in a way that gave the detectives a fascinating insight not only into the subject they were discussing but into another era, a period in recent history that only those who'd lived through it could perhaps fully appreciate. They were fascinated.

"Eh? Oh, sorry, Inspector. The memories, you know? They sort of bring those days all back to life for me, if you see what I mean. It all happened so long ago and yet, now I'm talking to you about it, it could all have taken place last week, it seems so real in my mind. Anyway, you asked about the meeting in the Red River, well, it was Phil and Brendan themselves who told us about it, mostly Phil, I'll admit, when he got in touch with me and Mickey soon after him and Brendan had met in the café."

"I see, and who did he call first, you or Mickey? Do you remember?"

"It was me, Inspector," Mickey spoke quietly. It was obvious from his demeanour and facial expression that Ronnie's recollections of the past had affected him too. "He called me a couple of days after he'd met with Brendan. It was actually me who told Ronnie about it, but Ronnie spoke to Phil after that, if I remember it right."

"Yes, that's right," said Ronnie, "you did tell me first, and I agreed to speak to Phil to arrange a meeting with him, Brendan and Marie. We agreed that it should be me who talked to Marie, us being closer back in those days."

"Yeah, she was always a bit awed by me, I think. Don't know why, Maybe it was just because I was the eldest, you know, big brother and all that?"

Ross had allowed the brothers to digress slightly, wanting them to feel at ease as he gradually teased the story from them, and now he moved to get them back on track.

"Alright, Ronnie, please, can we get back to the meeting with Brendan Kane and Phil Oxley? What happened next?"

"Yeah, right, Inspector, sorry. Well now, where was I? Right, yeah, well, Mickey and me agreed that I'd talk to Marie first, make sure she was up for it, and then make arrangements to meet up with Brendan and Phil."

"And how did Marie react when you approached her and told her you'd known about her affair with Brendan for quite some time, which I'm presuming you must have done?"

"She was bloody scared shitless... oops, sorry about that Sergeant," Ronnie said, apologising for his language to Izzie Drake who merely said,

"Don't let it worry you, Mr. Doyle. I hear far worse than that from our own people within these walls every day of the week, I can assure you. Please, go on with your story."

She smiled and Ronnie Doyle relaxed again and went on with his tale.

"Okay, like I said, she was scared shi... a bit scared at first, thinking me and Mickey were mad at her, and that we'd go round and knock seven shades of shit out of Brendan Kane."

"And did you feel like doing that?" Ross asked.

"For a second or two, yes, to tell the truth, Inspector. Mind you, Brendan was bigger and tougher than me so I really wouldn't have had much chance of doing him any damage, even if I'd wanted to. I was a bit like the typical seven stone weakling, physically in those days. I've filled out a bit now of course, middle age and all that."

"How about you, Mickey? Did you feel like thumping Brendan's lights out?"

"It might come as a surprise to you, Inspector, but no, I didn't. Ever hear of Woodstock?"

"You mean the place in Oxfordshire?" Izzie interjected.

"No lass, not the one in bloody Oxfordshire. I mean the Woodstock music festival in the USA."

"I've heard of it," said Ross. "What's that got to do with your relationship with your sister?"

"Well, Woodstock didn't happen for another few years, but what I'm saying, is that even back in sixty-six, I was already a believer in free love, peace and all that stuff, you know? I might not have liked what Brendan bloody Kane did to us over the group, but hell, if he wanted to shag me sister, and she wanted it too, then bloody good luck to the pair of 'em. That was my attitude Inspector. Just 'cos I'm a big bloke, doesn't make me a violent one. You shoulda seen me in me flower power hippy shirts, complete with beads after Woodstock took place and the hippy culture took me over."

Ronnie couldn't help laughing at his brother.

"He was a right sight, Inspector, I can tell you. All 'peace, man' and bloody weird hand gestures and long lank hair. Thank God he grew out of it."

"And when did that happen, Mickey, you growing out of the hippy lifestyle?"

"When my first wife Chrissie left me for another man, Inspector. We'd met at a concert and got married within six weeks, so you can see why I wouldn't be the type to be hard on my sister, but she left me for a bloody stockbroker she met at an art gallery of all things, and well, I just drifted out of the lifestyle. Mind you, I was thirty by then."

The two bothers laughed again and Ross groaned inwardly. These two were natural jokers and he needed to keep them deadly serious if he was going to get what he wanted from them. How soon, he wondered, would either Ronnie or Mickey realise the remains at the wharf were probably those of their friend, Brendan?

"Okay, point taken, Mickey. Now, Ronnie, the meeting with Brendan and your sister, *please*. Just where and when did it take place and exactly what happened? I know it was a long time ago but please try to remember as many of the details as you possibly can, it really is important."

"Alright, sorry. It's just funny thinking of Mickey the hippy. Anyway, yes, we arranged to meet with Brendan and Marie round at Brendan's flat a few days later. We all thought it best to go there as there'd be no way our parents would find out about it if we kept is private, like. Anyway, I remember most of it as if it were yesterday."

"So, go ahead, Ronnie, take us back to nineteen sixty-six again, please. You were all at Brendan's flat, and...?"

Chapter 17

BRENDAN KANE & THE PLANETS REUNITED

"So, here we are, all back together again. It's been a while, eh, lads?" Brendan Kane looked at the gathering of his old friends as they sat around the living room in his flat. He and Marie were seated side by side on the sofa, with Phil Oxley on the other side of Marie. Mickey and Ronnie had claimed an armchair each and after an uncomfortable couple of minutes following their arrival, Marie being already with him to greet them, it seemed as though a peaceful camaraderie had fallen over the room. They'd all spent a long time together as Brendan Kane and The Planets, and though their eventual split may have borne a deal of acrimony, all that seemed to be in the past and for the most part, everyone seemed pleased to be back in each other's company, much to Brendan's relief.

"Too long if you ask me," Ronnie replied.

"I thought you'd all hate my guts," said Brendan.

"We probably did, for a while," Mickey added, "but friends are friends, and we couldn't stay mad at you forever. Hell's bells, Brendan you were probably right. We'd never have made it anyway and at least we quit before the bookings dried up and we got booed off stage in some poky little working men's club somewhere."

"Hey, we weren't that bad," Brendan protested.

"Maybe not, but that's not why we're here tonight is it?"

"No, and I'm surprised you two don't want to knock my block off."

"Why?" Ronnie asked. "Just because you and Marie fell for each other? Hell, we all knew about you two ages ago, maybe not as much as we could have known, but enough to know there was something going on between you."

"So, you don't mind if we get married and if Marie comes to America with me?"

"We couldn't stop her if we tried, could we Marie?"

"No chance, Ronnie," Marie replied.

"Okay, but it's not that simple, is it, girl?" said big brother Mickey.

"I know. It's Mam and Dad isn't it? What can I do, Mickey?"

"Phil told me and Ronnie his idea, and I think that's the only way to do it."

"What, you mean me and Brendan elope to Gretna Green and then go to America as man and wife?"

"Yes, but, you've got to be really careful about how you do things. If Dad finds out what you're up to, he'll be mad as hell." Mickey fell silent and Ronnie, normally so quiet, took over again, his intellectual side clearly coming to the fore as he worked the problem out in his mind.

"Right, you arrange a short holiday in Scotland with a couple of your girlfriends, first. You can do that, yeah?" Marie nodded. "Good, you can use them as witnesses anyway. Once you've stayed there as long as you have to, you get married, and then you'll need to come back here and carry on with normal life until you can leave for the States."

"We couldn't do that, Ronnie," Marie exclaimed. "Once we're married, we want to be together, forever."

"It won't be for long, Marie. That's up to Brendan to make all the arrangements in advance."

"It all sounds a bit complicated to me," said Brendan. "I'd rather we just go one day and not come back,"

"Look, Brendan. It's up to you. We're just agreeing with Phil's plan, which sounds a good one if we want to keep it all nice and quiet so you too lovebirds can slip away without Dad finding out." Ronnie insisted.

"It's a good plan, Brendan, honest it is," said Phil.

"But it's just as easy for me and Marie to meet one day, and just board a plane or a ship or whatever and disappear from Liverpool, without going through all your cloak and dagger stuff, Phil. We can get married in America when we get there."

"And what do you think, Marie?" Phil asked the young woman.

"I just wanna be with Brendan," she answered.

The argument raged on for over an hour without any real decision being made. It was clear to the brothers that Marie would end up doing whatever Brendan wanted her to do. She was totally besotted with him and would truly follow him to the ends of the earth. They had to hope that good sense would eventually prevail. They knew that if Marie and Brendan were legally married in Scotland, their father could scream and bellow all he liked, but the marriage would be valid and they would both do their best to support their sister against their father's wrath.

The remainder of their time at Brendan's flat felt rather surreal to the Doyle brothers and to Phil Oxley. Brendan insisted on showing off his brand new Dansette record player, with it's facility to hold up to ten singles on its spindle, automatically dropping the next record in turn onto the turntable after the playing arm lifted from the record.

As the Searchers' *When You Walk In The Room* played in the background, Marie left the boys for a minute, returning soon afterwards with chilled bottles of Double Diamond from Brendan's fridge. The cold pale ale was refreshing and helped them all to relax, and the record ended, the needle rose magically and another disc dropped on to the turntable, this time The Rolling Stones, one of Mickey's favourite groups, with their smash hit, *It's All Over Now,* with the brilliant Brian Jones on lead guitar. Little did any of them imagine at the time that the superb guitarist would tragically be lost to the pop scene in July 1969, drowned in his swimming pool just a month after leaving the Rolling Stones. For now, though, Mickey Doyle idolized the young man who had formed the Stones in the first place and whose musical talents helped them become one of the biggest names in the British pop industry.

Soon, however, with the future as yet unresolved, the time came for the group to go their separate ways and the Doyle brothers patiently waited outside with Phil Oxley as Marie said goodnight to Brendan, obviously, according to the time taken, Ronnie commented, accompanied by much 'snogging and groping'. Mickey playfully slapped his younger brother across the back of his head, "That's our bloody sister you're talking about, you pillock."

"So! She's got the same equipment as other girls, hasn't she? Brendan's a red blooded guy and..."

Before he could say more the street door opened and Marie stepped out to join them, waving to the figure of Brendan Kane, hidden from the brother's view. After blowing him a kiss, she skipped across to where the others waited in a huddle on the footpath and quickly linked arms with her two brothers, smiling up at each in turn, then said, cheerfully,

"We going home then, or what?"

Chapter 18

BACK TO THE FUTURE

"And that, Inspector Ross, was honestly the last time I saw Brendan Kane," Ronnie said as he sighed and sagged a little in his chair, a rather wistful look on his face. Ross quite correctly guessed it had taken something out of Ronnie Doyle, going back in his mind to those long ago days of his youth, and the trauma of losing his sister, though he hadn't yet told Ross anything about what eventually happened when Brendan and Marie appeared to vanish from the face of the earth. It was time to be blunt, to hit Ronnie and Mickey with his theory.

Still directing his words in Ronnie's direction, Ross began.

"Ronnie, and you too, Mickey, I know you came here today to try and help us, and you thought the remains at Cole's Wharf might have been your sister, which we've been able to discount, but the reasons we asked to go into such detail about your sister's disappearance, and believe me, I want to know much more in a minute, are twofold. One, I do believe the remains at the wharf could be very closely connected to your sister's eventual disappearance, and two, I have strong reasons, based on what you've told me, and from other evidence we've discovered, to believe the remains at Cole's Wharf are those of your old friend, Brendan Kane."

Ronnie and Mickey Doyle both looked as if someone had hit them over the head with a cricket bat. Both Ross and Izzie Drake had no doubts that the news the inspector had just delivered had struck the brothers a real sledgehammer blow, and that neither man had up to now connected the dots, and worked out where Ross had been leading throughout the current interview. They were either totally innocent of any involvement in the disappearance and subsequent murder of Brendan Kane, or, one or both of the brothers was a very good actor. Ross had to consider the possibility that one of the men sitting before him could be a cold hearted and very clever sociopathic killer, emotionless and devoid of the emotion necessary to register true emotions, and therefore he had to take things slowly and carefully.

"You can't mean that, surely, Inspector Ross," Ronnie exclaimed.

"It's not possible," said Mickey, his voice rising almost to the point of shouting. Sudden realisation had dawned on the elder Doyle brother, even if, for the moment it had escaped his younger brother. "Brendan went to America, and Marie went with him. If the skeleton you found is Brendan then that means that Marie would well be..."

Mickey suddenly choked up with the emotion of the moment, unable to complete his sentence, but by now, Ronnie had caught on to the possibilities Ross's revelation had opened up.

"So she is dead. That's what you're saying, isn't it, Inspector? If Brendan died here in Liverpool all those years ago, there's no chance Marie made it to America on her own is there? After all, why would she go without Brendan? They were fucking inseparable."

It was only at that point that Ross realised the brothers still harboured hopes that Marie might be alive, that their search through endless newspaper articles over the years had been in truth, a sort of cathartic process of elimination. With each body that wasn't Marie, the more they hoped she may yet turn up alive sometime, somewhere. It was a 'syndrome' he'd witnessed once or twice in the past with relatives of missing persons, a form of positive denial, that led hopeful parents or, in this case, siblings to refuse to accept the inevitable as long as no body could be found. For now, though, he had to push the brothers in order to ascertain every fact he could squeeze from their memories.

Ross spoke firmly but gently once again, trying to convey a calmness that might enable the two men to begin to think clearly once more.

"Look, Mickey, Ronnie, as of right now we have no idea what happened to your sister. Until the pair of you walked in here today we had no idea she had anything to do with this case, and we had no firm proof that the remains were those of Brendan Kane. But you had suspicions that your sister might not have gone with him or why come here saying you thought the remains at the wharf might be Marie? What really made you think your sister might be dead?"

Ronnie Doyle thought for a few seconds before replying.

"Look, Inspector Ross, at first we'd no idea what had happened. Yes, me and Mickey thought she'd run off with Brendan but when we heard nothing from her, and then our Mam and Dad started worrying, we had to come clean and tell them what had been going on. Even so, me and Mickey took a long time to come round to the idea that something bad, and I mean really bad, might have happened to Marie. We started searching newspapers for stories about unidentified bodies or unsolved murders against unknown victims, and when we saw the article about the skeleton at the docks, we thought, well...you know what we thought."

Ross knew the time had come to be open and honest with the two brothers. Perhaps if he could first obtain conclusive proof that the remains at the wharf were those of Brendan Kane, he might then be able to ascertain if the death of the young musician and the disappearance of Marie Doyle were connected. He now felt it extremely unlikely they wouldn't be. First of all, of course, he needed to know more.

"Okay," he said. "You remember me asking you if Brendan had ever suffered a broken leg?"

The brothers nodded in unison, words failing them both for the moment.

"Well, our victim suffered just such an injury, and we're currently conducting a survey of dentists who may have been practicing in the city around the time of death, to confirm the identity of the remains through dental records, but so far, thanks to what you've revealed today, I have to say my thoughts are leaning towards the fact that this was in fact, Brendan Kane. I want to show you something and I want you to tell me if it has any significance for either of you." With that, Ross opened the top right hand draw of his desk and reached inside, his hand emerging holding a small Perspex packet. He passed the packet across the desk towards Ronnie, who looked at it as if it was about to bite him. He could see something within the packet and as it came closer to him, he realised what he was looking at.

"Oh, shit," he said, his face assuming a crestfallen look.

"What is it Ronnie? What's in there?" his brother asked, a quiver of fear creeping into his voice.

Ronnie picked up the packet with the tips of two fingers, as though it contained a human body part, and passed it to his brother.

"I take it you both know what that is?" Ross asked, as Izzie Drake moved to take the packet from Mickey's trembling hand. She passed it back to Ross who returned it to his desk drawer before he spoke once more.

"A plectrum. A broken guitar plectrum," Ronnie said, quietly.

"A tortoiseshell plectrum," Mickey added. "Brendan always used one just like it."

"I'm sorry if this has shocked you both," Ross said, "but now, I want you to really think back and tell me what took place, to the best of your knowledge, between the time you last saw Brendan, and your sister's disappearance."

Both men nodded again. Mickey Doyle appeared to be on the verge of tears. Ronnie was exerting great effort in an attempt not to join his brother on the point of breakdown.

Seeing the state of the men, Ross thought a break would be in order and he asked Izzie to organize tea and coffee for all four of them. She also sent in a uniformed officer who escorted Ronnie and Mickey to the men's toilets, allowing them to relieve themselves and splash some water on their faces in an attempt to refresh themselves a little before going on with what had now become, for both men, a frightening and potentially tragic interview with Detective Inspector Ross.

A few minutes later, the Doyle brothers were returned to the office where they were soon seated once again in the identical positions in front of Ross's desk. During the short break, Ross had ascertained that his sergeant had been totally in line with this thoughts and the line of his questioning from the moment he'd first suggested the remains may be those of their old friend. He was reassured by the fact that Drake was still able to almost read his mind and think along the same lines as he did. This ability to almost think in parallel was, he believed, one of the particular strengths of the working relationship between himself and Izzie Drake. Drake soon furnished the two men with cups of very strong tea, and Ross soon took up the thread of his questioning again. This time, he felt he had to really strike hard and make the brothers realise just where his line of inquiry had been leading.

"Right lads, I know you came here today thinking you might have found some answers about the disappearance of your sister, and to be honest, I'm going to do all I can to find out what happened to her, because, although you may not have caught on so far, I do believe your sister may have been closely connected with the remains unearthed at Cole's Wharf."

"But how, Inspector? What on earth could Marie have had to do with whatever happened down at the docks all those years ago?" It was Mickey who now seemed to have assumed the mantle of spokesman for the brothers. Ross paused for a moment, turning his head to look out of his office window. A darkness had fallen on the room, and Ross could see the cause, as a bank of dark, grey clouds were sweeping across the sky, obliterating the sunshine and turning the sky a strange mixture of purple and black. Somehow, it seemed fitting, bearing in mind the information he was about to divulge. Turning quickly back to face the brothers, he spoke again, in almost hushed tones.

"I don't know, Mikey but we need to find out," Ross continued.

"We believe someone either met or lured Brendan to that wharf, probably late at night, and cold-bloodedly murdered your friend, approximately thirty five years ago. Somehow, it now appears your sister may have been involved in what took place that night"

"Murdered?" This came from Ronnie. "But why? How? Inspector Ross, if that was Brendan you found at that wharf, how did he die? Can you tell, just from the bones? Don't you need the full body or something to get all that sort of information? And how could Marie have been involved?"

"Oh, we can tell alright, Ronnie. Forensic science is highly advanced nowadays. I can tell you our pathologists have determined that Brendan was probably shot in both kneecaps to incapacitate him, then someone struck him over the head with a hammer, not enough to have caused his death, and finally threw him into the water, as the river still flowed up to the dock in those days. In other words, he was shot, bludgeoned and thrown into the Mersey to drown."

Ross waited as his words hit home. Both brothers seemed incapable of speech for a few seconds, Mickey visibly blanched, and then Ronnie finally broke the awful silence that had descended on the room.

"But, that's bloody monstrous. Brendan never did anything to deserve anything like that. Do you know who did it yet, Inspector?"

"Of course he doesn't, Ronnie, you moron," said Mickey. "After thirty five bloody years? They haven't got a friggin' clue, have you, Inspector Ross?"

"Not yet, Mickey, no. But, I'm sorry to say that if it is indeed Brendan who was murdered at the wharf, bearing in mind the information you've brought to us today, it now leads us on to another, potentially unsavoury matter."

All of a sudden, the penny dropped, and both brothers exchanged a glance as Ross's words registered.

"Oh, my God," Mickey blurted out. "So you *do* believe Marie's dead too, don't you, Inspector? She must have been with Brendan and whoever killed him probably did the same to our sister. That's what you're thinking, isn't it? We came here thinking the bones might have been Marie's, we've thought she was dead for a long time, but now you've described what happened to poor Brendan, well, it looks like she might have been murdered too. That's not what we expected you know. We always thought she'd gone off with Brendan and maybe there'd been an accident or something or…"

Mickey halted in mid-sentence as his emotions overcame him and the big man suddenly slumped, silent, against the back of his chair. Ronnie took one last stab at denial.

"You still can't be sure it's Brendan, though, can you? I mean, a skeleton who broke a leg in the same place as Brendan and a broken guitar plectrum aren't exactly positive proof are they, Inspector?"

There it is again, thought Ross, *positive denial.*

"Until you two walked in here today, no, but after hearing what you've told us so far, Sergeant Drake and I are certain that the remains are those of your friend, and I'm certain the dental analysis of the skull will confirm it."

Ross didn't let on that they so far had no idea if they would actually find the dentist who'd worked on the victim.

"Maybe now you can see why it's so important that you tell us everything you can, every small detail you can recall about those last weeks when Marie still lived at home, right up until the time she and Brendan disappeared."

The brothers nodded in unison, and Ross continued.

"Okay, please carry on with your story and then, when you've done with that, I want to know precisely what happened when you reported Marie missing to the police. That would have been the Liverpool City police back in those days, wouldn't it?"

"Yeah, for what it was worth. Bloody useless lot if you ask me," Mickey grunted.

"Like I said, that's for later. For now, please, tell me about those last weeks. You said you never heard from Brendan again after the meeting at his flat, right?"

"No, Inspector," Ronnie corrected him. "We said we never *saw* him again. That's not the same as saying we never *heard* from him, which we did, about a week after the meeting. We spoke on the phone, didn't we, Mickey?"

"About a week, yeah, right," Mickey confirmed his brother's words.

"Okay, good. Right, let's hear it," said Ross.

Ronnie now took up the story once again.

"Well, the best I remember is it happened something like this, Inspector Ross. Please remember it was thirty-five years ago and it's not all as clear as it could be, but anyway, here goes…"

Chapter 19

The typing pool at the offices of BICC, (British Insulated Callendar's Cables), known locally simply as B.I. was its usual hubbub of sound, the constant clacking of typewriter keys interspersed with the chatter of the girls who manned the machines. Towards the back of the room, Marie Doyle sat busily typing invoices as to her right, her best friend, Clemmy (Clemency) De Souza sat at the neighbouring desk, typing letters for various departmental supervisors. Clemmy and Marie shared a love of music, and when she wasn't seeing Brendan, Marie could usually be found in the company of the olive-skinned, pretty girl whose father had been a Portuguese merchant seaman. He'd met and fallen in love with a local girl when his ship had been docked in the Port of Liverpool many years ago, and Clemmy had been the first-born offspring of the marriage.

Together, the two girls would shop together, visit the various clubs where live music could be heard, and would also spend many a happy Saturday morning in town, listening to the latest record releases, squeezed together in one of the listening booths in one or more of the many record shops that had blossomed across the city in keeping with the rise of the pop music industry.

In recent weeks, Clemmy had noticed a distinct change in her friend. Marie had become moody and rather withdrawn and Clemmy, though only the same age as Marie, had a feeling that something serious now weighed heavily on her friend's mind. As the two continued touch-typing, their fingers almost flying over their typewriter's keys, Clemmy first made sure that Mrs. Marley, the supervisor who sat at a desk at the front of the typing pool where she could survey her territory with a quick glance around the room, wasn't looking in their direction, she leaned to her left and spoke to Marie, just loud enough to be heard by her friend, though not by any of the other girls around them.

"Why won't you tell me what's wrong, Marie?"

"I keep telling you, there's nothing wrong, Clemmy, honest there isn't."

"Good God, girl. How long have we known each other? D'you not think your best friend knows when you've got a serious problem in that head of yours? I've been waiting for you to tell me, but now I'm going to ask you straight out, are you up the duff, Marie Doyle?"

Marie almost laughed out loud at Clemmy's words, but controlled herself, not wanting to attract Mrs. Marley's attention.

"Look, Clemmy, let's talk at lunchtime, okay? I'm not supposed to say anything, but, well, you are my best friend, and to be honest, I'm bursting with excitement, but I'm not allowed to show it, and by the way, no, I'm not bloody pregnant. What kind of girl do you take me for?"

Both girls found the next hour almost intolerable as they continued beating a tattoo on the keys of their rather out of date Imperial typewriters. B.I certainly needed to modernise their equipment if the girls were to achieve the level of productivity the company demanded of its workers. Clemmy desperately yearned to learn Marie's big secret and Marie, at last, felt she could tell Clemmy her big, big news.

Finally, the lunch break arrived and the two girls quickly made their way to the canteen, where they both obtained a lunch of sausage and mashed potato, garden peas and gravy, then found a table in a corner of the vast room, at a table with no other workers in close proximity to them. Satisfied that they'd achieved a modicum of privacy, Clemmy immediately pushed Marie to open up to her.

"A'right, girl, tell. If you're not bloody pregnant, just why have you been acting so funny lately?"

Taking a deep breath, and swallowing the last of a piece of sausage with a visible gulp, Marie replied.

"Me and Brendan's goin' to America, but you're not to breathe a word to anyone, d'you understand, Clemmy De Souza, not to *anyone*, especially not to your Mam and Dad."

"Bloody hell, Marie. What's this all about, girl? You've never said nothin' about America before. Is Brendan mad or what, wanting to take you all that way, when you've never been further than bloody Birkenhead in your life?"

"That's not true, Clemmy, and you know it. What about when Mam and Dad took us on that holiday to Blackpool, and to Spain a few years ago? Saved up for years to pay for that, they did."

"Oh, right, yeah, sorry. But, it's still only Blackpool and one trip to Spain isn't it? It's not exactly Las bleedin' Vegas, Marie. I'll change what I said to you've never been out of Lancashire except for once in your life, and you can't argue with that. So, why does your boyfriend suddenly want to whisk you off to America, and just where in America is he thinkin' of, by the way? You do have some idea how big that country is, don't you, girl?"

Marie leaned across the table towards her friend and lowered her voice to what she felt was a nicely conspiratorial level.

"Keep your voice down, Clemmy, please. Look, he thinks his singing career might have a better chance of taking off in America. The music scene in Liverpool has grown a bit stale, so he says, and solo singers like him seem to have more success over there. You've only got to look at the U.S charts and all the big names over the last few years, like Bobby Darin, Bobby Vee, Elvis Presley, Ricky Nelson. There's hardly been one really big solo singer over here, not counting Cilla of course, and she's a girl."

"Get away," said Clemmy, sarcastically. "I'd never have known that, if you hadn't told me."

Marie waved a derisory hand at her friend and then continued.

"Anyway, he wants us to go as soon as possible, but nobody, not a soul, has to know what we're doing. The lads from the group know, and they've all agreed to keep quiet until after we've gone, at least, I think they have."

"Oh come on, Marie. You're trying to keep a secret and you've let your brothers and Phil Oxley into it already. Why don't you just tell half of Liverpool and then mention, "Oh, by the way, please don't tell me Mam and Dad. And what's to say your precious Brendan won't take you over there and then dump you if things don't go well for him and he runs out of money or meets some rich yank bird or whatever?"

"He won't do that, Clemmy. He's asked me to marry him. I'm going to be Mrs. Brendan Kane."

"God, no wonder you've been all edgy lately. Just when is all this going to happen?"

"As soon he's made all the arrangements. And my brothers won't say a word. They've known me and Brendan have been sweet on each other for a long time, so it seems, and they just want me to be happy."

"You know your Dad'll go bloody mad if he finds out, don't you?"

"But he won't Clemmy. None of the boys will say anything and I'm telling you because you're my best friend and I just felt I needed to tell, well, someone, or I'd have burst, you know?"

Clemmy fell silent for a few seconds, and after contemplating her friend's revelation, finally spoke again.

"Well, there's not much I can say, is there? You know I love you and want you to be happy too, but, by God, I'll miss having you around. Who'll I go shoppin' with on a Saturday now, or go dancing with?"

Marie's face fell for a second, as though she hadn't really considered not seeing her best friend again once she and Brendan left the country, then said,

"Look here, once we get settled over there, maybe you can come and see us, like, for a visit now and then."

"Don't be daft, Marie Doyle. When would I ever get the money to pay for a holiday in bloody America? I only work for B.I. you know; I don't friggin' own the place."

Marie reached a hand across the table, and took Clemmy's hand in hers.

"We can write to each other, Clemmy, can't we? We don't have to forget each other. I'll never have a better friend than you, I know I won't."

A small tear formed and slowly ran down Clemmy's face and she quickly wiped it away.

"Aw, give over, look what you're doing. You'll have me crying like a baby in a minute. Look, we'd better hurry up or we'll be late back from lunch and we don't want to get a tongue lashing from bloody Mrs. Marley do we?"

* * *

"You did what, Marie?"

"I told Clemmy what me and Brendan are going to do. She's my best friend, Mickey. She won't tell anyone. She promised."

"Are you crazy? Clemmy De Souza is a total airhead. She couldn't keep a secret if her life depended on it. Half of bloody Liverpool will know all about you and Brendan going to America by this time next week."

Mickey could scarcely believe his sister had told Clemmy about her and Brendan's plans. Since the meeting at Brendan's flat, he and Ronnie had carefully avoided saying anything about America to Marie when their parents were around. They restricted any discussion on the subject to the times when their parents were out of the house or when they might meet Marie for a drink in the pub or to share a coffee in the local café.

"She's not an airhead, Mickey. She promised not to tell and I believe her."

"Look, Marie, me and Ronnie's gone out on a limb for you, girl, helping you and Brendan and keeping everything quiet as far as Mam and Dad are concerned. Last thing we need is big mouth Clemmy lettin' the world know about everything. How d'you think Dad would carry on if he found out all three of us have been keeping secrets from him, especially one as big as this? I'm going to tell Ronnie and we'll see what he thinks about it."

"Go ahead, Mickey, but what do you expect Ronnie to do? Whether you like it or not, I've told me best friend, and she's promised not to tell anyone, and that's all there is to it."

Three hours later, after coming home from work to find a worried and irritable Mickey waiting for him, and having placated his fretting brother somewhat, Ronnie Doyle took a walk to the phone box at the end of the street, where he first made sure no one was around, and then lifted the phone and rang Brendan's number. The conversation that followed was short and sweet. Ronnie explained his and Mickey's worries but Brendan simply replied, "Don't make a big fuss about it, Ronnie. Marie should know if she can trust her best friend or not. If Clemmy says she'll keep the secret than that's good enough for me."

"You're sure, Brendan? There could be big bother for all of us if Dad finds out what you and Marie are planning."

"I'm sure. Biggest problem right now is this green card thing the Americans are talking about."

"Eh?"

"Something to do with their immigration rules. I don't get it myself. I'm trying to work something out even if it's just a tourist visa to get us into the country to begin with."

"Listen, Brendan, don't you go letting our little sister down, you hear me?"

"There's no way I'd do that, mate. You should know that. Look, Ronnie, I've gotta go, man. I'm doing a gig in Southport and I need to get on the road."

"Well, okay, but be careful, Brendan, you hear me?"

"I hear you, see you, Ronnie."

With those few words, Brendan ended the conversation, Ronnie finding himself left holding a silent phone in his right hand. Replacing the phone on its cradle, he pushed the door of the phone box open, made his way home, and on seeing his father in the sitting room, watching the television with his brother, he simply nodded to Mickey to indicate he'd dealt with the matter in hand. They'd talk later when they had a degree of privacy. Marie, it transpired, was out, enjoying a night at the cinema with Clemmy, the two girls excitedly having ventured to The Odeon to see the newly released *Alfie,* starring Marie's favourite actor, Michael Caine. Both girls had bought the single of the theme song sung by Cilla Black and released earlier in the year, and had been mortified when they found the title theme for the movie had been sung by Cher, rather than local girl, Cilla.

Ronnie walked through the hallway and entered the kitchen, where his mother sat in her fireside chair near the small coal fire, darning her husband's work socks, and listening and laughing along to a repeated episode of *The Clitheroe Kid* on the radio. Hot as the kitchen felt, it was necessary to keep a small fire burning in order to provide heat to the boiler which in turn ensured they had hot water provision in the house. Winter or summer, the fire would be kept burning and the kitchen at all times stood out as the warmest room in the home, uncomfortable as it might feel in the heat of high summer. Ronnie leaned down, giving her a brief hug where she sat, then lit the gas on the stove and put the kettle on. A cup of tea would be just the thing to settle his nerves, he thought.

"Hope you're making me one, too," his Mum said softly, without looking up from her darning.

"Of course I am, Mam," he replied as he waited for the kettle to boil. In a couple of minutes, the kettle began to whistle, Ronnie set about the time-honoured English ritual of first warming the pot, then brewing the tea, his Dad's favourite, PG Tips, and, to all intents and purposes, life in the Doyle household appeared a picture of domestic normality. Future events would soon prove otherwise.

Chapter 20

A DEAD END?

"That's it? That's all the contact you had with Brendan after the time you'd met at the flat?"

Andy Ross had hoped Ronnie's recollection of the last contact between the Doyle brothers and Brendan Kane might prove to be a little more revealing. In truth, he found it rather odd that the brothers appeared to have had minimal contact in the run-up to their little sister's perceived departure for the New World. He said as much to Ronnie, who replied,

"Honest, Inspector, that's all, right Mickey?" his elder brother nodded in confirmation and added to his brother's words. "We wanted to go and see him again. We were a bit worried by these 'problems' he was supposedly having with the whole emigration thing. We thought we might be able to help him, but Marie said it was best not to keep going round there, to his flat that is, in case someone saw him and Ronnie going there a lot and maybe word got back to Dad. She told us she'd pass on any messages between us and Brendan, and that Phil Oxley was doing what he could to help. He was good at paperwork, filling in forms and stuff like that, was Phil."

Ross shook his head and fell silent. He found it hard to accept some of the Doyle brothers' story, but then remembered that back in the nineteen sixties the world, and Liverpool in particular was a very different place to today's fast-paced, technology driven metropolis. There had been a naiveté, a sense of being involved in the beginnings of a brave new world, almost, as the rapid rise of the British pop music industry walked side-by-side with the technological and lifestyle revolutions that went along with it. For people like the Doyle brothers and Brendan Kane, all children of the immediate post-war years, a set of old-fashioned values and standards, alien in many ways to those of a similar age as the millennium dawned, were the norm, and despite their claim to the contrary, the teenagers and young adults of those days were in fact far less 'street-wise' than their modern-day counterparts. Perhaps the current familiarity of the music and the groups who made the Liverpool of the sixties such a throbbing, vibrant environment in which to grow up somehow masked some of the realities of those times. Andy Ross just couldn't imagine the kids of today being quite so 'unworldly' as the boys from Brendan Kane and The Planets appeared to have been back then. Today, a few minutes on the internet, a few calls on the phone, and today's youth would have all the information they needed at their fingertips.

"Sir? Do you have any more questions?"

Izzie Drake broke into Ross's reverie. The inspector hadn't realized he'd allowed himself to drift away from the conversation and he quickly pulled himself together again and faced Ronnie Doyle.

"Yes, sorry Sergeant, sorry gentlemen. I was lost in thought for a minute there. Thinking about what you've told me so far. So, Ronnie, I'm presuming things went along quite normally from that time until Brendan and Marie suddenly disappeared, right?"

"Yeah, well, no, not really 'normal', Inspector. Over the next couple of weeks, we could see Marie was getting edgy, nervous, like. I tried to get her to tell me exactly what Brendan had arranged but she was a bit…what's the word? Evasive, that's it."

"In what way?" Ross asked.

"She just kept saying that Brendan was taking care of things and we'd know about it all when the time was right. I know Mickey tried as well, to get her to talk to us, but she just clammed up and we both thought things weren't going just as they were supposed to. Tell you the truth, we, that's me and Mickey, we thought perhaps the whole plan had fallen through, didn't we, Mickey?"

"Yeah, we did," the elder brother agreed. "I phoned Phil Oxley the next day, and he said he'd been in touch with Brendan, helping him to get things sorted out. He said he didn't think Brendan's plans were workable but he was trying to help Brendan get tourist visas for him and Marie. Brendan thought he might still find a record company or producer to represent him even if he was only there for a short time. If he succeeded, according to Phil, a U.S record company would be able to help him get whatever permits he needed to live and work over there. A couple of weeks later, me and Ronnie knew something was in the offing. Marie was definitely acting odd, like, and I waited outside her work one day and met her when she knocked off. I told her I wasn't going to just leave things as they were, and that even Mam and Dad had mentioned she was acting weird. Dad even wondered if she'd got herself pregnant by 'some scally' as he put it. She just laughed and told me not to worry about things, that she and Brendan wouldn't be around much longer, and then, just a week after that, she went out late one afternoon, a Saturday, I remember, and that was it. We never saw our little sister again after that day."

Mickey fell silent, looked at his brother, and the two men seemed to be sharing an intense sadness as the recollection of the last time they'd seen their sister came flooding back to haunt their collective memories. To Andy Ross, none of this seemed to add up., however. Even back in the nineteen sixties, people rarely just vanished without leaving a single piece of trace evidence behind them. How could Marie Doyle and Brendan Kane simply disappear from the face of the earth? Of course, Ross now felt sure he knew what had happened to Brendan, but what the hell had happened to Marie, and why hadn't the police at the time of their disappearance done more to try and find them? It was time to move on. Despite his interest in the saga that the Doyle brothers had laid out before him, he needed more if he was going to solve the murder of Brendan Kane and the disappearance and perhaps also the murder of Marie Doyle. For now, he didn't want to raise that spectre too highly in the two Doyle's minds. He turned to Ronnie again, and decided to move on to the alleged lack of investigation by the old Liverpool City Police.

* * *

"Ronnie, I want you to tell me why you first became suspicious that something was wrong, and why you went to the police, and then, please try to recall exactly what happened when the police became involved. Take your time. Gather your thoughts. I know it all took place a long time ago, but anything you can tell us could be important, even now."

Ronnie Doyle nodded and pursed his lips as he once again allowed his mind to wander back in time. Ross waited patiently as Ronnie's brow furrowed as he concentrated hard, doing his best to dredge up even more details of events that took place over thirty years previously. At last, after an interminable pause, and after taking a deep breath, he began.

"Well, Inspector Ross, you need to understand that when Marie didn't come home that night, me and Mickey didn't think she'd run off with Brendan, not at first. We thought she'd maybe been with a friend, and missed the last bus home or something, and maybe stayed overnight at the friend's house, didn't we, Mickey?"

Mickey nodded his agreement but remained silent.

"So, Marie didn't come home, and Mam and Dad were going frantic. They were convinced she'd been raped or murdered by a nutter or something, you know? Anyway, they wanted me and Mickey to go look for her, so we did. We went to Clemmy's house first, on Huyton Road. Marie hadn't told either of us where she'd been going that night, no hint that she wouldn't be coming home, or that she'd be seeing Brendan, anything like that. Looking back, that's what she must have done of course, but we didn't know it then. Clemmy said she hadn't seen her all day, but said that when she'd seen her the day before, Marie had seemed excited and on edge at the same time. Clemmy asked her if she and Brendan had made their plans but Marie clammed up. We knocked on a couple more doors of friends of hers, but no one had seen her that day.

We found a phone box and called Phil, but he hadn't seen either Marie or Brendan that day. He admitted he'd been a bit worried about Brendan lately, that he didn't seem to accept that going to America wasn't as easy as he'd thought at first. He kept telling Phil he was going to make it one way or another and Phil was getting exasperated with him. I was running out of coins so instead, agreed to meet Phil in person the next day. We couldn't do any more that night, we had no more money and so couldn't ring Brendan's number, though Phil said he'd try and make sure Marie contacted us somehow if she was with Brendan.

Our parents worried all night, and Dad was ready to call for the police right away, but we knew the police wouldn't do anything about someone who hadn't even been missing twelve hours. Next day, I went alone to see Phil, 'cause Mickey had to go to work. We met on the waterfront in the city, and sat on a bench outside The Cunard Building. I thought Phil looked uncomfortable, but that was maybe because he'd worked in that place until a few months earlier, but had been made redundant when Cunard moved their centre of operations from Liverpool to Southampton. Poor old Phil wasn't enjoying unemployment, but work wasn't easy to come by. Thank God he had the part-time job in the dance band in the evenings, or he'd have been stony broke. Anyway, we sat there for a few minutes, watching the world go by, feeling a bit uncomfortable with each other. Then, Phil sort of coughed, and then told me he'd tried ringing Brendan the previous night and received no answer, so he'd been round to the flat first thing that morning. He'd knocked, rung the doorbell and knocked again, but no one answered. He'd had to assume there was no one at home after knocking on the door of Brendan's flat, then tried the flat next door, and the woman who answered the door said she hadn't seen or

heard anything of Brendan for a couple of days. Phil admitted he felt
a bit guilty by that time, for helping Brendan, who he now believed
had 'lost the plot' a bit. You can imagine how I felt when he said that,
Inspector. My sister was, as far as I knew; with a man who Phil thought
might be so obsessed with his American dream that he'd maybe lost
touch with reality."

Ronnie paused at that point, and appeared to Ross to be struggling
to control his emotions. Ross asked a question at that point, in an effort
to take some of the pressure off Ronnie and give him a break from his
retelling of his sister's disappearance.

"Mickey, tell me, do you know if Phil Oxley is still living in Liverpool? Are either of you still in contact with him?"

"Haven't seen or heard from him for years, Inspector Ross. Last I
heard, he was living in Fazakerley somewhere. Don't know if Ronnie's
heard from him."

"Not for a long time. I saw him in town about five years ago, as he
was leaving the main post office. I tried to cross over and say hello but
by the time I got there, he'd disappeared into the crowd of shoppers
and pedestrians," said Ronnie.

"You're sure it was Oxley?" said Ross.

"You don't forget someone you've known since you were about six
years old, Inspector Ross. He'd lost a lot of hair over the years, but his
face hadn't altered much at all, and he had a way of walking that was
pretty unmistakable. I think it was something to do with the way he
used to sit at his drum kit. He walks kind of bow-legged. It was Phil
alright, I'm sure of it."

"Right," said Ross, "we've established that Phil Oxley is still somewhere in the local area. Sergeant Drake?"

"I'll get someone on it as soon as we're done here, sir." Drake replied.
Izzie knew McLennan would soon be able to find an address for Oxley,
probably from the local electoral roll.

"Ronnie, go on with what happened next, please," Ross prompted
Ronnie to continue his story.

"We waited two days, Inspector," Ronnie quickly went on, eager to get things out in the open. "Two full days and not a bloody word from her. Mam and Dad were going out of their minds with worry and us two were mad at Marie and Brendan for just taking off without a word after we'd kept their secret for them. In the end, me Da insisted on going to the police station to report our Marie as missing, and it was Mickey, not me who went with him. Tell the inspector about it, Mickey, what happened at the cop shop."

"Yes, Mickey, and please, try to remember everything that was said to you at the time, and what action, if any, the police took at the time," said Ross.

A little like his brother before him, Mickey took a couple of seconds to compose himself, his mind working on recalling the events that had transpired over thirty years in the past. Before he began, Izzie Drake interrupted the flow of the interview with a question of her own.

"Just one question before you carry on, Mickey. Do either of you know if Brendan's parents are still alive, or if he has any other family in the area? If I'm going to try and locate Phil Oxley, I can search for Brendan's family at the same time."

"Good idea, Sergeant," Ross added. "Anything you can tell us, lads? Mickey replied instantly.

"Brendan's Dad was already ill at the time he left Liverpool, Inspector. We heard it was cancer, and he died about a year after Brendan disappeared. His Mum never got over Brendan leaving home and then losing her husband within a year and I saw her death notice in the Echo one night about five years after that. When we were growing up together, Brendan always told us he had no other family in the city. His grandparents died during the war in an air raid, and he apparently had an Uncle Michael in the Royal Navy who died when H.M.S. Hood was sunk by the Bismarck. Me and Ronnie spent quite some time with his Mum and Dad after Brendan and Marie disappeared. They were as worried as we were, and I think his Dad died sooner than he should have from the worry of it all. Honest, nobody could understand why Brendan and Marie never got in touch with anybody."

Ross nodded as Mickey fell silent again.

"Right then, Sergeant, just Oxley to locate if you can."

"Yes, sir," Izzie replied. "Sorry for the interruption Mickey, please carry on with what you were about to tell us."

"Oh yeah, right, the police back in sixty-six. There was a big row at home before we went to the police. Me and Ronnie couldn't keep the secret any longer and we came clean to Mam and Dad. I thought Da was going explode when he realized we'd misled and deceived him, as he put it. Me Mam cried and cried, and told me and Ronnie she was ashamed of us, that we couldn't be trusted any more. We couldn't blame them, deceiving them like that and all. We only meant to help Marie, Inspector, we never thought it through properly, I suppose. We sure as hell never meant to hurt our Mam and Dad. Anyway, they calmed down eventually and we were surprised that Da seemed to be the first to accept what we'd done, but he told us that there was now no alternative to going to the police. He said it was obvious that Marie had run off and something had to be done to find her. I can remember he went upstairs to the bathroom and a few minutes later he came back down to the kitchen. He'd changed into his best suit, his only suit to tell the truth and had his best white Sunday shirt and tie on, that he normally only wore to church, or maybe for weddings and funerals. Not that we got invited to many weddings, and we certainly didn't go to many funerals in those days, not at our ages, anyway. He'd shaved and even used some of Ronnie's after shave, a bit too much as I remember. When he walked in the room the smell of Old Spice nearly knocked us out.

I remember going to the police station with me Dad on the bus. I think it was on St Annes Road or something like that. They kept us waiting ages, even though Da told 'em we were reporting a missing person. Eventually a sergeant came out and saw us and took us into an interview room."

"Was this a detective or a uniformed officer?" Ross asked.

"He was in uniform. Big bloke, name was Carson. I remember he had a mustache, looked a bit like a bloody RAF Wing Commander in a war movie. He asked us a few questions, well, he asked Dad mostly. I felt bad for Dad. He hardly said a word."

"Okay then, Mickey, in your own words, try to tell me everything you remember about that interview with Sergeant Carson and what subsequently took place following the day you and your father made the initial report."

"Eh?" Mickey sounded a little nonplussed by Ross's terminology. Ronnie decided to help his brother out.

"He means, tell him what happened when you and Dad met with Carson and then as much as you can remember about everything the cops did from that day onwards, for what it was worth."

"Oh, yeah, right. Got it. I were never right impressed with Sergeant bloody Carson, inspector, right from the start. Sorry, I know he was one of your lot, but that's the plain truth of the matter. The bloke was friggin' useless, so he was."

Ross simply nodded in response to Mickey's remark and replied

"Don't apologise, Mickey. If the investigation wasn't carried out properly back then, I need to know about it. Try and recall any details that come into your mind, however small and insignificant you think they might be. It could be important today in helping us ascertain what happened to your sister and to Brendan Kane."

Ross turned to Izzie Drake.

"Could you please organise some more tea and coffee please, Sergeant, and maybe some biscuits? I think we could all do with a little refreshment before we continue."

Drake nodded and closed her notebook, placing it on Ross's desk as she moved to the door.

"Right sir, won't be long." She smiled at Mickey Doyle, having decided there was something rather likeable about the elder Doyle brother. Despite his rough and ready exterior she sensed a vulnerability about Mickey, a fragility of temperament his brother Ronnie certainly didn't suffer from. From the moment the brothers had begun relating their story to Ross and herself, Izzie had been using her intuitive prowess to weigh up and analyze the two men. Both she and Ross were aware that it wouldn't be the first time a potentially psychotic murderer had walked into the hands of the police, often with a view to taunting the law by appearing to help the investigation, inserting themselves into the case as willing witnesses while at the same time using their inside connection to discover how much the police knew, and often being able to deflect the investigation from the truth. After over an hour spent in the company of Ronnie and Mickey Doyle she felt reasonably certain that neither of the brothers had been involved in the murder of their friend, Brendan Kane, or the subsequent disappearance of their sister. If anything, she thought they'd been naïve and a little too trusting of their friend and of the so far unknown quantity that was Phil Oxley, but she could feel no malignant hostility coming from either brother. Returning to Ross's office soon afterwards with a tray containing the requested beverages and a packet of chocolate digestive biscuits, Ross's favourites, Izzie poured drinks for all of them, and pulled a stool from under the computer desk in the corner of Ross's office and sat down, her feet growing tired of standing as she listened to the men's story. Izzie took up her notebook from where she'd left it on the desk, looked up and out of the window, where the earlier clouds had given way to heavy rain, falling in almost horizontal sheets, driven by a strong wind blowing in from the Irish Sea. She felt the weather suited the mood of the interview they were conducting. Ross took a drink of his coffee allowing the hot liquid to refresh his throat before speaking again.

"Right Mickey, I apologise this is taking so long, but I'm sure you both realize by now how important your information is proving to be. Please, take your time, clear your mind again and then, do your best to take me back to the interview with Sergeant Carson."

Mickey Doyle nodded, coughed once and cleared his throat, and allowed his mind to once more return to nineteen sixty-six, as Ross and Drake listened intently to the next installment of the story of Brendan and Marie.

Chapter 21

MISSING PERSONS, 1966

Sergeant Robert Carson sat quietly observing the two men, father and son, who'd just spent half an hour relating an almost unbelievable tale to him. Now, he had to decide just what, if anything, he intended to do in relation to their story. Looking at the notes he'd made on the form that sat on the table in front of him, he decided to first of all recap the details of what they'd told him.

"So, Mr. Doyle, and Michael, you insist Marie had every intention of leaving the city with her boyfriend, this Brendan Kane character, correct?"

James, (Jimmy) Doyle replied with exasperation in his voice.

"That's what we've been telling you for the last thirty minutes. And I told you I knew nothing about Marie wanting to run off with the lad until just before we left home, when Mickey and Ronnie told me and their Mother all about it."

"Ah yes," said Carson, "quite a little conspiracy of secrecy, wouldn't you say?"

"What the fuck d'you mean by that? What conspiracy?" young Mickey snapped at the sergeant.

Carson puffed his chest out, a visible display of his own self-importance. Aged fifty-three, and close to retirement, the dapper sergeant, with his knife edge creases in his uniform, and crisply starched collar, firmly believed in his own ability to tell truth from lies, or to know when his time was being wasted on trivia when there were more serious crimes out there waiting to be solved. Sadly, even his own superiors saw another side to him, that of a man too set in his ways and unable to accept change readily, thereby holding him back and being among the reasons he'd never managed to pass his inspector's exams. Carson had held the rank of sergeant for fifteen years, and would remain in his rank until the day of his retirement. The Doyles, of course knew none of this. To them he was 'The Police' the man they'd been introduced to by the desk sergeant as being the officer available to help in their search for their daughter and sister. He now responded to Mickey's angry comment. Maybe he'd used the wrong word?

"Whoa there, young fellow," he said to Mickey." I meant nothing sinister by my use of the word. Just that it seems to me you and your brother and your mate Oxley seemed to be the only ones in on the secret of this planned move to America. You all played it very close to the chest to ensure your Dad here, and your Mother, knew nothing about it."

"Hang on a minute," said Mickey, "Clemmy knew too."

"Clemmy?"

"Marie's best friend, Clemency De Souza. Marie told me and Ronnie she'd told Clemmy about it, a while ago. She swore her to secrecy."

"Ah, right, I see," Carson nodded his head in mock understanding at Mickey's explanation. "Tell me, has it ever entered your head that Marie and this boyfriend of hers might have been spinning you a line?"

"How d'you mean?" Mickey asked the apparently all-knowing experienced officer sitting looking sternly at him.

"Well, in my experience, I've often found that when young folks want to do a disappearing act, they often tell people one thing, and then up and do something totally different. Have you considered the fact that your sister and her fella might have told you they were planning to go to America, while they secretly made plans to go somewhere different entirely?"

Carson leaned back in his chair with a self-satisfied smile on his face as he watched his words take effect.

"But, why would they do that?" Mickey asked, incredulously. "She knew me and Ronnie were on her side," he said, rather sheepishly as he felt his father's eyes boring into him, his and Ronnie's earlier deception rising high in Jimmy's thoughts once again.

"And you fell for it, didn't you?" Carson went on. "You believed every word. They even got this Oxley lad to go along with their plans, have him make all sorts of inquiries about how to go about getting to America, as you've told me. What better way to throw everyone off their true scent than by creating a clever fantasy that you all fell for? You told me, Mr. Doyle, that Marie is almost twenty one, and there's no law that says a couple can't up sticks and move away from home without telling their parents about it, you know. Also, from what you and your son here have told me, it seems you'd have been none too pleased if you'd known they were planning to run off and elope together."

Both Doyles, senior and junior, appeared quite nonplussed by Carson's theory. Jimmy Doyle appeared lost and unable to respond to Carson, but eventually replied,

"Yeah, well, that's true enough. I don't hold with mixed marriages."

Now it was Carson's turn to look nonplussed, not quite able to grasp Doyle senior's meaning at first.

"Mixed marriages? Are you telling me Brendan Kane is foreign, Asian, or West Indian or something? Is it because you wouldn't want your daughter marrying a coloured person?"

"Colour's got nothing to do with it," said Jimmy Doyle, forcefully. "Brendan Kane is a bloody proddie, a protestant, Sergeant. We're good Catholics, so we are, and I'll not have my daughter marrying a bloody proddie."

Carson almost choked at the man's bigoted words, unable to really grasp such feelings.

"Mr. Doyle," he said. "This is the nineteen sixties. Surely you can see such ideas and attitudes are out of date? If you must know, I happen to be Catholic myself, and I've been happily married to my wife, a 'proddie' as you'd call her, for over thirty years. This is England, Mr. Doyle, not Northern Ireland, though I suspect from your name and your attitude you may have connections over the water."

"I do indeed, Sergeant. I have many cousins and uncles and aunts in Belfast and Derry. As for you and your wife, that's your business. I've no interest in you and your marriage. Like I said, I'd not let any child of mine marry outside our own faith. It's not right and that's all there is to it."

Carson was almost lost for words. He was well aware of the problems that existed across the Irish Sea in Northern Ireland, but had never seen or heard such a display of outright bigotry here in his home town. He could see from the look on Mickey's face that the younger man felt totally embarrassed by his father's outburst and tried to reach out to the father again.

"If you feel so strongly about it, Mr. Doyle, how come you let your sons appear in the pop group with Kane, and let your daughter help them?"

"Aye, well, we don't have a lot of choice in this day and age, do we? We might have to work with people of the other side, but that doesn't mean we marry them and raise kids who don't know the true faith."

Carson had just about had enough of Jimmy Doyle, and any sympathy he felt towards the family's plight now switched entirely to the worried-looking Mickey, who now looked totally uncomfortable in response to his father's outburst.

"Look, here's what I propose. I'll make some inquiries among their friends and social circle. I'll speak to Mr. Oxley, and go along to Brendan Kane's flat, and speak to his parents. Like I said, this whole America thing may have been a total red herring, concocted to make sure you and anyone else couldn't follow them or find them wherever it is they've really gone."

Jimmy and Mickey Doyle left the police station a few minutes later, arriving home half an hour later, soaked to the skin after a very wet walk to the house from the nearest bus stop. Marie's mother, Connie, waiting impatiently in the kitchen, was anxious to hear the outcome of their visit to the police, but became very angry and agitated when Mickey told her about his father's religious outburst to the sergeant. She'd been baptized forty four years earlier as Concepta O'Malley, a good, old-fashioned Irish Catholic name, but one she'd hated since childhood, always preferring the more modern and as far as she was concerned, secular name of Connie. Unlike Jimmy, who was Liverpool born and bred, Connie had actually been born in Lisburn on the outskirts of Belfast, her parents having moved to Liverpool when she was ten years old, themselves sick and tired of what her father referred to as the 'medieval' attitudes towards alternative religions that existed in the Northern Irish community. She'd met and fallen in love with a young, handsome Jimmy Doyle when she was eighteen and he'd been a year older, and they were married a year later. The football loving, weekend fisherman she'd fallen for hadn't displayed his latent tendencies towards religious intolerance until some years later, and she certainly didn't share her husband's religious bigotry, and often found it embarrassing to hear his outdated views on religious affiliations.

"In the name of God and the Holy Virgin, James Doyle, why'd you have to behave in that way in front of the police? Marie's missing, and a young man too, and all you can do is turn it into a speech on marriage between Catholics and Protestants. You're a disgrace, man, so you are."

"D'you think I care what happens to a little scally like Brendan Kane? He's probably already had his way with our Marie and spoiled her for a proper marriage in the future. Then he's enticed her away from her home and family and our two stupid sons went so far as to help them keep it all under wraps. They knew what I'd say if I found out, and so did Marie. That Oxley boy's just as bad, conspiring with them to deceive us."

"He's not a boy, he's a young man, same as Mickey and Ronnie, and he didn't conspire against us, as you put it. He just helped his friends, Jimmy, same as you probably would have done at their age."

"That's where you're wrong, woman. There's no way I'd have disrespected my parents like that."

"Of, for crying out loud, Jimmy, hush your mouth for a minute. I want to know what they said at the police station. You tell me, Mickey. You'll make more sense than your father, to be sure."

Jimmy Doyle gave a kind of growl from deep in his throat, but at least he fell silent and walked across the kitchen, where he took up residence in Connie's comfortable fireside chair, knowing it would irritate his wife as he did so. Connie chose to ignore him as Mickey quickly filled his mother in on their conversation with Sergeant Carson.

"That's all he'd say for now, Ma," Mickey said as he came to the end of relating the story of their interview to his mother. "The sergeant did say he'd be in touch with us after he's made some inquiries and asked around a bit, but I don't think he was really all that interested in what we had to say."

Mickey's back was to his father as he spoke and he managed to gesture with a sideways glance that his mother correctly interpreted as him indicating that his father definitely hadn't helped matters.

Connie Doyle managed to hide her simmering anger towards her husband over the following days, though the atmosphere in the Doyle household deteriorated until it was almost possible to cut it with a knife. Jimmy spent every spare minute at the pub, drowning his sorrows in beer, while Mickey and Ronnie did their best to avoid both their parents. Instead of joining their father at the Red Rose as they would normally have done, they found a haven of relative peace at the local billiard hall, where they did their best to work off their anxiety and frustrations over endless games of snooker and billiards. John Pullman had successfully defended his World Championship status in a series of challenge matches with Fred Davis at the City Hall in Liverpool, and the two brothers had developed a love for the game from watching some of the matches on television. Days passed almost interminably, with no word from Marie or Brendan as to their whereabouts. When the loud knocking that could only be that of a police officer interrupted the family's early evening six days later, it almost came as a form of relief when Connie opened the door and admitted Sergeant Carson to her home, showing him into the sitting room, where she invited him to sit down, introduced him to her younger son, Ronnie, and then together with her husband and sons, nervously awaited his news. Carson sat in one of the two armchairs in the room and politely refused Connie's offer of a cup of tea. Having developed a dislike for Jimmy Doyle at their first meeting, he wanted to keep his visit to the Doyle home as short as possible. Opening his notebook, the sergeant began his report to the expectant Doyle family, delivering his words towards Jimmy Doyle, as the head of the family.

"As I attempted to explain to you when you visited me at the station, Mr. Doyle, bearing in mind the circumstances surrounding this matter, there isn't an awful lot the police can effectively do..."

"So what the fuck do we pay your bloody wages for?" Jimmy Doyle almost exploded at the sergeant.

"For crying out loud, Jimmy, will you just let the man speak?" Connie snapped at her husband, instantly winning the respect of Sergeant Carson. In a quieter voice she continued, "Please go on Sergeant, and forgive my husband's rude and uncouth outburst."

For once, Jimmy Doyle found himself on the receiving end of a tongue lashing, and he made a gruff sound in his throat, stood up and walked across the room to the fireplace, where he stood leaning against the mantelpiece as Carson continued. Even Mickey and Ronnie appeared impressed as their mother at long last appeared to have found the courage to assert herself over her domineering husband.

"Yes, right, thank you, Mrs. Doyle. As I was saying, we don't have many options open to us, I'm sorry to say. I have visited Mr. Kane's parents, your friend, Mr. Phillip Oxley and your daughter's friend, Clemency De Souza, and obtained statements from each of them. I followed this up by reporting the case as you yourselves, Mr. Doyle and Mickey presented it to me, to my boss, and it is Inspector Ledden's opinion that none of the people interviewed, and this includes yourselves, have been able to show that any threat existed against the couple. In other words, nobody has been able to say with even a hint of certainty that they believed Marie and her boyfriend to be in any imminent danger, either from each other or from any other person or persons, known or unknown. There is absolutely no evidence to suggest that this is anything other then a case of two young people, both over and above the age of consent, and of legal voting age, deciding to leave their homes and make a fresh start somewhere else."

"That's a load of bollocks, Sergeant Carson," Mickey cut in. "Me Dad and me only came to see you because we were worried about them disappearing without leaving word. It was totally not like them to do that, especially after making their plans to go to America."

Connie Doyle shot a glance at Mickey that he instantly recognized and responded to.

"Er, sorry about the bad language, Sergeant, sorry, Mam."

"Yes, well, where was I?" Carson almost smiled at the tiny domestic cameo that had just played out before his eyes. "Oh, yes, so, we have a situation where Marie and Brendan Kane appear to have produced an elaborate plan to run away to America, but as your mate Phillip Oxley told us, Brendan Kane knew he couldn't just waltz into the United States without going through a lengthy immigration process, so my boss concluded that they must have got tired of waiting, and have gone somewhere else entirely. There are lots of places in the world that don't have such strict rules about who they allow into their countries. I take it Marie has a passport?"

"Yes, she does," Connie replied.

"Listen, Mrs. Doyle, it's been my experience over the years that most missing adults go missing because they want to do so, whatever the reason or the rights and wrongs of the matter, that's a simple fact. If they don't want to be found, there are many ways for them to remain hidden, often in plain sight in another town or country, but by the same token, many of them will simply turn up after a few days, or weeks perhaps, when things don't go quite the way they expect them to. You know, the old 'grass isn't greener on the other side' thing. If there had been any evidence of foul play here, rest assured we would have thrown the weight of the force behind a search for them, but as it stands, no one can substantiate the merest hint of a threat to their safety. No crime has been committed and the inspector simply won't sanction the number of man hours required for an extensive country-wide search for a couple who everyone admits had planned to leave town anyway."

A pall of desperation hung heavy in the Doyle's living room as the sergeant's words struck home to each member of the family. Jimmy Doyle at last found his voice once again.

"So that's it? That's all the police can do for us? What about that scally's flat? Did you even bother going round there?"

"I did go there, as a matter of fact, Mr. Doyle. There was nobody at home, and I looked up the landlords of the building, and they told me they received a letter from Kane just two days ago, saying he was leaving town, and enclosing a month's rent in the envelope, along with instruction to sell his things, as he wouldn't be coming back to Liverpool."

"But, that's rubbish," Ronnie said in response to the news of the letter. "He'd never do that, not leave all his things behind, not Brendan. I mean, there was his new record player, his guitar, all that kind of stuff. Did you ask if his guitar was gone or still in the flat?"

"Ronnie, love, I know you're upset. We all are, but you mustn't badger the sergeant like that, really you mustn't," Connie Doyle said to her son. Connie retained a good old-fashioned healthy respect for the police and didn't like to see and hear her son acting in a belligerent manner towards a member of the force.

Ronnie shook his head in exasperation.

"Yeah, right, sorry Mam, sorry Sergeant," he apologised.

With great dignity, Connie Doyle rose from her chair by the fire and walked slowly to the polished wooden sideboard at the opposite side of the room, and picked up a small, yellow plastic transistor radio from behind a large school photograph of Marie, taken when she was fourteen. Holding it as though it were an item of inestimable value she held it up so Carson could see it clearly.

"This, Sergeant Carson, is my daughter's most treasured possession. It cost her two shillings on Kirkby Market. Expensive? No, but valuable beyond words to Marie. She loves music, Sergeant, and if she was going anywhere important, or for any length of time, this little radio would have gone with her. That's why I know something's very wrong, and that my little girl is in trouble of some kind."

"Look," said Carson, "I've personally distributed your daughter and Brendan Kane's descriptions to other police forces in the country. If any officer sees and recognizes them they will report it back to us here in Liverpool and I promise to let you know if that happens. The case file will remain open, but for now, there's not much more I can do for you. I'm sorry"

"Yeah, I just bet you are," said Jimmy Doyle, his voice heavy with sarcasm.

"I have to go, I'm afraid," Carson said, now in a hurry to be gone from the Doyle house. "If I hear anything, I'll be in touch."

Connie Doyle saw the sergeant out and as he disappeared down the street to the spot where he'd parked his sleek, white, Ford Zephyr 6 patrol car, she slowly closed the front door, somehow knowing in her heart of hearts that she would probably never see her little girl again.

Chapter 22

CONFIRMATION

"That was it, Inspector Ross" said Ronnie Doyle with a look of intense sadness on his face. "The police did virtually sod all to try and find Marie or Brendan for that matter."

"Are you telling me you never heard from the police again after the visit from Sergeant Carson?" Ross asked Ronnie.

"Well, we did get another visit a few weeks later. Sergeant Carson came to the house one morning. Me and Mickey were at work and Dad was out, I can't remember where. Me Mam told us later that Carson had done a routine follow-up on our report of Marie's disappearance and that there'd been no word from any of the flyers he'd sent to other forces and there'd also been no reports of any 'victims of violence' as he put it, being found anywhere in the country. That was his nice way of saying murder, I reckon, and not wanting to upset me Mam. He told her he'd checked with the airports and docks and found no reference to either Brendan or Marie attempting to leave the country. I think, by that time, me Mam had resigned herself to Marie not coming back, but I remember her sitting crying very quietly to herself that night. I left her to her own thoughts, because I didn't want to upset her even more and to be honest, I wouldn't have known what to say to her, Inspector. She cried a lot after that, usually when she thought no one could hear her, but we did, often."

Andy Ross sat, deep in thought for a few seconds after Ronnie finished his story. He could understand why the Doyles felt less than satisfied with the response of the old Liverpool City Police in nineteen sixty-six, but knew that Sergeant Carson, by all accounts, though not sounding like the most dynamic officer he'd ever experienced, had probably done his best under the circumstances. In addition, Carson was only human and his reaction to James Doyle's outburst of blatant religious bigotry had probably been entirely justified, bearing in mind his own personal circumstances. Favouritism was frowned upon in the police service but no one could be blamed for not being entirely sympathetic to someone like the elder Doyle. Without doing his best to make some attempt to look into the investigation that took place at the time of Marie's original disappearance, he certainly wasn't going to buy into the Doyle brothers' account of the rights or wrong of the way the police handled their complaint at the time, or make any criticism of Carson or anyone else involved. Based on what they'd just told him, Ross knew something the brothers weren't aware of, something that might add a little sensitivity to the way he approached his research into the past, but now wasn't the right time to mention it. He needed to try and communicate that to them in a way that wouldn't alienate his best, in fact his only witnesses to the final days of Brendan Kane. He quickly decided on his next move and after allowing Ronnie a brief respite, Ross said,

"Look, Ronnie, you too Mickey. It's been a long interview and you've both been very helpful. I know today hasn't gone exactly as you expected when you walked into the station earlier but you really have given me a lot to work with. We now know with reasonable certainty that the remains found at Coles' Wharf are those of your friend, Brendan Kane and thanks to you, we now know about the disappearance of your sister, which I assure you, I'm going to follow up on, as I feel both cases are closely connected. We'll speak to everyone we can find from those days, Phil Oxley, Clemmy De Souza and whoever has a good recollection of either of the two. I forgot to ask if your mother and father are still alive?"

"Yes, they are," Ronnie replied. "Dad is eighty now, but still fit as a fiddle, Inspector. Hardly had a day's illness in his life. Our Mother is only about a year behind him but not as well as she was. She has severe arthritis and has coronary heart disease, but still lives in hope that one day she'll find out just what happened to our Marie."

"Okay, that's good to know. I will of course need to speak to both your parents in due course. I hope their powers of recollection are as good as yours."

"I wouldn't count on it, Inspector. They are getting on a bit, you know, said Mickey. "I know they're great for their age, but Mam especially is a bit forgetful these days."

"Understood," Ross replied, "but whatever they can remember may prove useful. Please make sure you give Sergeant Drake both of your telephone numbers and that of your parents before you leave, so we can get in touch with you quickly if we need to."

Both men provided Izzie Drake with the required numbers and Izzie herself showed the Doyles from the premises a few minutes later, then returning to Ross's office where the inspector and his sergeant sat quietly and began to confer on the events and the information they'd received in what had been a rather long two hour interview with the brothers.

* * *

"Wow, that was a bit of a marathon session, sir," Drake commented.

"It was indeed, Izzie," Ross replied, "and totally unexpected. Who'd have expected those two to walk in off the streets and give us the vital link we needed to identify our victim?"

"You're sure the remains are those of Brendan Kane, then, sir?"

"Everything they told us seems to fit with what we already have, which admittedly wasn't much up until now."

"But what about the missing sister, sir? Where do we go with that one?"

"I must say, Izzie, I'm not too sure at the moment. It adds another, highly sinister element to the case we already have. I'm going to have to talk to the boss. D.C.I Porteous will have to allow us a little extra manpower I think. I want a few uniforms available to help us with the footwork that I envisage we'll need to go deeper into the affairs of nineteen sixty-six."

"Do you believe everything the brothers told us, sir?"

"They came here believing we may have found the remains of their sister. They had no reason to lie to us and I believe they were genuinely shocked when we suggested the bones could be those of their friend. I think they both firmly believe Marie is dead, and in light of what they've told us, I must admit I tend to subscribe to that theory too."

"But why, sir? Why would anyone want to murder a young couple who, as far as we can ascertain, hurt no-one and whose only fault appears to have been the fact they fell in love and wanted to start a new life somewhere else?"

"Well, according to the brothers, their father was certainly bigoted enough to want Brendan Kane out of the way, but, would he have harboured sufficient hatred to murder his own daughter too? Somehow, I just don't see that happening. He seems to have been a hundred percent family orientated, though we'll know more about him when we interview the man. Plus, if Marie Doyle was murdered at the same time as her boyfriend, how come her body has never been found?"

"It's taken over thirty years for Brendan's remains to turn up, with all due respect sir."

"Yes, of course it has, Izzie. Thanks for reminding me." Ross smiled at Drake as he accepted his sergeant's mild rebuke. "It's always possible they were killed together and Marie's body simply got carried away by the tide, and ended up as fish food somewhere between Liverpool and the Irish Sea."

As the two detectives continued bouncing ideas back and forth between them, the afternoon began to grow darker, as the overhead storm clouds grew in intensity and the view outside Ross's window became even more depressing than it had been during the visit of the

Doyle brothers. Ross stood, pushed his chair back and walked to the window, peering out into the sheets of almost horizontal rain that were lashing down, presenting a grim picture of the world outside to go with the grim task he and Drake were involved in.

He walked across the room and flicked the light switch. A few clicks from overhead heralded the coming of the light from the long fluorescent tubes, which burst into full life after a few hesitant seconds of flickering. Andy Ross re-took his seat, and just as he was about to continue his discourse with Izzie Drake, the telephone on his desk began ringing. Ross lifted the receiver.

"D.I. Ross," he announced to the caller, and then, "McLennan, why are you phoning me from the other end of the office?" He listened to the young detective constable for a few seconds, and then with an amused look on his face, he replied, "Oh yes, right, I see, the door was closed and you thought it best not to disturb me by knocking on my door, so I presume you thought it best to disturb me by phoning me instead?"

Before Derek McLennan could say any more, Ross said, "If you have news for us, better get yourself in here now, McLennan. Don't keep me waiting, there's a good lad."

"You can be a cruel sod, sir, if you don't mind me saying so. He's a good lad, and trying to impress you whenever he can, you know?"

"I know, Izzie. Can't help winding the lad up sometimes. In a way he reminds me of me at his age, intense and doing everything by the book, trying to please the boss, until one day I realized the way to get on was just to be myself, do my best and sod the consequences. He'll get there one day. He's got the makings of a first class detective and..."

A knock on the door interrupted Ross's words and as the door opened, Derek McLennan strode into the room, a very big smile on his face, and a sheet of A4 paper in his hand.

"From the look on your face, I'd say you come bearing tidings of great joy, Constable McLennan", said Ross, returning the smile.

"Yes sir, very good news, I'd say. We have a positive I.D on the dental records of our skeletal remains. A firm of dentists in town, Ledger and

Crowe, they've been in business for donkey's years, and the current Mr. Ledger is the grandson of the original owner. Seems dentistry runs in the family and anyway, they were able to put a name to the remains from the photographs Doctor Nugent and his people gave us."

Ross couldn't stop himself.

"Brendan Kane, unless I'm very much mistaken, eh, young Derek?"

McLennan's jaw dropped, surprise clearly evident on his face at Ross's apparent wizardry in coming out with the name on his sheet of paper.

"Well, yes, that's right, sir, but how the heck did you know that? I've only had the confirmation myself for ten minutes."

"Don't fret yourself, lad. Believe it or not, Sergeant Drake and I have just finished a grueling two hour interview with two brothers who gave us the name in connection with the disappearance of their sister around the same time. I took a chance on asking if their friend had broken his leg as a boy, they said yes, and the rest just fell into place."

"Oh, I see, sir. That's great then, isn't it?"

"Yes, and well done on tracking the dental records down too. I'm not stealing your thunder, because if the Doyle brothers hadn't come in to see me today, the dental evidence would be the only identifying evidence we have, which in reality it still is. You've done well."

"Thank you, sir," said McLennan, holding out the sheet of paper and passing it to the D.I. Here's the faxed confirmation from Ledger and Crowe, absolute one hundred percent certainty that the teeth are those of Brendan Kane."

"Right then, here's what I want you to do next. Sergeant Drake has some things to check while I go and have a word with the D.C.I. In the meantime, I'd like you to run a criminal records check on these two men," and he passed a piece of paper bearing the names and addresses of the two Doyle brothers to McLennan. "It doesn't hurt to be thorough, and this case has just expanded greatly, so I want to be sure our two witnesses are all they appear to be."

McLennan grasped the piece of paper and was gone in a few seconds, eager to play his part in the gathering intensity of the case.

"Er, before we go our separate ways, sir, just one question, if I may?" said Drake after they were alone again.

"Go on, Izzie, what's on your mind?"

"You said there was something you'd tell me later, sir, when we were with the brothers. Well, is this 'later' enough?"

"Oh yes," Ross smiled at her. "You remember the Doyles mentioned an inspector, Sergeant Carson's boss by all accounts?"

Quickly flicking back through her notes, Drake replied,

"Inspector Ledden; that was the name, sir."

"Yes, that's right. I didn't want to appear too hasty in any condemnation of the previous investigation into Marie Doyle's disappearance, because, if I'm right, the Inspector Ledden they were speaking of is now Detective Chief Superintendent Bernard Ledden, head of the Regional Drug Squad. If so, I don't want to go treading on toes that can be avoided if you know what I mean, at least, not at this stage of our investigation."

Drake nodded her head in agreement.

"Oh yes, sir, I see very well indeed. I'd best be getting on with looking for these addresses for now then hadn't I?"

"Yes, you do that, Izzie. I'll be with the boss for a while, please fix up a mini-conference for the two of us, McLennan and Paul Ferris for eight o'clock in the morning. Then tell them to finish what they're doing and go home. I won't be out of the boss's office for at least an hour, so we can't do much more today, but I want everyone bright and fresh in the morning. We're going to have a lot of work to do in the next few days. We can then discuss where we go from here after I've spoken with the D.C.I. See you when I get back," and with that, he rushed out of the office to report the new developments to D.C.I. Porteous. Izzie tidied Ross's desk, and left to do her own assigned tasks before talking to the team and leaving for home. Tomorrow promised to be an interesting day.

Chapter 23

CASE CONFERENCE, LIVERPOOL, 1999

Although he'd told Izzie Drake to arrange the operational conference for eight a.m. Andy Ross made sure he arrived at the station a half hour earlier. The two reasons for his early arrival followed him into the conference room soon after, and were closely followed by Drake, Ferris and McLennan, who may have been surprised to see two new faces in their midst, but waited for Ross to explain. After inviting all those present to be seated, Ross took up a position at the head of the grandly sounding, but actually quite functional and cheap wooden conference table, this being the city of Liverpool after all, not a gentlemen's club in Mayfair. Various nods and quiet hellos were spoken and then, Ross gave a polite cough to catch everyone's attention before speaking.

"Good morning, everyone," he began. "As you can see, we have two new faces with us this morning. After my meeting with D.C.I. Porteous yesterday afternoon, and after he agreed that, as the local bad boys are not giving us too hard a time at present, he generously allotted us a little extra manpower. Let me introduce you to Detective Constables Nick Dodds and Samantha Gable."

Another series of more formal welcomes and hellos followed and as silence fell once more, Ross continued.

"Nick comes to us from the burglary squad, and Sam has just completed a year working the vice squad. Both are experienced officers and I have to stress that, following my talk with the gaffer yesterday, he agrees there is more depth to this case than the original discovery of the skeletal remains suggested."

Ross gave a brief resumé of the initial discovery of the remains at the wharf, mostly for the benefit of the newcomers, followed by a detailed run through on the interview he and Drake had conducted with Mickey and Ronnie Drake the previous day, ending with the confirmation of Brendan Kane's identity from his dental records, miraculously still available after over thirty years, a lucky break if ever they needed one.

A soft knock at the conference room door followed, and the door opened to admit a well-dressed man in a grey pin-stripe suit, sporting a blue silk tie, aged somewhere in his forties. The man issued a brief apology for being late, and Ross quickly introduced the newcomer.

"Ah yes, no problem, George. Everyone, I'd like you all to meet George Thompson. George is the Headquarters' Press Liaison Officer. D.C.I. Porteous wants us to keep George in the loop on the case, now that it's expanded beyond its original parameters. Seems there's likely to be a fair bit of local interest in this one, with young Brendan Kane having been something of a relatively minor local celebrity among the growing rock and pop music fraternity in the early days of the sixties. Add in a young girl, his sweetheart, missing for over thirty years, and the boss wants George to be able to keep any press interest on track and avoid the force coming under any unduly harsh criticism for its handling of the case either then or now. Anything you'd like to add, George?"

Clearing his throat, George Thompson moved round the table to sit at the opposite end of the table to Ross.

"Just that it's good to meet you all. I promise you that despite what you may hear sometimes, as PLO I'm here to act as a back up to the work you do, not to do anything that might hinder your investigation. I want to portray the force in a good light of course, but I also want to make sure that I can help the case wherever possible by passing sound bites or articles to the local and if necessary, the national press that might assist in your inquiries. Any appeals you guys want out there, I'll be happy to put them together in a way that they look and sound good and reach the target audience. So please, don't see me as a hindrance, but rather, use me and my expertise in my field as a useable asset in your approach to solving the case. As D.I. Ross just said, there is likely to be some media interest and it's my job to deal with it, and to protect your backs from any mud slinging that might begin when the facts of the case come out. I'll be putting out a press release in the next day or two, detailing the identification of Kane's remains and the connection with the long-forgotten disappearance of a girl called Marie Doyle. Hopefully, it might jog a few memories and maybe bring in one or two pieces of useful information. That's all for now, everyone, and thanks for listening to me."

Ross in turn thanked Thompson for his time and invited him to remain in the meeting until its conclusion, so he could understand just what Ross and his team was initially trying to achieve. George Thompson sat listening as Ross brought the team planning conference towards its conclusion.

"There's one other thing that arose as a result of the visit by the Doyle brothers yesterday. They still feel the police at the time of their original complaint failed to take the disappearance of Marie Doyle seriously enough and didn't do enough to find her, and it would appear the officer in charge at the time was an Inspector Bernard Ledden, who just happens to still be with the force and is now a Detective Chief Superintendent, in charge of the Regional Drug Squad."

After a few murmurs from those around the table, Ross continued.

"Yes, a potentially sensitive issue, as I'm sure you can appreciate. I can't exactly go marching in to the office of a D.C.S and accuse him of failing in his duty thirty three years ago. The D.C.I has given me the go ahead to go and talk to Ledden, with the proviso I tread carefully and avoid making any unsubstantiated allegations of dereliction of duty towards him or his team at the time. I phoned yesterday and I've an appointment with D.C.S. Ledden later this morning. In the meantime, Sergeant Drake has obtained certain addresses of those people I need interviewing in connection with the two cases, which I now want us to regard as part and parcel of one, wider reaching case. I agree that coincidences happen, but the fact that Marie Doyle and Brendan Kane disappeared from sight at the same time all those years ago is just stretching coincidence too far. Ferris, you're a good man on computers so I want you to be our case coordinator and collator, any and all information you all obtain comes back to Ferris who will keep me updated at all times. Spend an hour or so this morning setting up your case files while we're out, okay?"

Nods of agreement from Ferris and the others followed and Ross then proceeded to hand out individual assignments.

"Sergeant Drake will visit Phillip Oxley this morning. Sam, I'd like to you visit the last known address we have for Marie's former best friend, Clemency De Souza, and Nick, I want you to accompany Sergeant Drake and after interviewing Oxley, I want you to pay a call on James and Connie Doyle. I'd like to meet this old man myself but at present, it's important we move swiftly to try and get a handle on exactly what we're dealing with. If these two young people were simply a pair of runaways, I fail to see how Brendan Kane ended up with two bullet wounds in his knees and his head bashed in, and then, what the hell happened to Marie? We have questions that require answers, and I don't care how long ago this all took place, as far as I'm concerned it's an open murder inquiry, and we're going to work hard at finding those answers. Everybody got that?"

Everyone gave more nods and words of agreement as Ross brought the case conference to a close. After sending his now expanded team off to deal with their allotted tasks, Ross made his way to conduct his interview with Detective Chief Constable Ledden.

* * *

"Detective Inspector Ross, pleased to meet you," said D.C.S. Bernard Ledden, rising from behind his large, highly polished mahogany desk after Ross had been shown in to his office by Claire, his secretary. He offered an outstretched hand as he reached across his desk and the two men shook hands. Ross was impressed by his first impressions of the man. Tall, just over six feet, his uniform immaculately pressed and a face that seemed to exude a look of confidence born of many years experience in the job. There appeared to be no pomposity about the man, something Ross had seen in all too many officers of senior rank over the years.

"Please, sit," said Ledden, gesturing to a large, comfortable looking leather upholstered chair to the left of his desk. Ross sat as requested, and realized the layout of the office; the positioning of the chair he sat in was intended not to intimidate Ledden's visitors, but to put them more at ease with man. Sitting directly opposite from the Chief Superintendent would have increased any junior officer's tension at such a meeting. As it was, Ledden was making Ross feel welcome, on a more equal footing than he actually occupied.

"D.C.I. Porteous spoke very highly of you when he phoned me yesterday. Apparently you have some questions to put to me about a case I may have been involved in back in my days as an inspector?"

"That's correct, sir. It's about a missing persons case from thirty three years ago, one that we've only just tied to the murder of a young man whose remains were recently discovered in a dried up part of the river bed beside an old wharf undergoing redevelopment."

"Ah, yes, I saw something about that case in the Echo, and then caught something about it in a recent newsletter that landed on my desk. Please, tell me how you believe I can be of help in your investigation."

With Porteous's words about being diplomatic and non-confrontational ringing in his ears, Ross first passed the Chief Superintendent a file containing the pertinent facts of both cases and then tried, in the best way he could, to lay out the case before the D.C.S as briefly as possible, knowing that senior officers such as Ledden appreciated brevity and keeping to the point. When he'd finished, he breathed a sigh a relief and waited as Ledden assimilated the information Ross had presented to him, both verbally and in print.

After what felt like an age, but was only about a minute, during which Ross barely drew a breath, Chief Superintendent Ledden looked up, closed the file on his desk, and delivered his reply.

"Well, you've certainly painted quite a picture here, Inspector. From a pile of old bones barely two weeks ago to an unsolved murder, an identified victim and a girl missing for over thirty years, really quite something. You and your team have done well."

"Thank you sir. My team will be pleased to hear that."

"It's true. A lot of officers wouldn't have put such effort into a case like this and would have left it on the unsolved pile rather than go digging like this, but that shows what a diligent police officer you are. Now, as for the Marie Doyle case, there's not a lot I can really tell you. Yes, Bob Carson was a sergeant under my command, and he was a good man in his younger days, though he did kind of let things slide a bit as he moved towards retirement, as I recall. He was tenacious in his own way though, and from what these two brothers have told you, he appears to have ticked all the boxes, without going too far beyond the basics. I won't knock him for that, Inspector, as I don't honestly recall the case, but if he'd thought there was a case to investigate at the time, and he'd recommended further investigation to me, I would have given the go-ahead, I can assure you. My God, there were so many cases that fell under my purview in those days, and if I had any knowledge of this Marie Doyle, I'd share it with you, please have no doubt about that, but thirty three years is a long time, Inspector."

"Yes, sir, I do understand that. I wasn't expecting miracles but I hope you understand why I needed to at least ask if you had any memory of the case?"

"Of course, and credit to you for making the effort. Anything else I can help you with, while you're here, Inspector?"

"One question, sir. Would you happen to know if Sergeant Carson is still alive? It might help if I could talk to him, maybe jog his memory and see if he can remember something that might help me."

Ledden slowly shook his head and a grave look crossed his face before he replied.

"I'm sorry, Ross, but Carson died about three years after he retired. Bloody tragic. Just beginning to enjoy some quality time with his wife and they took a holiday in Thailand, I think it was and he picked up some heinous tropical disease. Poor chap died within two weeks of returning to the UK. I attended his funeral. Poor Emma, his wife was totally devastated I can tell you."

"Well, sir, thank you for being honest with me and for giving up your time. I know you're a very busy man."

"Not a problem, Inspector Ross. Listen, let me tell you something. I've been a police officer in this city almost all my working life. I joined the old Liverpool City Police as a probationary constable when I was twenty years old, and by the time the force was amalgamated with the Bootle Borough Police in nineteen sixty-seven, I'd made it to Inspector. Liverpool and Bootle didn't last long, Ross, and in nineteen seventy-four, the powers that be decided to change things again, and took large slices of the old Cheshire and Lancashire Constabularies to form what we have now, under this grand title we have of Merseyside Police. You probably know the history of the force from your own time with the force, but my point is that over all those years, and through all the reorganizations and amalgamations, I've seen a lot of good coppers come and go and known a few bent ones in my time. I have never allowed a bent copper to escape if it was in my power to do something about it and the same thing goes for any officer who didn't apply due diligence and professionalism to any inquiry. Bob Carson was neither bent, nor unprofessional, despite what these two brothers have intimated in their statement. The worst accusation you could have made against him was that he slowed down a little as retirement approached, and that is something that applies to many long-serving uniformed officers, as I'm sure you're aware. Now, having said that, I'm only sorry I couldn't be of more help to you, but I do wish you good luck in your efforts to try and solve this one. It would be quite a feather in your cap if you could solve a thirty-three year old murder and disappearance at the same time. I'll keep a watching brief on your progress, and wish you the best of luck."

Knowing the meeting had reached its natural ending, Ross stood and prepared to leave the Chief Superintendent's office. Ledden also stood and walked around the large mahogany desk, and stood facing Ross as he first shook his hand warmly and then passed the file Ross had brought, back to him, adding a few parting words before allowing Ross to depart.

"I know you probably thought you'd find evidence of a failed or botched investigation, Ross, but believe me, Bob Carson might not have been *'Columbo'*, but he wouldn't have let the case of a missing girl slip past him if he'd thought there was anything sinister going on. He was a husband and father himself you know, and he must have genuinely believed this girl had simply run off with her boyfriend. Have you found anything that suggests otherwise in your new investigation, so far?"

"No, sir, we haven't, and I wasn't insinuating anything untoward had taken place in the original investigation. But, I did want to know if everything that could have been done, was done. I hope you understand my reasoning."

"I do, Inspector, and I appreciate you being candid with me. Your honesty is refreshing. There are too many 'yes men' around nowadays. Now, go catch yourself a murderer, if you can after all this time, and if you do find what happened to the girl, as it was my case once upon a time, please do me the courtesy of letting me know."

"I will, sir, and thanks again for seeing me," said Ross as he took his leave of the Detective Chief Superintendent.

* * *

A sense of relief washed over Andy Ross as he sat behind his desk, back in his own office once again. Being in the rarefied atmosphere of the office of one of the upper echelon of the city's senior officers had made Ross slightly uncomfortable. D.C.S. Ledden had come across as far more 'human' than Ross had expected and had seemed to be open and honest with him. Yes, it had been over thirty years since the Marie

Doyle investigation, and it was true that Ledden must have overseen thousands of cases in his years on the force, so Ross agreed in his mind that it had been impractical to expect the man to remember each and every one that landed on his desk. However, he did feel that more could have been done on the original inquiry and that Ledden himself, as the inspector in charge at the time, could have pushed Carson to take his inquiries further. Perhaps, he surmised, they had other, more pressing cases on their books at the time, cases with identifiable victims and perpetrators, or with more at stake either personally or financially for those involved. Whether that excused a slight lack of application to the Doyle case, he couldn't truly decide. After all, he'd have had to be there at the time to make such a judgement. For now, he knew he had to accept Ledden's word for things, and press on with his own inquiry.

Knowing his own ineptitude at remembering important family dates, he immediately picked up the phone, making a call to Maria's favourite restaurant and reserving a table for two for the night of her special day. A second call to the florists also ensured a delivery of red roses in the late afternoon of her birthday. He'd already checked and knew she'd be working the early shift at the surgery that day. The similarity in Christian names drew his thoughts back to Marie Doyle. Somehow, the two Doyle brothers and their story had touched Ross in a way he'd never have expected. Over thirty years had passed and yet her brothers had never given up hope of finding out what had happened to their little sister. Such loyalty, Ross had inwardly decided, deserved rewarding and if he hadn't already done so, he now made himself a mental promise that, one way or another, he'd do everything possible to achieve a result, to find not only the murderer of the young Brendan Kane, but also to discover exactly what fate had befallen Marie Doyle.

His reverie was interrupted by a knock on his half open door, followed by the appearance of the Press Liaison Officer, George Thompson, who entered the office, briefcase in hand.

"Got a minute, Andy?" Thompson asked.

"Sure, George. What can I do for you?" Ross replied.

"I've composed a new press release, and wanted to let you read and comment on it and suggest any changes you feel may be appropriate before I let it out to the newshounds."

Having worked with Thompson on a couple of previous occasions, one of the things Ross liked about the man was that, unlike some P.L.Os, George Thompson never lost sight of the fact he was part of a team, and whatever he did could have a major bearing on the results of any inquiry he became involved with. The man was devoid of what Ross saw as the curse of many a Press Officer, that being a sense of self-importance that could lead to conflict with the investigating officers. In short, he rather liked the man.

"Thanks, George. I appreciate that. Let's see what you've got for me then."

George Thompson opened his slim leather briefcase, slowly removed a sheet of A4 sized paper and passed the printed, proposed Press Release to Ross.

"Sit down for a minute, won't you, while I read through it, George?"

Thompson sat in the chair in front of Ross's desk and remained silent as Ross read:

'Skeleton Identified, - Police Seek Missing Woman!'

Following the recent discovery of the skeletal remains of a young man in the river bed adjacent to a dried up, disused warehouse in the old docklands area of the city, Merseyside Police have now been able to positively identify the remains as being those of twenty one year old Brendan Kane, a one-time musician and book store worker in the city. It is known that Mr. Kane, once the lead singer and a guitarist with the early sixties pop group, Brendan Kane and the Planets, had planned to leave the city together with his girlfriend, twenty year old Marie Doyle, in the summer or autumn of nineteen sixty-six. Pathologists have determined that Mr. Kane was the victim of a vicious attack prior to his body being deposited in what, at the time would have been a watery grave in the Mersey, close to the disused Coles' Wharf, in the old docklands area of the city. Miss Doyle is reported as having disappeared either simultaneously with the murder of Mr. Kane or at some time close to his death and has not been seen or heard from since that time. Anyone with information they feel might assist the police in this inquiry should contact Merseyside Police on. . . (phone numbers).

"Looks good to me, George," said Ross. "One small point though. Shouldn't we be a little more specific regarding approximate dates and times etc? You know, try to get people to focus on what they were doing right about the time both people disappeared?"

"In my experience, Andy, it's usually best not to be too date-specific with this type of appeal. If you try to pin people down to, for example, 'between the dates of 10th-20th August, you tend to find they will mentally ignore anything that might have occurred before or after that time, but that may still be relevant to the inquiry. Better to be deliberately vague so that anyone who thinks they might have seen or heard something prior to, or after the time of the double disappearance, won't be put off contacting us because they fear their information may not be relevant or important."

"I see what you mean, George," Ross replied, impressed with the Press Officer's thought processes. "I'd never have thought of it like that. I'm glad we've got a real professional on the job."

Thompson accepted the compliment gracefully.

"Just doing my job, Andy. I only hope it produces results for you and your team, though, after over thirty years, I wouldn't be too optimistic. A lot of folks who may have been around then with any knowledge of your case could well be dead and buried by now."

Ross nodded his head slowly, almost ruefully.

"I know," he said. "That's my biggest fear, too. We could be chasing ghosts in this case, people who just aren't around any longer to help us."

"Well, good luck with it, anyway. I'll get this to *The Echo* today, and copy it to all the nationals by tomorrow. It might help to have full coverage in the dailies as well as the local press. People move around a lot more these days. We may find witnesses in other areas who lived here way back when."

"Thanks again, George," said Ross as Thompson closed his briefcase and got up to leave, the copy of the press release left on the desk for Ross to show to his team later.

"My pleasure, Andy," said Thompson, who closed the door quietly as he left, leaving Ross alone with his thoughts once more.

Chapter 24

A STEP IN TIME

Izzie Drake pulled up on the street about five doors away from the home of James and Connie Doyle. An earlier visit to the address Izzie had found for Phil Oxley had proved fruitless, with no reply to their knocking at the door and ringing the doorbell, so she'd decided to try the Doyle home first and return to Oxley's later. The two detectives exited the car, and as Drake pointed the remote at the vehicle, activating the central locking system, Nick Dodds looked up and down the street and commented on his first impressions.

"My God, Sarge, this place looks as if it's hardly altered since the nineteen-sixties, at least from pictures I've seen of those days, me being a bit young to have been around then."

"Oh, the wisdom of youth, what are you, a child of the seventies?" Drake quipped, and then, also looking at their immediate surroundings, "But yes, you're right. Red brick terraces, back to back gardens, all we need is a bomb site at the end of the street with dirty-kneed kids in short pants kicking a ball around among the rubble and we could be in another time, Nick, for sure."

Grafton Street, where Mickey and Ronnie Doyle had grown up and spent their early adult years had indeed retained much of the way it must have looked thirty to forty years ago. Though many owner-residents had invested their money in improving their properties, with new, uPVC double glazing, and new front doors, others, perhaps those still owned by absent landlords and rented out as cheap, low income housing, seemed to bravely carry the scars of years of at least partial neglect, with peeling paintwork on window ledges and doors, and faulty pointing in brickwork and the occasional missing roof tile. It really did represent a place out of time, a throwback to another age, and a million light years away from some of the ultra-modern apartment complexes and other new developments taking place in various, more desirable parts of the city. In place of the bomb site Drake had joked about, at the end of the street stood a nineteen-eighties built community centre and library, perhaps the local council's attempt to help create some sense of belonging and identity among residents, most of whom had probably lived in the surrounding streets for much shorter durations then older families like the Doyles. The graffiti-covered walls of the community centre were perhaps a measure of the project's success.

As the two officers arrived at the door to number 26, the sound of loud reggae music could be clearly heard from an upstairs bedroom of the house next door. Having heard about James Doyle from his two sons, Izzie had a feeling he might not be too enamoured of his current next-door neighbours. She nodded to Nick Dodds and the constable knocked firmly on the front door, which Drake could swear she saw shaking on its hinges as he did so. A few seconds later the door opened, just a crack, and a voice, female and frail-sounding asked, "Yes, who's there?"

"Mrs. Doyle?" Izzie asked.

"Yes, and who are you?" the old lady asked.

"My name is Detective Sergeant Clarissa Drake, Merseyside Police, and this is Detective Constable Dodds. We'd like to talk to you about your daughter, Marie, Mrs. Doyle."

The door opened fully as the old woman gasped and almost fell forward into Izzie's arms. Izzie reached out to steady the woman, not having prepared herself for such a reaction.

"Oh my, what is it? Have you found my little girl after all this time?" gasped Connie Doyle, pulling herself upright as she recovered from her initial shock.

"No, not exactly, but look, can we come in, please, Mrs. Doyle? I'm sure you don't want to talk about this on your front doorstep?"

"Oh, sorry, of course. Please, come in. You must excuse the place. I haven't finished the housework yet you see and..."

"Please don't apologise, we didn't exactly make an appointment did we?" said Izzie, feeling a little sorry for the woman, who looked as frail as she sounded.

Connie Doyle looked ill, thought Izzie, her skin having a rather dull, lifeless pallor, though the woman's blonde hair retained much of its life and was well-styled. Mrs. Doyle cared about her appearance and probably paid regular visits to her hairdresser. Her floral patterned dress looked clean and ironed and her pale yellow cardigan was of good quality and hung unfastened on her shoulders.

"Would you like to come into the kitchen?" Connie asked the officers. "I was just making some tea when you knocked on the door."

"That would be nice, thank you." said Drake as she and Dodds followed Connie Doyle along the hallway and into the small but surprisingly clean and well appointed kitchen, the centerpiece of which appeared to be an old, but beautifully maintained sideboard, the wood polished to a high gloss and the brass handles on the drawers and doors gleaming like new. Izzie couldn't help noticing a photograph subtly placed to the rear of the sideboard, quite clearly the photo of Marie she'd heard about the previous day. She'd wait a little while before asking to see it.

As Connie busied herself boiling the kettle and brewing the tea, Drake and Dodds used their eyes to take in every aspect of the room. The kitchen table and chairs were, like the sideboard, definitely from a previous age, but again superbly looked after. By contrast, all the major appliances, washing machine, gas cooker, fridge freezer and microwave oven all looked quite new. Drake quickly noticed that the fireplace which would once have burned brightly with a welcoming coal fire now contained a 'living flame' gas fire, eminently practical but somehow an indictment on modernisation in Drake's mind.

Tea made, and the three of them seated at the kitchen table, Drake asked Connie, "Is your husband at home, Mrs. Doyle? We'd like to speak to both of you at the same time, if possible."

"Oh, sorry, yes of course, silly me," said Connie with an almost girlish giggle that Drake found particularly engaging. "He's in the garden. Seems he's always in the garden nowadays, so he is. The Holy Virgin herself must know what he does out there, all day. It's no bigger than a postage stamp."

Connie's accent betrayed her Irish upbringing, now intermingled with a liberal dose of the local Scouse dialect. Izzie thought it quite endearing.

Rising from her seat at the table, Connie walked to the back door, opened it and called to the unseen James Doyle. "Jimmy Doyle, get yerself in here this minute. There's two bobbies here wanting to have a wee word with you."

Drake smiled to herself. It had been a long time since she'd heard anyone refer to her as a 'bobby', a term of endearment for a policeman that, like Connie Doyle, belonged to a happier, previous age. A few seconds passed before the back door opened and James, (Jimmy) Doyle walked in, only as far as the large Hessian door mat that awaited anyone entering the house, where he stood and removed a pair of mud-stained brown boots, turned round and placed them outside the door on the doorstep, turned again and closed the door. Only now did the large man with thinning grey hair bother to look at and acknowledge the two police officers who sat drinking tea in his kitchen.

"I know why youse are here," said Doyle, looking at Dodds. "Your lot did fuck all about finding Marie thirty three years ago, so what chance d'you think you have now? I don't know why those idiot sons of mine had to go running to the police just because a few bones got dug up."

Izzie felt an instant dislike for Doyle. She'd already heard him described as a religious bigot, and a possible racist. Now, his immediate direction of his words to Nick Dodds indicated an in-built sexism too. A woman couldn't possibly be in charge, could she?

"I'm Detective Sergeant Drake, Mr. Doyle, and this is Detective Constable Dodds. Those 'few bones' you mention happen to be the mortal remains of Brendan Kane, your daughter's boyfriend at the time of her disappearance. I'd have thought you might show a little concern that he's been found dead after all this time, particularly as his death may bear a strong connection to what happened to Marie all those years ago."

"Hmm, sergeant eh?" Doyle pronounced the word with a heavy hint of sarcasm. "Well, in the first place, I'll shed no tears for the man who took my daughter away from me and secondly, why should you finding his bones have anything to do with my Marie?"

"Mr. Doyle," Izzie replied, "You can't seriously think it was a pure coincidence that Marie and Brendan disappeared at the same time? They'd made plans to run away and start a new life together, as you well know."

"Aye, thanks to my sons helping her to deceive her poor Mam and Dad."

Nick Dodds stepped in with a question of his own before Izzie could speak again, part of a strategy they'd agreed on earlier.

"And why do you think they did that, Mr. Doyle? I presume you felt they should have shown loyalty to you and told you their secret long before the couple disappeared."

"So they should have," Doyle snapped back at Dodds.

"Could it have had anything to do with your dislike of Brendan Kane?" Dodds pressed his point home.

"I'd no particular liking or dislike of the man."

"But you didn't like a protestant, a 'proddie' being so romantically involved with your daughter, did you?"

"Bah," Doyle mumbled. "All he wanted was to get in her knickers and have his way with her, turn her into his tart."

Connie Doyle now exploded at her husband. Frail or not, Connie possessed a temper worthy of her Irish roots.

"James Doyle, how can you say that about your own daughter? Marie was a good girl, you know she was. And Phil Oxley told us a long time ago that they truly loved and cared for each other."

"Oxley? Another scally like his pal, Kane, if you ask me. I heard he helped them plan it all,"

"He helped his friends, Mr. Doyle. Isn't that what friends do?"

Izzie Drake now came back into the conversation as Doyle blustered and hesitated.

"You didn't seem to have any objections to your sons and daughter being involved in the pop group though, did you?"

"Look, Sergeant, playing music together is one thing, marrying someone outside your faith is different to my mind, okay?"

"Faith, Mr. Doyle? I thought Protestants and Catholics were all of the Christian faith, or is that wrong?"

Doyle again fell silent, not wanting to be drawn by Drake's line of questioning. Izzie instead turned to Connie Doyle.

"Is that a photo of Marie on your sideboard, Mrs. Doyle? May I see it?"

Connie proudly walked across to the sideboard, picked up the framed photo and passed it to Izzie.

"She was a very pretty girl, wasn't she, Sergeant?" Connie said, proudly.

"She certainly was," Izzie replied.

"Do you think she's dead?" Connie asked suddenly, with tears beginning to form in her eyes.

"I'm being honest when I say I just don't know, Mrs. Doyle. Until a couple of days ago we knew nothing about Marie or her involvement with the case. We were focused on identifying the remains that have turned out to be those of Brendan Kane and thanks to your sons, we've been able to confirm that identification and we now know about Marie so we'll be treating the whole affair as one case. Trust me; we'll do all we can to discover what happened to your daughter."

Connie pulled a small lady's hanky from the sleeve of her cardigan and dabbed at her eyes, as she placed a hand on Izzie's arm and sniffed, "thank you."

Izzie's eyes caught sight of another object on the sideboard, previously hidden by the photograph. Connie saw her looking and picked up the small, yellow plastic, nineteen sixties transistor radio.

"It was Marie's," she said. "She used to take it almost everywhere with her. She loved music, Sergeant. That's how she got involved with Brendan and the group in the first place. She had a driving licence and used to help out by driving them to and from their performances sometimes. Mr. Oxley, Phil's dad would lend them his van until his business went bust."

Connie turned a dial on the side of the radio and Izzie was surprised to hear the sounds of Radio One coming from the tiny speaker.

"I make sure it always has new batteries in it, you know, just in case Marie ever…"

Connie let her words hang and Izzie nodded and took the old lady's hand in her own. Words failed her for a few seconds, but eventually she looked across the room at Nick Dodds, who nodded back at her and she brought the interview to an end.

"Thank you both for your time. We wanted you to know that we're seriously looking into Marie's case and would appreciate you getting in touch with us if you can think of anything that might help us with our inquiries."

Passing a card bearing her phone number at the station to Connie, she turned to Jimmy Doyle.

"Thank you for your time, Mr. Doyle. We'll be in touch."

"Yeah, sometime never, I'll bet," Doyle replied.

"Manners, Jimmy, please," Connie pleaded, but Doyle simply stood his ground and maintained a silent pose, by the back door.

Connie saw the two detectives to the front door and just before they took their leave of her, said,

"Please don't think too badly of my husband, Sergeant. He's getting on in years and he's very set in his ways. He talks tough, but he's never got over Marie leaving as she did. He's not half as bad as he sounds."

"Yes, well, thanks, Mrs. Doyle. Like I said, we'll be in touch."

As the front door closed behind them, the pair walked briskly to their car and were soon motoring back in the direction of the last known address of Phil Oxley, Nick Dodds at the wheel.

"Any thoughts, Nick?" she asked the constable as the streets of the city sped past the car windows.

"Nice old lady, bitter and twisted old man," Nick Dodds replied without hesitation.

"My thoughts exactly," Izzie concurred.

"Why the hell does someone stay with a bloke like him for all those years?"

"That's an easy one to answer, Nick," she replied. "First of all, they're from a generation where husbands and wives stuck together through thick and thin, the 'for better and for worse' bit of the marriage vows, I suppose, but, more importantly to them at any rate, is the fact that they're obviously staunch Roman Catholics, and for them, divorce is one massive taboo, a great big no-no."

"But couldn't she just have left him, gone somewhere else and lived on her own, without getting a divorce?"

"And gone where, Nick? She probably couldn't have managed financially or emotionally without her family around her. A case of 'better the devil you know,' I think. But, do you think either of them knows more than they're telling us about Marie's disappearance?"

"I doubt the mother knows anything, and though he seems a right old bastard to me, I can't see her father doing anything to hurt his own kids, especially if, as you say, the whole concept of family means so much to them."

"I tend to agree. We'll see what the boss thinks when we meet up later."

"Yeah," said Dodds. "I wonder if this Oxley chap can tell us anything new, once we get hold of him?"

"We'll soon find out," Drake replied as Nick turned into Phil Oxley's street for the second time that day.

Chapter 25

SURPRISE, SURPRISE!

As Dodds pulled up a couple of doors away from Phil Oxley's address they saw a couple unloading bags of shopping from the rear of a Vauxhall Astra hatchback, parked directly in front of the Oxley address. In contrast with the home of James and Connie Doyle, this street, though composed of similarly aged terraced homes, had a far greater upmarket feel to it. All the houses were in excellent repair, with much modernisation having been applied to virtually every property in the street. Obviously no absent landlords here, and lots of middle earning blue collar types in residence, Izzie thought to herself.

Izzie exited the car and left Dodds to lock up as she approached the middle–aged couple who were intent on their unloading and who hadn't noticed the car pull up not far from their own.

"Excuse me? Are you by any chance Mr. Phillip Oxley?" she asked the man, who had turned instinctively towards her as she'd got closer to the couple.

"And who wants to know?" the man replied.

Izzie flashed her warrant card and introduced herself and Nick Dodds, who'd joined her by now.

"Oh, I see. Hello, Sergeant, Constable. How can I help you?"

"Could we go inside, please, Mr. Oxley? We have a few questions we'd like to ask about something that happened a long time ago, and we think you may be able to fill in a few gaps for us."

A knowing look appeared on Oxley's face and he nodded slowly.

"Well, yes, of course, do come in. I don't know how I can help you, but you can tell me inside."

"Let me help you with these bags," Dodds said, as he moved to take a couple of obviously heavy bags from the woman accompanying Phil Oxley. "Mrs. Oxley is it?"

"Yes, I'm Phil's wife, and thank you," the woman replied, allowing Nick Dodds to help with the laden shopping bags.

Minutes later, Phil Oxley was seated in his favourite armchair in his and his wife's beautifully decorated and clean living room. The two detectives sat side by side on the sofa, and the three managed to make small talk for a minute or two until Mrs. Oxley entered the room with a tray, loaded with cups of coffee and a selection of biscuits. Although she must have been around fifty years old, Mrs. Oxley looked and dressed at least ten years younger. She was very pretty, with long, dark, wavy hair that framed her face perfectly, with a figure some twenty year olds would kill for, and now that she'd divested herself of her coat, was dressed in a cream, pleated blouse and a navy pleated skirt that ended just above the knee. After ensuring everyone was served with drinks and had helped themselves to biscuits, the petite and well dressed wife of Phil Oxley seated herself in the room's remaining armchair and her husband said, "Now, Sergeant, you have our full attention. Please tell me how we can help you."

Izzie Drake wanted to complete the introductions first.

"Yes, of course, Mr. Oxley..."

"Please call me Phil," Oxley interrupted.

"Right, thanks. Can I please just ask your full name, Mrs. Oxley, for the record?"

"Yes, Sergeant. It's Clemency Anna Oxley."

Izzie Drake was stunned as Phil Oxley's wife gave her name, and even Nick Dodds' pencil seemed to hover in shock over his notebook. Drake was the first to react.

"Clemency, as in Clemmy De Souza?"

"Why, yes," Clemmy replied, equally surprised that the police sergeant knew both her nickname and her maiden name. "But, how did you know?"

"Perhaps I'd better explain exactly why we're here," Drake said to the couple.

"Might be a good idea, Sergeant Drake," said Phil Oxley.

Izzie Drake spent the next ten minutes bringing the couple up to date on everything, from the original discovery of the skeletal remains at the old wharf, through the process of attempting to identify the bones, and the visit of the Doyle brothers to the police station, where they provided information that not only helped to identify Brendan Kane as a murder victim, but also brought the name of Marie Doyle into the investigation for the first time. Obviously, she explained, both Phil and Clemmy had been mentioned in the course of Mickey and Ronnie's statement to the police about events surrounding the eventual disappearance of the couple. When she finished telling the Oxleys the story so far, she waited for a response, Clemmy looked on the verge of tears, but Phil Oxley didn't hesitate.

"My God! We read the story in the Echo about the bones being found during a regeneration project. We'd no idea it could have been poor Brendan. All these years, I believed he and Marie had gone off somewhere together and were living a happy ever life far away from here, and now here you are, telling me poor Brendan never left Liverpool, and that someone actually murdered him. Who the hell could have hated him so much that they'd shoot him, beat him and throw him into the river?"

With his final words, Clemmy couldn't hold the tears back any longer, and her shoulders drooped and her face became a mask of tears. Phil quickly moved to comfort his wife, sitting on the arm of her chair and placing a comforting arm around her shoulder.

"I'm sorry to have had to break it to you like this," said Drake, "but there's never an easy way to communicate these things."

"It's alright, Sergeant," Phil replied. "I think deep down, we maybe knew we'd never see him again. It was always odd that he never got in touch after he left, especially after all I did to help them get away in the first place, but I can't believe he was murdered. Who ever'd do such a thing? He was only a young man. We all were, little more than kids, really."

Nick Dodds changed tack a little to allow them to recover their composure.

"And you two fell in love and got married? Brendan's best friend and Marie's best friend. That's nice for you, isn't it, Sarge?"

"Yes, very romantic," Izzie agreed. "How did that come about, if you don't mind telling us?"

Clemmy had managed to control her tears, and though she appeared pale and shocked, she replied to the question before her husband could say anything.

"It was romantic, really. When everyone first realised that Brendan and Marie had gone missing, I think either Mickey or Ronnie went to the police with Mr. Doyle to report Marie as a missing person. The two lads had been to my house, to see if I'd heard from Marie, which I hadn't, and then a couple of days later, Mr. Doyle came round to talk to me and started to get a bit angry, saying I was her best friend and that if anyone knew where she was, it should be me. My Dad got mad at him for bullying me, Sergeant, and my Dad was a big man, and he got tough with Mr. Doyle and virtually threw him out of our house. I didn't like him at all, and don't know how Marie put up with living with him for so long, but he was her Dad, after all, so I suppose she loved him in her own way, and didn't know any other way of life, until she met Brendan, of course. Anyway, after Mr. Doyle's visit to our house, I was really worried about Marie and I knew from what she'd told me that Phil was doing his best to help Brendan find a way to get to America, so I went to see him a few days later and we got talking about everything. We started meeting in coffee shops and for the odd drink in the pub and gradually we became closer and closer.

Anyway, the longer Marie and Brendan were gone, the more we felt they'd finally got sick of waiting and Brendan had somehow found a place for them to go while he got things sorted properly. I know Marie would've followed him to the ends of the earth, Sergeant. She loved him so much. Me and Phil dated for a few months, and then, like young people do, we sort of drifted apart, and we split up and went our separate ways. We didn't see each other again until about ten years later, when Phil walked into the record shop where I was working. We got talking, and Phil asked me to meet him for a drink after work. To cut a long story short, we started seeing each other regularly again and this time, one thing led to another, we fell for each other big time and we were married a year after meeting up for the second time. Two years later we had a child, our daughter, Carrie Anne. She pointed to a framed school photograph of a young girl, probably about the age of Marie in the photo her mother kept on the sideboard of their home. She goes to the same school where Phil teaches music, Our Lady of Sorrows. It's a private Catholic School for Girls in Walton."

"I know the school," said Izzie Drake. "I remember playing hockey against them when I was at school. So you're still involved with music, Phil?"

"Yes, I became a teacher when Carrie Anne was still a toddler. Clemmy was a big fan of The Hollies in the sixties, in case you're wondering," Phil explained. "She named our baby after one of their hit records." The detectives nodded and smiled and Clemmy continued from where she was before Phil's interruption.

"In the early days we'd talk about those days with Brendan and Marie and wondered what might have happened to them, but over the years they faded into the background of our lives, and now, well, I'm so sorry and upset to hear about poor Brendan. I don't suppose you know what happened to Marie, do you?"

"Not at present, Clemmy," Drake answered her honestly." We hoped Phil might be able to help us, and we'd planned to seek you out next to talk to you too. Finding you here together has been a lucky break for us, really."

Talking to Drake had produced the effect of calming Clemmy down and Phil now took his arm from her shoulder, rose and took a seat in his previous armchair. Scratching his head in thought for a few seconds, he seemed to be weighing up what he might or might not know that could be helpful and then said, "I'm not sure how I can help much after all these years. Is there anything specific I can tell you?"

"According to Mickey and Ronnie Doyle, you did a lot of the research for Brendan in finding ways to emigrate to America, is that correct? Drake asked.

"Yes, quite true. Brendan was useless at anything like that. I think he had a bit of a mental block when it came to dealing with forms and official documents. I can even remember him getting flustered when he first applied for a provisional driving licence. Anyway, I eventually told him it would take a couple of years at least for him to fill the requirements for immigration into the USA, and he couldn't work over there without a Green Card. You have to understand, Sergeant, that Brendan really was quite talented and it was a shame we didn't make the breakthrough over here, but he just might have made it in The States, which is why I was happy to help him as much as I could."

"We'd heard something about that from Ronnie and Mickey," said Drake. "How did your attempts to help end up?"

"Well, after a lot of research and some phone calls, I managed to convince Brendan of the most practical option left open to him if he was serious about making a new start in the music business in America."

"Which was?"

"First of all, we contacted several music producers and record companies in the States, giving them information about Brendan and his career so far, and also sent copies of the demo disc we'd made as a group. I contacted the U.S. Immigration Service on advice from someone at the embassy in London, who told me that if, while on a holiday in the USA, Brendan received an offer of work or a contract with a U.S. recording company, they would view an application for residence favourably. A couple of the recording companies and music producers got back to us saying they would be happy to audition Brendan if he contacted them once he arrived Stateside. It was the best, and probably the only chance he would ever have, and he seemed to accept that. One night, I sat with him and Marie at his flat and together we completed applications for tourist visas for them both. He'd saved enough money to allow them to spend at least four weeks over there, and we applied for the visas to take effect from late October, I think. It's a long time ago, I can't be sure of dates and things, you know?

"That's alright, Phil. Thanks for that information. We weren't aware of any such applications being made. Tell me, did they receive their visas?"

"Yes, they did. I remember Marie being excited when she and Brendan showed them to me on another evening visit to his flat."

"And she told me about it too," added Clemmy. "They had passports, too, Sergeant."

"That's right," said Phil. "All the lads in the group had passports of course, from when we first started out, in case we got any bookings on the continent, you know? Like The Beatles used to do Hamburg and that in the early days?"

Clemmy added, "Yeah, and people used to joke that Marie had never been out of Liverpool, but she had, once. A couple of years earlier, their parents took her and the boys on a self-catering holiday in Benidorm, so they all had their own passports."

Nick Dodds quickly added their observations to his notes and now asked, "Did you tell the police about this at the time they talked to you after Marie had been reported missing?"

"Yes," Phil replied. "A Sergeant came round in a big Ford Zephyr police car, like they had on *Z Cars* on TV. He seemed to think my information just confirmed his thoughts that they'd done a runner, left town and gone off to start a new life together."

Drake took over again, turning to Clemmy.

"Clemmy, one of the brothers told us he thought Marie was a little preoccupied, or on edge in the week or two before she disappeared. He assumed it was because she and Brendan were planning their sudden getaway from Liverpool. Can you think of any other reason why she might have felt worried or preoccupied?"

Clemmy Oxley thought about the question for a few seconds before replying.

"Now you come to mention it, she was a bit edgy around that time. I think it was mostly to do with her uncle."

"What uncle would that be?" Drake asked.

"Well, he wasn't really her uncle, he was her Dad's cousin from Ireland, so strictly speaking I suppose that made him her second cousin, but because he was a lot older than Marie and the lads, they all called him Uncle Patrick. His name was Price or Bryce I think. Marie didn't like him. She said he was bit of a bully, and really full of himself and what she called his 'silly tales' about what he called 'the old country'. Marie was just happy he wasn't staying at their house. He had a room at a B & B somewhere but was round at their house a lot she said, talking about all sorts of stuff she didn't understand with her father."

Drake was more than interested in this piece of information, as it placed another, previously unknown name into the mix, and could maybe open up another line of inquiry. She couldn't help but wonder why one of James Doyle's Irish cousins had suddenly appeared on the scene prior to the double disappearance. Coincidence? Maybe. Relevance? Quite possibly. She was certain this was something Ross would find of interest.

Another ten minutes passed by, with the Oxleys merely seeming to reinforce what the police already knew, until, just as Izzie was about to bring the interview to an end, she had a thought, like a light bulb flashing on in her mind.

"Just one more question, Phil," she began.

"Yes, Sergeant?"

"We've been told that Brendan had a car, is that correct?"

"Yes he did, an old Hillman or Humber, something like that. I'm not too sure after all this time."

"That's okay. My question is, do you have any idea what happened to it? I mean, when he disappeared, was the car left parked near his flat, or at his work, or whatever? You see, he must have either used the car to get to the docks, if he was meeting someone there, or else he caught a bus into town. Now, if you had a car, would you bother using a bus if you could get to where you where going in the comfort of your own vehicle?"

"Good point, Sergeant, and I'm sorry I can't give you an answer," Oxley replied. "I'm sure the police must have spoken to Brendan's parents and probably asked about the car, but after they'd interviewed me at the time, they didn't come again or tell me anything about any other lines if inquiry they were following. Confidentiality I suppose."

"Yes, of course, thank you Phil. I just thought I'd ask. Oh yes, another thought just sprang to mind. Clemmy, you worked with Marie, didn't you?"

"Yes, in the typing pool at BICC."

"Do you know if Marie gave her employers any notice she was about to leave?"

"No, I don't know for sure, but if she had, I'm sure she'd have told me. You see, Sergeant, a lot of her Dad's mates worked at B.I. too, and she wouldn't have wanted to risk one of them finding out what she was planning and then telling her Dad, would she?"

"That's true, thank you, Clemmy. Do you have anything else you'd like to ask, Constable?" Izzie said, thinking Nick Dodds may have also thought of something she could have omitted. Dodds thought for a second or two, and then his brow furrowed and he said,

"Well yes. We have on record that Brendan Kane apparently left his landlord a typewritten note saying he'd left the flat, and that he wouldn't be coming back and saying the landlord could sell off anything he'd left behind. Now, knowing him as you did, would you say that was typical of the man, and do you know if Brendan owned a typewriter?"

"D'you know? I heard about the letter, and always thought it a bit weird at the time," Phil replied. "First of all, in all the time I spent at his flat, I never saw a typewriter, and I doubt very much whether he could type anyway. I sort of thought that if it was a typewritten note then Marie must have typed it for him. That was her job after all."

"Yes, that makes sense," said Dodds. "Do either of you know the name of Brendan's landlord back then?

"No, sorry," said Phil and Clemmy shook her head. "But I can give you the address of the flat. If they haven't bulldozed the place to make way for more urban redevelopment the place might still be standing and maybe someone in the area might be able to help you."

"That might be helpful. Thank you," said Dodds and the two officers waited while Phil Oxley wrote Brendan Kane's old address on a yellow post-it from a pad by the phone, which he gave to Dodds.

Taking their leave of the couple, Drake and Dodds were soon motoring back across the city to headquarters. "First impressions of our lovebirds?" Drake asked Dodds as he drove.

"Well, Sarge, bit of a shock to find two of our persons of interest together like that. Saves us some time for sure. I liked them both though. I got the feeling they were both incredibly shocked to hear about Kane's murder, and in Mrs. Oxley's case, I think that knowledge only served to heightened her fears that Marie Doyle is probably also long dead. I don't think they could tell us any more than they did. It all happened so long ago that I doubt anyone has a really accurate recollection of what took place at the time. You know how people's memories degrade over time."

"And there lies the crux of the problem with this case, Nick. Time, or rather the passage of time, has created so many barriers that we have to overcome if we're ever going to solve this one, but I tell you now, D.I. Ross is determined to solve this case and if know him, together with the rest of us, that's just what he'll do, despite whatever obstacles we might come up against."

"Is he really that good, Sarge? I've heard he's like a dog with a bone when he gets his teeth into an inquiry. Do you think we can solve the case, even after all these years?"

"Short answer, Nick? Yes, he is that good, and yes, I really think with him in charge of the investigation, we'll solve this case, and find justice for Brendan Kane at the very least."

"And Marie Doyle?"

"You've got me there, Nick, I'm afraid. I just don't know how to answer that one, at least, not yet."

Chapter 26

BITS AND PIECES

"Okay everyone, gather round. I want us to take a long, hard look at where we are with this case. Let's see if we can start to add some of the pieces together."

Detective Inspector Andy Ross and his team were assembled in the small murder squad conference room. The team had spent three days assembling and collating every scrap of information they could find on both Brendan Kane and Marie Doyle. As Izzie Drake had pointed out to her boss shortly before the team meeting, trying to 'join the dots' as she put it, to a case so old, with no witnesses and with those involved at the time not necessarily able to trust their memories, they really were chasing shadows, with little hope of being able to pull the whole thing together.

"I'm well aware of that, Izzie," Ross had replied in response to her quite valid point. "The thing is, I feel as if we're missing something, something that may be so simple we just don't recognize it yet. When we do, I think the case will open up before us and we'll be able to put together all these small bits and pieces to form a complete picture of what took place thirty three years ago."

"You know, sir, if there's one thing I hate, it's a bloody mystery without clues to follow."

"Ah, but that's just it," said Ross. "The clues are there, Izzie. It's just that we don't see them yet."

"Oh, very cryptic, sir. You been doing the Daily Telegraph crossword again?"

They both laughed, the mood lightening for a few vital moments before they returned to the serious business of unsolved murder and a young woman missing for over thirty years.

Now, they stood either side of a large white board, with Nick Dodds, Sam Gable, Paul Ferris and Derek McLennan seated in the uncomfortable plastic chairs around the white-topped table which occupied the centre of the room. At the back of the room, Press Liaison Officer, George Thompson stood, nonchalantly leaning against the pale green painted wall, his briefcase positioned at his feet, resembling an obedient puppy, waiting for its master's next instruction.

On the left hand side of the white board, Izzie had taped a large blown up photograph of Brendan Kane. Paul Ferris had worked hard, managing to find an old and faded photo of Brendan Kane and the Planets in a now ancient copy of the *Echo*, taken when they'd won a talent contest in their early days. He'd used computer technology to isolate the head of Kane, and had blown it up as large as was possible without losing too much definition. At least the picture gave Brendan a more 'human' face than the photo displayed side by side with it, of the skeletal remains that were all that remained of the one-time pop singer and guitarist. Displayed on the opposite side of the board was a photo that depicted an eighteen-year old Marie Doyle, pictured in a happy pose with her best friend, Clemmy De Souza, now of course known to be the wife of Phil Oxley. Sam Gable had borrowed the photo from Clemmy's parents during her abortive trip to find and talk to Marie's best friend. Clemmy's Mother had explained that it was taken on the occasion of her eighteenth birthday, when the two girls celebrated by visiting their local Berni Inn Steak House, where Clemmy enjoyed her first legal alcoholic drink. Apart from growing her hair an inch or so longer, Marie hardly changed at all over the next two years, Clemmy had explained, so the photo was a good representation of how she would have looked at the time of her disappearance.

Beneath the photos, Paul Ferris had noted down all the relevant facts relating to each of the couple in one column and items of conjecture or open questions in another. Unfortunately, for the moment, the conjecture column contained a lot more than the factual one.

Ross surveyed the faces in the room as they waited expectantly for his next words. He knew from past experience that this was the type of case that could soon breed frustration, due mostly to the age of the case, the lack of direct witnesses, few clues as to motive for murder and even fewer clues relating to the disappearance of a young woman who seemed to have everything to live for. He'd admitted to himself that in all probability, Marie Doyle was dead, quite possibly murdered and her body disposed of at the same time as Brendan Kane met his death. He was loathe to voice that thought to his team, however. Better that, for now, they kept an open mind and worked on the very faint possibility that the girl had survived, but, if she did, then what the hell had become of her? Choosing his words carefully, he began the morning briefing.

"Good morning," he began, receiving in turn various acknowledgements and greetings from the members of his team. "As you can see, our collator has been hard at work. Well done, Ferris. You've done well here, given us a good background to both victims, if indeed we want to view Marie Doyle as a victim. For now, I'd prefer we did just that, until we know otherwise. How's that boy of yours by the way?"

"He's doing okay, thank you, sir," Ferris replied, grateful that his boss had taken a few seconds to think of him and his son, still waiting patiently for the kidney transplant that might never come. "I tried to put as much relevant info on the board as I could find, without muddying the waters with pure speculations."

"Yes, like I said, good job. I like the fact you've got a photo representation of Brendan up there. I want you all to look hard at that picture, and remember this was a young man, healthy and ambitious at the time of his death, who was brutally murdered, and not just a pile of bones as he was when the builders dug up his remains."

"Sam," he said next, looking directly at D.C Gable, "I'm sorry you had a wasted trip to try to find Clemmy De Souza, but at least Sergeant Drake and D.C. Dodds got lucky, finding her married to Phil Oxley. And, you did get the photo of her and Marie from Clemmy's parents, plus a little more background information on the girls."

"Thank you, sir. Yes, I must say I was shocked when Mrs. De Souza told me her daughter was married to Phillip Oxley, but she was very helpful in answering my questions, not that her information will go far towards helping us find a solution to the mystery. She did say that Marie was a very pretty girl, with a sweet and trusting nature. She added that Marie could be a little naïve at times, easily taken in, and could understand how she'd be enthusiastic about Brendan's plans to go to America. Clemmy had told her that Marie was besotted with Brendan, and would go along with whatever he suggested. Clemmy was disappointed that her best friend was planning to leave Liverpool, so she said, and was even more crestfallen when it appeared Marie had left without even saying goodbye. Mrs. De Souza's enduring memory was that for weeks after Marie's disappearance, Clemmy moped around the house, both worried she hadn't heard from Marie, and angry that Marie might have run off without a word."

"Okay, Sam, try following up with Mrs. Oxley. See if she or Marie had any other close friends, someone either of them might have confided in. Also, ask if there were any particular places that meant something special to her or Marie, somewhere Marie might have run to if she was in trouble or needed to get away from home for a while."

"Okay, sir," Gable replied.

Ross moved on to the information gathered by Drake and Dodds so far.

"You two seem to have made some progress in your talk with Marie's parents."

"We do?" Drake said, surprised her boss thought that way.

"Yes," Ross replied. "I've been thinking through everything you were told, and it strikes me that the mother was very close to the girl, but the father was more of an old fashioned patriarchal figure, and liked to rule the household with something approaching a rod of iron, pushing his own principles and beliefs onto his children. The two boys, Mickey and Ronnie appear to have been tough enough to live their lives around their father's code of discipline, but I believe Marie may have retreated into a kind of fantasy world of her own as a kind of coping mechanism. Hence her love of music, the fact she carried her transistor radio almost everywhere, and also, perhaps why she fell for Brendan's almost impossible scheme to emigrate to the USA and become a huge rock star. That fits with what Sam heard from Mrs. De Souza, and is probably the first piece of tangible and substantiated evidence we've received about her state of mind at the time."

"There's something else about old James Doyle that's bugging me, sir," Drake said.

"Go on, Sergeant. Let's hear it."

"Well, I think D.C. Dodds will agree that James Doyle is not a particularly nice person," Izzie said, and Nick Dodds immediately agreed, saying, "You can say that again. What a bigoted and objectionable bastard he is, for sure."

"Yes, but sadly we can't arrest the man for being a bigot, at least not yet," Ross laughed. "Tell me what it is you find unsettling about the man, Izzie."

"Well, he obviously didn't give a damn about what happened to Brendan Kane, even though he was his daughter's boyfriend, and in all likelihood Marie suffered the same fate as Kane. If it was me in his place, I'd want to know just what happened to young Brendan, but all he seemed bothered about was his daughter being romantically involved with a protestant. The man's a real religious dinosaur. He belongs in the middle ages."

"Or on the Falls Road in Belfast," Dodds quipped, referring to one of the notorious areas of sectarian violence in Northern Ireland.

"Funny you should say that," Drake went on. "Clemmy De Souza, sorry, Oxley, told us one of Doyle's Irish cousins, who Marie referred to as 'Uncle Patrick' came to Liverpool a week or two before Clemmy's disappearance. Clemmy told us Marie didn't like the man and was glad he wasn't staying at the house with them. Patrick stayed in a B & B or hotel as far as she knew. The thought just struck me, I wonder if this 'Uncle Patrick' could have had anything to do with both the murder and Marie's disappearance?"

Ross suddenly realized that Drake and Dodds might have stumbled on an important clue.

"Did Clemmy have a surname for this 'Uncle Patrick' character?" he asked.

"Yes, sir," Dodds spoke up, as he referred to his notebook. "Mrs. De Souza thinks it might have been Price, or Bryce, something like that."

"Ferris," said Ross, and Paul Ferris looked up expectantly, "when we're done here, I'd like you to run a full criminal records check on anyone with the names Patrick Price or Bryce, or any similar sounding names you can think of, probably from the Belfast area. Let's just see what comes up when we go looking for Uncle Patrick."

"Right you are, sir. I'll get on to it as soon as we're finished here."

"Good man," said Ross, who now turned his attention to young D.C. McLennan.

"I've got a tricky little job for you, McLennan. I want you to do your best to go back in time and find out if any cars, possibly Hillman or Vauxhalls, were either reported abandoned, or were picked up and impounded by the old City Police between August and September in sixty-six. It means wading through lots of old records and you might not find anything, but Brendan Kane owned a vehicle that, as far as anyone knows, simply disappeared along with its owner on the night of his murder. That car must have ended up somewhere. See if you can find it."

"Okay, sir," McLennan replied. "Er, sir?"

"Yes?"

"What's a Hillman, sir?"

Ross laughed and said, "A bit before your time. Great cars, My Dad had one once, a Hillman Hunter, I think. Try the Hillman Minx. That was a popular model back then. Look it up, Derek."

"Right, sir"

"If you need help with all that, ask D.C. Ferris. He'll probably know exactly where you should be looking for the information we need, isn't that right, Ferris?"

Paul Ferris nodded and said, "I'm here if you need me, Derek."

McLennan thanked him as Ross carried on,

"Dodds, I want you to look into the backgrounds of both Mickey and Ronnie Doyle. They're not out of the woods yet, in my book."

"But sir, they'd hardly have walked in here saying they thought the skeletal remains were Marie's if they'd killed Kane and left him there, would they?"

"Think about it for a minute," said Ross. "It's possible one of them is guilty and the other innocent. Let's say the innocent brother sees the newspaper article and wants to come and see us because he thinks it might be Marie. Now, if you're the other, guilty brother, what do you do?"

Dodds hardly hesitated before replying:

"Go along with the innocent one, sir. Pretend you're as innocent as he is, and play it clever. That way, you not only make yourself look innocent, you also find out how much the police know, if you're lucky."

"Good. I see you're thinking, that's great. Check 'em out, make sure neither of them's hiding any skeletons of their own in their cupboards, okay?"

"I've got it sir."

"Izzie, you're with me," he said to Drake. "We're going to see your friend, James Doyle. I have a feeling the time has come for me to meet this cantankerous, bigoted old man. There's something 'off' about him from what everyone's telling me. And don't forget the kneecapping. Maybe, just maybe, Doyle and his Irish connection had something to do with all this."

"You have anything to say, George?" he asked, as all eyes in the room turned to look in the direction of George Thompson.

"Not at present, thanks Andy. I just wanted to keep up to date myself. I only hope the press releases bring you something useful eventually."

"Me too, George, me too," said Ross, bringing the briefing to a close. When the others had left the room he said to Drake, "Well, Izzie, we've got a real mix of unrelated odds and ends, bits and pieces here, and we have to pull them all together. When we do, we're going to find a killer, I mean it."

"I hope you're right, sir," she replied. "It would be a pity for Brendan Kane's remains to resurface after all this time and still fail to find justice."

"That's where we come in, Izzie. We're going to be the instrument of that justice, I promise you. I intend to do what I can to find out if those visas issued to Brendan and Marie were ever used. I know it's a long shot, but the Americans may have records that go back that far."

"But, why, sir? We know Kane never got to the USA, so what's the point?" Drake asked.

"Because, it's possible someone killed the pair and then faked their own identities, became Brendan and Marie, and used those visas to effect a very clever getaway."

Drake looked impressed at her boss's line of thought, and said so.

"I'd never have thought of that, sir. Rather an inspired piece of thinking."

"Thanks, but it is just a long shot, though we seem restricted to those at present."

"What about me, sir? Anything specific you want me to follow up?"

"Yes, Izzie. Gretna Green has been mentioned more than once. I'd like you to check back and find out if a marriage was recorded at any time during nineteen sixty six, between our couple. I haven't had time to check on the actual residence period required back then. It's possible they intended to go to Scotland and get married before doing a runner, and maybe they did or did not make it."

"Will do, sir. I'll get started then, if there's nothing else?"

"Carry on, Sergeant," said Ross. "I'm going to get on the phone to our American cousins and try out my long shot, or maybe I should I call it my *very* long shot."

Chapter 27

HELPING HANDS

"Inspector Ross? Good morning to you. My name is Ethan Tiffen. The lady on the switchboard tells me you're seeking some information on Visa applications?"

The voice on the telephone immediately reminded Ross of New York, having spent a holiday there himself a couple of years previously with Maria. It was rare for them both to be able to secure a week away from work at the same time, so their brief time in The Big Apple remained firmly embedded in his mind, as did the unmistakable accent of a native New Yorker.

"Yes, well, something like that, Mr. Tiffen," said Ross in reply to Tiffen's cheerful voice.

"Hey, please call me Ethan, Inspector, and tell me exactly how the United States Immigration Service can help the police up there in Liverpool, I think Deirdre said?"

"My name's Andy, and yes, I'm in Liverpool, with Merseyside Police," said Ross. "I'm not sure if or how you can help…"

"Try me, Andy," Tiffen interrupted.

"Okay, here goes. I need to know if a pair of tourist visas issued to two British citizens were ever used in order to gain entry into the USA."

"Sounds doable," Tiffen replied. "When exactly were these visas issued, Andy"

Andy Ross paused, took a deep breath, and then allowed the words to pour out.

"That's the thing, Ethan," he said. "These visas were originally issued sometime in nineteen sixty-six."

"Whoa, there, buddy," a rather shocked-sounding Tiffen responded. "You're talking about another world, another time, another place, Vietnam, Civil Rights marches, Peter, Paul and Mary protest songs, and long haired hippies. I guess this request of yours is important, but then, I doubt you'd be asking such a question if it wasn't, am I right?"

"Yes, it's very important," Ross said. "I'm investigating a murder that took place in sixty-six, together with the disappearance of a young woman at the same time. The skeleton of the murder victim, a young man, a musician with a local band, a pop group, was only recently discovered by a contractor carrying out an urban redevelopment project, and the missing girl, his girlfriend, hasn't been seen or heard of since the time of his own disappearance."

"Hell, that's a long time to be missing. How old was the girl when she went missing?"

"Nearly twenty-one, and the boyfriend was almost twenty-two."

"Andy, I have a daughter almost the same age. I can't imagine losing her like that, not knowing where she is, or what happened to her."

"Look, I know it's a very, very long shot, and your records may not go back that far, and I'll understand if you can't do anything to help, but anything you can do will be greatly appreciated."

"Now, just hold up there, Andy, my new friend. I never said I couldn't help, did I? Just let me think a minute, okay?"

The line fell silent for what seemed an interminably long few seconds and Andy Ross wondered if he'd been cut off, when the sound of the phone being picked up at the other end rattled his eardrum.

"Sorry to be so long," Tiffen apologised. "Just needed a quick word with one of my people here. Seems we do keep records going back a long, long time, to well before the advent of computers, in fact. Thing is, it might take some time to track down the original issue of the visas and then it'll need another search to find out if those visas were ever used, or cancelled, or just disappeared."

"Did that happen often, visas just not being used and disappearing, never to be heard of again?"

"Hell, yes, more than you'd imagine. People would apply for a visa, then change their minds or their holiday plans at the last minute and just throw the darned things in the trash. Still happens today, Andy."

"But you might be able to help me, is that what you're saying?"

"That's what I'm saying, Andy, sure. Now, what I need from you is all the details you can give me. I need the names of your couple, including middle names if they had any, addresses at the time of application, dates of birth, and, if you have them, photographs of each of them. A good written description would be good also. I know this is pushing it, but if you or their families have their passports, then the passport numbers would be a big help too. Probably be a good idea if you can fax them to me so I can get the ball rolling here at my end, and then maybe mail me copies of the documentation as soon as you can."

"I don't know what to say, Ethan. I wasn't expecting such a helpful response to an old case like this. I'm grateful to you, I really am."

"Hey, better save your thanks until we see if I come up with anything helpful. I can't give you any guarantees, like I said. Oh, yes, and please be sure and send me an official request so I can reconcile this with our people here at the embassy."

"Consider it done, Ethan, and thank you. I'll have all the relevant information with you within the next hour or two, as soon as I can get my collator to pull it all together for you."

The two men exchanged their direct line telephone numbers and fax numbers as well as, in Ross's case, the number for the main switchboard at Merseyside Police Headquarters. He gave Tiffen the names of Izzie Drake and D.C. Paul Ferris, telling the Immigration Officer he could be reached through either of them if he wasn't at his desk if the American needed to speak to him again.

Ross knew he'd just played a very unlikely long shot, but even a negative response to his inquiry might serve useful in terms of eliminating other theories, no matter how improbable or outlandish they might seem. As he explained to Paul Ferris while outlining the information and documentation he needed collating and sending to Tiffen, the whole frustrating part of investigating a mystery was in not knowing what information may or may not bear relevance to the case. Every avenue, no matter how vague, had to be investigated and followed to its conclusion, with the majority of such investigations almost inevitably leading to dead ends. What he fervently hoped of course, was that by following each and every blind alley, they would eventually hit on the one course of action that would suddenly unlock the whole case and lead him to its eventual solution.

Leaving Paul Ferris to do what he did best; Ross went looking for Izzie Drake, wondering how she'd got on in her attempts to track down marriage records from Gretna Green. He found her in the canteen, doing her best to look as if she was enjoying a limp-looking cheese and ham sandwich and a cup of something that he thought vaguely resembled coffee.

* * *

"Looks almost edible," Ross quipped as he pulled up a chair and seated himself opposite his sergeant.

"Almost, being the operative word," Drake replied, a wry smile on her face. "They ought to make it a criminal offence you know, trying to slowly poison police officers through the administering of noxious sandwiches."

"Couldn't agree more," Ross agreed. "Give me a bag of nice, greasy chips, liberally doused with salt and vinegar from Rothwell's Fish Bar over the road, any day. Any luck with Gretna Green?"

Swallowing a chunk of plastic-looking cheese, almost choking in the process, Drake cleared her throat before replying. "Well, we can forget any romantic runaway wedding for a start, sir. Just didn't happen. A nice, kind old lady, well, she sounded old, up at the Gretna Register office kindly looked it up for me. No Brendan Kane, and no Marie

Doyle, at any time in sixty-six. She was very thorough, old Mrs. Burns, checked every month that year. She also informed me that there was a fifteen day residency rule, before anyone could get married at Gretna so, with the timeline we have, our couple just couldn't have done it anyway, unless they'd gone after leaving Liverpool, which, with Brendan lying dead in the water was impossibility. Dead end, I'm afraid, sir."

"That's alright, Izzie. I really didn't expect there would be any marriage in Gretna, but we had to check. It's all adding up to something less than we might have expected, and as much as someone might want us to think the answer lies in some transatlantic musical dream, I think we'll find our answers much closer to home."

"You do, sir? Want to share your thinking with me?"

"Sure. Look, we have lots of conjecture surrounding the fact that Brendan and Marie wanted to go to America. Phil Oxley did his best to help Brendan in his quest for a means of entry to the States. I've got a U.S Immigration Service official checking, even now, to see if the visas issued to the couple were ever used. I doubt he'll find anything. We have no real evidence to link anyone with the murder of Brendan Kane, but a few of the people we've come across in recent days could have had a vague motive for wanting him dead."

"Okay, sir, I'm hooked. Go on, please."

"We know there was bad blood between the group members and Brendan when he decided to go solo, so any one, or combination of two or three of the band members might have felt aggrieved enough to take out a form of revenge, especially if they thought Kane was going to America and stood a chance of real stardom, after they'd all struggled along on the local circuit for years. Then, there's Marie's father. James Doyle would have gone mad if he knew his daughter planned to run off with a protestant lad. Mickey and Ronnie Doyle told us they broke the news to their parents about Brendan and Marie just before going to the police station to report her missing. That puts their father in the clear, on paper, but what if he already knew about the couple?"

"How, sir?"

"I don't know. I'm just brainstorming, speculating. You'll just have to humour me, Izzie, okay?"

"Okay," Drake replied. "So, that makes four potential suspects. Any more to add to the list?"

"Ah, that's just it, isn't it? We're assuming this is all to do with the group in some way. We know so little about the lives of both Kane and Marie. If this was a fresh murder case, we'd be interviewing families, friends, everyone who knew the couple. Because it took place so long ago, we're denied that luxury, so we are kind of left with a very narrow track to follow, hoping it'll lead us somewhere."

"And is it, sir? Leading anywhere, I mean?"

"I have a feeling it's about to, Izzie. For now, I want you to drive me over to James Doyle's house. I really want to meet, and talk to this cantankerous old bastard myself. A real charmer, according to you and Dodds, and also it would seem, in the memory of Clemmy Oxley."

"You want to go now, sir? I can't take any more of this bloody sandwich anyway."

Ross laughed as he and Drake rose and left the canteen, casting mock salutes at poor old Doris, the canteen supervisor who stood behind the servery, a look of confusion on her face.

Chapter 28

COMING TOGETHER

Before Ross and Drake left headquarters, they were called over by D.C. Ferris, sitting as usual at his desk, his fingers dancing over the keys of his computer keyboard.

"You have anything for me, yet, Ferris?"

"I do indeed, sir. I was about to come and find you. You asked me to look into this relative of James Doyle?"

"That's right, Bryce, or Price, wasn't it?"

"It was Bryce actually, sir. Patrick Bryce. Born in Belfast in 1941. Lots of petty crime in his teens, four arrests, three convictions and was first suspected of being a member of the Provisional IRA in nineteen sixty three. Like a lot of those suspected of involvement in the troubles over there, the Royal Ulster Constabulary could never pin a thing on him. He was thought to be involved in at least a dozen sectarian murders but fell off the authorities' radar in the early nineties."

"Well, well, well," said Ross, slowly and deliberately as the gears of his investigative brain kicked in. "Looks like our friend James Doyle has a few questions to answer."

Izzie Drake added, "I should say so, sir. The man has a potential IRA man in his family and Bryce was apparently in Liverpool just before Marie went missing."

"And more importantly, just before Brendan Kane was killed, if the timeline holds firm," said Ross.

"Makes the kneecap shootings fall into place, sir," Ferris added.

"It does, Ferris. And it also possibly reveals just why Doyle is such a religious bigot. If his philosophy is the same as the IRA's, it's bloody easy to see why he was so set against Brendan Kane and his daughter Marie being romantically involved."

"But James Doyle was born here in Liverpool, sir. Why the hell would he subscribe to such sectarian rubbish when he'd never lived in Ireland in his life?"

"Because his family is rooted in Ireland, Ferris. I don't know why, but it seems Liverpool in the sixties was still quite a divided city in terms of religion. Most folk couldn't care less, but in certain areas of the city people still clung to the old divisions. You're too young to remember Scottie Road in its heyday. Loads of Irish Catholics settled there in the eighteenth century and it almost became a city within a city. Even later generations kept up the old religious divides well into the sixties, when modernisation gradually dragged Scotland Road kicking and screaming into the twentieth century, over half a century too late. The place you see today is nothing like it once was, with all the old red brick terraces stretching for miles along the A59. Did you know, Cilla Black was raised on Scottie Road?"

"No, I didn't know that, sir," said Ferris. "So in a way, it's hardly surprising there are people like James Doyle around, even today. His ancestors probably came over and possible lived in the Scottie Road area over a hundred years ago, and a few of them have obviously perpetuated the old hatreds. It's almost unbelievable."

Ross nodded and replied, "Sounds crazy, I know, but it was there, just under the surface. It was never extreme though, as far as I know, and certainly the nineteen sixties helped bring all that sort of nonsense to an end. You've done well, Ferris. Any word from the others?"

"Yes, sir. Derek McLennan has had no luck trying to determine what happened to Brendan Kane's car. It was a pretty thankless exercise really, given that we had no registration number for the vehicle. He even tried DVLA in Swansea but they couldn't do a thing without either a registration number or a vin number."

"Well, he tried, and I didn't expect much after all these years, but it was worth a go. How about D.C. Gable?"

"Still out sir, probably talking to the Oxleys again as you ordered."

"Good, we'll see what, if anything she comes up with when we meet up later. If the boss or anyone wants to know where we are, Sergeant Drake and I are going to talk with James Doyle again. It's time for him to be a little more honest with us, I think."

As Ross and Drake motored across town to the home of James and Connie Doyle, the inspector confided his private thoughts to Drake.

"Right from the beginning, something has bugged me about the kneecapping of Brendan Kane. It was typical IRA justice, but we could find no connection at all between Kane and the terrorists. It was never something that criminals on this side of the water went in for, not even the London gangs, so there had to be something, somewhere, even though no evidence existed to confirm it. I think we dismissed it all too easily after the anti-terrorist boys told us they had no information relating to IRA activity in the city at that time. Even Porteous virtually told me to leave that avenue of investigation alone, not wanting to add a political angle to the case."

"And you think there may have been such a connection, now, sir, is that it?"

"Not quite, Izzie. I've said all along that I thought the solution to this case lay much closer to home than we all thought. I don't think Brendan Kane had any links to terrorism or the IRA or any so-called 'Loyalist' organization, but I do think that we might just have uncovered a personal reason for what happened on that wharf. I'm speculating now, but let's say, knowing James Doyle's bigotry towards the prospect of Protestants having anything to do with his daughter on a romantic level, that he brought his cousin Patrick over here to 'sort' Kane out, scare him off, or give him a warning."

"But, isn't shooting a young man in the kneecaps a bit of an extreme way of warning him off, sir, especially as it would probably lead to someone making an instant connection to IRA involvement?"

"But it didn't, did it, Izzie, because we never found Kane's body, at least until now? Maybe killing him was an accident, I don't know, but I'm sure as hell going to put some pressure on bloody James Doyle, until we get the truth out of the old bastard."

"But, even if you're right, it doesn't do anything to explain Marie's disappearance, does it, sir?"

"No, it doesn't, Izzie. You're quite right, and that's the side of the puzzle that's confounding me a bit. I'm pretty sure Doyle wouldn't have hurt his own daughter, so we're still in the dark there. Maybe when we talk to him, we'll find a clue or two to what happened to that poor girl."

"We're here, sir," said Drake, as she pulled over and parked as close to the Doyle's house as she could.

"Right," said Ross, his face set in an impassive mask. "Let's see if we can get some truth out of Mr. James Bloody Doyle, shall we?"

Chapter 29

JIMMY DOYLE

Sister Mary Dominique stood quietly on the corner of Jubilee Street and St. Michael's Road, where they formed a three-way junction with Grafton Street. She'd seen the black Ford Mondeo arrive some minutes earlier, and seen the two police officers alight from the vehicle and make their way to the house in the centre of the terrace on the opposite side of the street. She knew they were police officers. Their bearing, the way they walked, even the way the younger of the two officers, the woman, held the thin file folder spoke to the world and announced them as officers of the law. If that wasn't enough, the way the light fell on the car it was possible to make out the red and blue flashing lights, situated behind the radiator grille, which clearly identified the Mondeo as an unmarked police car.

Mary Dominique had waited for some time in her position on the corner, before the arrival of the police car and its occupants. She was warm, too warm, and Mary Dominique let up a prayer of gratitude to The Lord Jesus and to The Holy Virgin, for the fact that the order she belonged to, The Sisters of The Virgin, Blessed, had long ago eschewed the use of the old, heavy, black cloth habits, so typical of Orders all over the world. Instead, Mary Dominique wore a neat, white blouse, with a high collar and a fairly lightweight grey pinafore dress with a hem that fell chastely just below the knee, and a grey and white half-wimple that complimented the rest of the habit. Her shoes were of plain black leather, functional but not too heavy, but still, she felt overdressed for the purposes of standing on a street corner in the heat of the day.

Seeing the two police officers being granted entry to the house halfway along the street on the opposite side of the road from her vantage point, she debated what to do next. Should she stay, and wait to see what happened next, or should she simply leave, and come back later, or perhaps another day, or then again, maybe not return at all? After all, if she hadn't seen the article in the Daily Mail during a recent visit to her local library, she wouldn't be here at all. The things she knew, the things she'd seen, surely could result in her knowledge of the past hurting the innocent as much as the guilty. It all happened such a long time ago. At first, she'd been all fired up with the thought that she ought to tell someone what she knew, maybe the police, or someone at the newspaper, she wasn't sure, and so, here she stood, in the heat of the day, watching and wondering, unable to decide her next move. The thought crossed her mind that maybe she'd never be believed anyway. Then again, would anyone have the temerity to accuse a nun of lying?

* * *

"You, Mr. Doyle, are a liar."

Ross had decided to take an aggressive stance with James Doyle from the moment he walked into the man's house. Despite his age, James Doyle appeared to be well capable of putting up stern resistance to Ross's line of questioning.

"What right do you have to come into a man's house and call him a liar?" Doyle snapped back at the inspector.

"The law gives me that right," Ross replied. "As I've already stated, I don't believe your story that your cousin, Patrick Bryce, visited you in nineteen sixty-six purely to look for work in Liverpool. It's also my belief that you have always been aware of his connections to the

Provisional IRA and that in fact you are a wholehearted supporter of their beliefs."

"That's nonsense," Doyle replied. "You're talking as if I'm some sort of terrorist. Connie, tell them, in the name of God, that I'm no terrorist." He directed his plea at this wife, seated in the opposite armchair to himself.

Connie Doyle had listened patiently as her husband had conducted his verbal sparring session with the inspector, but suddenly, the old lady seemed to snap, as though some long pent up frustrations couldn't be held in any longer.

"In the name of God Almighty, James Doyle, why don't you grow up at last, before you're too old to do so? I'll tell the inspector the truth, if you won't."

"You'll shut your mouth, woman, that's what you'll do."

"No, Jimmy, no I won't. No more. Inspector, let me tell you, that damned cousin of his was never anything but trouble. I don't know how or why my husband ever grew so close to him, but I'll tell you this, he wishes he never had. When Patrick came over here in sixty-six, my husband was afraid of him, Inspector Ross. You only had to see them together to know that. My husband wouldn't say no to him. It was me that told Patrick he wasn't welcome in my home. I couldn't stand him near me, and neither could Marie. I made him find a room in a bed and breakfast place. What he and Jimmy got up to when they met up in the evenings I can't say, but I will say this, my husband is a bigoted old fool, and he acts like he's a big, tough guy, but he isn't. There's no way he would have allowed himself to be dragged into anything to do with the IRA, I'm sure of it."

"I'm not necessarily saying he had anything to do with the IRA, at least, not intentionally, Mrs. Doyle." Ross said, quietly.

"Then what do you…oh, in the name of Heaven, please don't say you think he had something to do with Marie's disappearance? He loved her, Inspector. Marie was his pride and joy. He'd never have hurt her."

Izzie Drake was the one who replied, "Not Marie, Mrs. Doyle."

She allowed the words to hang for a second, and then, Connie Doyles eyes seemed to fill first with realization and then with tears as she gasped,

"No, you can't mean you think he had something to do with Brendan's death?"

"That's precisely what I do mean, Mrs. Doyle," said Ross, forcefully. "Why don't you own up, Jimmy? Come on, be a man for once, tell us the truth, like your poor wife here asked you to."

Jimmy Doyle had turned red in the face as the others talked around and about him for those few seconds. He was fighting to control the rage that was building up inside him.

"For cryin' out loud," he screamed at Ross, "I've bloody told you I had nothin' to do with that lad's death, I didn't. How many times do I have to tell you?"

"You can keep telling me until Hell freezes over," said Ross, his anger barely under control. He truly believed he was now face to face with a potential murderer. He had to forget James Doyle was an old man in his eighth decade, and remember that at the time of Brendan Kane's death, he'd have been a strong and fit forty-something, and easily motivated enough by hatred to carry out the evil task of cold-blooded murder. "Come on, out with it, Jimmy. Did you ask your IRA hitman cousin to help you get rid of your daughter's 'proddie' boyfriend? Or, maybe you just wanted Bryce to put the fear of god into young Brendan, to scare him off, keep him away from Marie. I'll bet he'd have loved that, wouldn't he? Is that why he was over here in the first place, Jimmy? Did you invite him to do you the favour because maybe you didn't have the guts to do it yourself? It's not that easy to kill a man in cold blood, is it, Jimmy?"

"I didn't do it," Doyle shouted at Ross, and now, for the first time, the two detectives could see tears forming in the old man's eyes. "Please, listen to me. I didn't do it. I didn't."

"I'm sorry we have caused you upset in your home, Mrs. Doyle," said Ross, quickly rising from his seat. Izzie Drake followed his lead and stood at the same time.

Connie Doyle looked shocked at the abrupt move and Jimmy Doyle, equally surprised gazed almost robotically at Ross and half spluttered, half gasped, "That's it? You believe me, then, you're leaving?"

"We're leaving, for now, Jimmy, and no, I don't believe you, and I certainly haven't finished with you, so don't think for one minute you're off the hook. Next time we meet, you'll probably be under arrest and in an interview room at Merseyside Police Headquarters."

Doyle looked on, speechless, as the two detectives walked from the room, closely followed by Connie Doyle. As they stood at the front door and prepared to leave, as part of their pre-arranged strategy, Drake opened the file she'd carried with her all this time and took out a photograph, which she handed to Connie for her to look at. Connie Doyle peered closely at the black and white print, gasped and said, "Holy Mother of God. Is that all that was left of that poor boy?"

"That's it, Connie," said Drake, gently removing the photo of the remains of Brendan Kane as they'd first been found at the old disused wharf. "All that's left to testify to the life of a young man, a man who loved your daughter, and may have paid for that love with his life."

"And Marie? What about my little girl? Do you still have no clues at what happened to her?" Connie sniffed as the tears slowly dripped from her eyes.

Andy Ross placed a hand on her arm, and softly said, "Not yet, Mrs. Doyle, but I'm going to find out for you, that's a promise."

No further words were spoken as Ross and Drake left the house, leaving Connie with her thoughts, and Jimmy Doyle, hopefully, panicked enough to do something that would give himself away in the next day or two. Ross would have Dodds and McLennan shadow the man in one shift, with Ferris and Gable taking over in watching over the old man, who, Ross firmly believed, was still a potentially dangerous and slippery character.

As they climbed back into the car, satisfied with their strategy so far, Drake turned to her boss and said, "You do know we were being watched when we walked from the car to the house, don't you, sir?"

"We were?"

"Yes, by a nun. I saw her on the street corner as we pulled into the street."

"And you think she was watching us?"

"Well, she looked towards us as we walked from the car."

"Probably thought we were interfering with her door to door work, you know, selling copies of the War Cry or something."

"Oh, sir, the War Cry is The Salvation Army, not the Catholic Church, I thought you knew that."

Ross laughed. "Of course I know that, Izzie, just joking, that's all. Anyway, I wouldn't have thought we'd be of much interest to a nun, would we? She was probably waiting for someone and we were probably the only moving thing to catch her eye in the street when we parked up and walked to the Doyle's house."

"Yes, you're probably right sir. Just thought I'd mention it, that's all."

"Right, let's get back to base then, and we'll set up the surveillance on Jimmy Doyle. I don't trust that old bastard as far as I can throw him."

"Okay, sir. I think you did a good job in there, if you don't mind me saying so."

"Why, thank you, Sergeant. Yes, we put the fear of God Almighty into Jimmy, I hope, and with luck, Connie will work on him in the home. Now she knows our suspicions, she'll want the truth from her husband, if it has anything to do with the disappearance of Marie. Connie Doyle could be our best bet for obtaining the truth in this case, if we play our cards right."

As they drove round the corner at the end of the street, Sister Mary Dominique stepped out of the small café on the next street after enjoying a nice cup of tea and a Bakewell tart, and watched as the police car disappeared from sight, lost in the general rush of traffic heading towards the city centre. She was still far too warm and headed away from the area towards her next port of call at a slow but steady pace, the pain from her arthritic knees forcing her to pace herself carefully as she walked.

Chapter 30

CLOSING IN

D.C. Paul Ferris, having added all the latest information to the white board in the squad's small conference room, and having heard Ross's plan for surveillance on James Doyle, took advantage of Ross's "Any questions?" to ask,

"So you really do think James Doyle is our man, sir, especially in the murder of Brendan Kane?"

"I certainly think he's involved, yes," Ross replied. "At the very least, even if he didn't pull the trigger, or bludgeon Kane about the head, I'm pretty sure Doyle was, in some way, complicit in the murder."

Sam Gable produced the next question.

"But what about Marie, sir? Do you really think James Doyle would have been so foolish or so filled with sectarian hatred that he'd put his own daughter at risk, or, worse still, do something to harm her?"

"That's the part of the puzzle that's evading me. He seemed genuinely affronted that I'd had the temerity to suggest he may have had something to with his daughter's disappearance. That's the problem with mysteries, I'm afraid, especially one this old. I have to be honest and say we've all done bloody well so far to piece together what we've achieved so far, with no real evidence, witnesses or solid clues to go on. Did your fishing expedition with Marie's old friends throw up anything of interest?" he asked as he finished his speech, knowing in advance the probable answer. If Sam Gable had found anything relevant, she'd have reported it to him by now, he was certain.

"No, sir. I'm sorry. Those I was able to trace and speak to mostly came up with the same kind of answers, you know the sort of things I mean, "*I can't remember back that far*," or "*I didn't know her that well*", and "*Wasn't it a shame? Have you found her then?*" If you ask me, most of Marie's so-called friends probably forgot all about the poor girl about a month after she'd gone. Apart from Clemency De Souza, no-one really admitted to being that close to her."

"Nothing less than I expected, but thanks for trying," said Ross. "I want to let James Doyle stew for a day or two before we have another crack at him. I'm hoping his wife puts a heap of pressure on him to come clean about whatever he's hiding, and I'm certain he *is* hiding something."

"So, what do we do in the meantime, sir?" Drake asked.

"We still have to do what we can to try and discover what became of Marie Doyle. If, as he insists, James Doyle had nothing to do with his daughter's disappearance, it leaves us still pretty much in the dark where she's concerned. We need to push for information on Marie. Sam has done her best, but while we wait to interview Doyle senior, I want us to try and tap in to the only other sources of information we have on the girl. Dodds and McLennan, I'd like you to go and talk to each of the Doyle brothers, individually and see if they can give us something, anything that they may have forgotten previously. Can they suggest a favourite place, for example, where she might have felt safe if she did escape the same fate as her boyfriend? We need a trail to follow, but unless we can come up with a starting point, we're just running around chasing our tails, and getting nowhere. Sam, I'd like you to go and do the same with Clemmy Oxley and her husband. Perhaps, Clemmy, of all people might know if Marie had, or maybe the two of them shared a secret place, or dreamed of visiting a place, like, oh, I don't know, like London, or the wilds of Cornwall. You'd probably know more about the way young girls and women think and you might be able to jog some sort of memory from Clemmy."

With the team briefed, they sat down with Paul Ferris, who, as collator had worked out just how they could fit their new assignments in with the task of shadowing James Doyle over the next couple of days. As he pointed out, the interviews of the Doyle brothers and Clemmy and Phil Oxley wouldn't take too long so could be fitted in around the surveillance operation. As the detectives left the room, Ross turned to Ferris. He had something else in mind for his collator. Ross had come to realize over the last few days just how much he valued the quiet, but highly intelligent D.C. Ferris. If anyone could be counted on to give maximum attention to a particular problem, it was Ferris. Ross appreciated how much strain the young detective must be under at home, with the worry about the health of his son always lurking at the back of his mind. Ross found himself sincerely hoping it wouldn't be long before the health service found a kidney donor for the lad. His wife, Maria, had told Ross just how difficult it was to find donors for a patient so young, and she'd expressed her own admiration for the medical staff who worked on such cases, where quite often the end result could have tragic consequences for a family. She was glad she was, as she put it, 'just an ordinary doctor' and not one specializing in such a high risk area. For now, though, Ross put such thoughts aside and stood in front of the white board as Paul Ferris updated it with the latest assignments and information, such as it was.

"When you did that check on Patrick Bryce, you said he'd dropped off the R.U.C's radar a while ago, but, I'm guessing that whoever you spoke to was only looking into known or suspected criminal activity, right?

"Yes, that's right, sir," Ferris replied.

"Okay, here's what I want you to do. Get back in touch with our friends in the R.U.C. and ask them to look for Bryce's last known address, and also try and see if they can find any legitimate references to him. He'll be getting on in years too, now, like Doyle, so maybe he really is legit these days. He may appear on an electoral register somewhere, or even had or still has a business of some kind. Somebody, somewhere in bloody Northern Ireland must know where Patrick Bryce is. Wherever he is, I want to speak with him, sooner rather than later."

"Right sir. I'll contact the R.U.C. but there may be an easier route."

"Go on, I'm listening," said Ross.

"If he's over sixty-five, there's a good chance the guy is drawing his old-age pension sir. If he is, the pensions people will have him on record, his address, where he collects his pension and so on. Could be just a matter of calling them and seeing if he's registered for his pension, sir."

Ross smiled a broad expansive smile.

"You're a genius, Ferris. Go to it, lad. See what you can dig up for me."

"Consider it done, sir," Ferris replied, as he began tapping keys on his computer keyboard.

Confident that he was close to a solution to the case, and that solving the murder of Brendan Kane would lead to the solution of the mystery surrounding Marie Doyle's disappearance, he left Ferris to his task as he made his way to the office of D.C.I. Porteous. It was time to update the boss.

Chapter 31

PROOF, WHAT PROOF?

Sister Mary Dominique stood just where she'd stood yesterday and the day before that, and the day before that, when the police officers had visited the house halfway down the street. She could see more police officers today, though, like yesterday, these two officers made no attempt to enter the house. Sister Mary knew they were police officers. Who else would sit for hours on end in a car, drinking tea or coffee from a flask occasionally, and trying not to look obvious each time the door of the house opened? It appeared to the nun that the police were only interested in the man in the house. They'd made no attempt to follow the lady of the house on the occasions she'd left the house alone. But, she felt sure the two men in the car would soon be on their way if the man left alone or in the company of his wife.

Mary Dominique decided to move from the street corner. If she stayed there too long, she felt sure the police officers would be certain to notice her, and in fact, was surprised they hadn't noticed her as yet. Then again, with their attention focused on the house occupied by Mr. and Mrs. James Doyle, they probably wouldn't notice her if she walked past their car half naked.

Carefully looking both ways, she ensured the road was free of traffic, then crossed the street, walking close to but behind the police car, and then made her way along the small passageway that led to the alley that ran the length of the rear of the houses in the street. She walked the full length of the street along the rear alley, coming out at the other end, where she found a new position, close to a betting shop built in a converted terraced house at the end of the street. Just like the street she'd grown up in as a girl. She chuckled to herself, as she thought of the effect her dress would have on some of the regulars at the bookies. Nuns and horse racing just didn't quite go together.

At that moment, Jimmy and Connie Doyle exited from the front door of their home and climbed into their Vauxhall Astra, parked immediately outside the house. Connie carried a collection of carrier bags under her arm, and this was obviously a shopping trip. The officers in the police car saw Jimmy Doyle say something to his wife, who appeared to answer him with a stony gaze. Even from a distance, it was easy to pick up the coldness of the atmosphere emanating from Connie towards her husband.

"Looks like things are a bit frosty in the Doyle household," Nick Dodds commented, as Derek McLennan started the unmarked police car and readied himself to follow the Doyles at a subtle distance.

"Yeah," McLennan replied. "Even from here, I'd say you could cut the atmosphere between them with a knife. Looks like the inspector's ploy to set the old lady against her husband is working. Where d'you think we're headed, Nick?"

"Tesco or Sainsbury's, I'd guess, looking at the bags she's carrying," Dodds replied. "Well, will you look at that?" he commented as they turned the corner at the end of the street, McLennan keeping a respectful distance between the two cars.

"Eh, what?" said McLennan.

"A bloody nun, Derek, right outside the bookies on the corner. She's just standing there, like she's waiting for someone. I'd place a bet of my own she'll be doing a great job of driving the punters away from that little den of iniquity."

McLennan, focusing his attention on the car they were following caught the merest of glimpses of the nun in his rear view mirror and then she was lost from his sight as they followed the bend in the road towards their destination, wherever that maybe.

* * *

Ross was at his desk, sipping coffee and reviewing his files on the case, when he was interrupted by the telephone on his desk, ringing loudly and demanding his attention. Knowing there was no escape, he picked up the receiver.

"D.I. Ross," he spoke into the phone.

"Well, hi there, Andy." The cheerful sound of the unmistakable Ethan Tiffen of the U.S. immigration Service assaulted his eardrum and he found himself holding the phone slightly away from his ear. "Didn't I tell you I'd get back to you real soon?"

"Hello, Ethan. Yes, you did. How are you, and how have your inquiries gone?"

"I'm fine buddy, just fine, thanks, and hope the same goes for you and your guys up there in little old Liverpool. Now, as for my inquiry into your visas from long ago, there's not really what you could call good news, I'm sad to say."

"That's what I was afraid of, Ethan, so look, don't worry about it. I didn't really expect you to find anything, to be brutally honest with you."

"Well, let me just tell you what I did find," said Tiffen, and Ross listened.

"I was able to track back all those years, and found the records of the original visa applications and the eventual issue of three month tourist visas to your Brendan Kane and Marie Doyle. I'll not go into dates on the phone as I'm having everything faxed to you when we get off the phone. It was as you suspected, Andy, we have no record of those visas ever being used, and certainly no record of anyone with either of those two names entering the States legally through any of the major ports or airports during that year. If your couple, or even just one of them, did find their way over to Uncle Sam, they did so as ghosts."

"Ghosts?"

"Yeah, ghosts, illegals, under the radar, you with me? You get your fair share of illegal immigrants over here too, don't you?"

"Yes of course we do, as you must read of from time to time in the news, Ethan."

Ethan Tiffen let out a quiet, diplomatic cough.

"Sure do, Andy, sure do. It's a shame your government can't seem to control the influx of immigrants into your great little country, and I don't mean that as an insult. This here is an island nation you live in, buddy, and it surely can only hold a finite number of people. If things go on like this, one day soon you guys are going to have to hang a 'full up' sign at all your points of entry. Your whole island might just fall into the sea if it gets too overcrowded."

There was little more Tiffen could say that would help Ross's investigation. At least he'd kicked into touch the idea, slim though it had been anyway, that someone had stolen the visas and used them to enter the USA, though, as Tiffen had pointed out, it didn't preclude anyone entering the States illegally. Ross knew Brendan hadn't done so, his body had been lying at the bottom of the river, but could Marie, perhaps with help, have joined the many thousands of illegal immigrants who flood into the United States every year?

Ross and Tiffen exchanged pleasantries for a minute, with Ross thanking the American for his attempts to assist his investigation, and expressing his admiration for Tiffen's dogged determination in seeking and resurrecting the records of those visa applications from thirty three years ago. Tiffen, in return, issued a well meant and genuine invitation for Andy and his wife, Maria, to join Tiffen and his wife for dinner, maybe spend a weekend as their guests in London, one day soon. Ross thanked him profusely, whilst doubting such a time would feasibly come up in the foreseeable future.

Hanging up the phone, Ross sat and shuffled the papers on his desk aimlessly for a few seconds, as he allowed his thoughts free rein. He was fairly sure Marie Doyle died at the time of Brendan Kane's murder, but whether her father James had been a party to her death, he still couldn't decide. Either way, he felt he and his team were on the cusp of identifying the murderer, or murderers, of Brendan Kane. The problem, as he knew only too well, was that knowing who did it, and being able to prove it sufficiently well to present to a court of law, were two very different things. He thought he knew who'd done it, but did he have any evidence that would convince the Crown Prosecution Service to launch a prosecution against those responsible? No! He knew it only too well, and the thought caused him to slam his fist down hard on the desk, so hard that he actually issued a cry of pain.

"Damn!" he exclaimed and then again, "Damn, damn, damn."

Chapter 32

THE TAPE

Just as he was about to leave his office, and take Sergeant Izzie Drake for a well-deserved coffee, a knock on his door signalled the arrival of Press Liaison Officer, George Thompson, accompanied by another man, who, without introduction, Ross immediately sensed was a member of the fourth estate, a reporter. The newcomer wore a well-used brown check jacket, with leather reinforcements on the elbows and his pale grey trousers looked as if they'd last been ironed around the time of the Queen's silver jubilee. His dark brown hair was neat but a little long over his collar, and he simply smelled of 'press' to Ross, who guessed the man's age at around fifty to fifty-five.

"Hello, George. Come on in," Ross said, wondering what information, if any, George and the newcomer might be bearing for him.

"Andy, hello," Thompson replied. "This is Terry Wallace, from the *Echo*. He received a phone call earlier today and thought it best to get in touch with us right away. We've known each other for quite some years and he thought contacting me would be the quickest way to get to you and be taken seriously."

"Looks like he was right," Ross smiled and gestured for the two men to take a seat. As they did, he spoke his first words to Wallace. "Mr. Wallace, good to meet you. I've read one or two of your pieces in the past. I must say they're a bit better than the usual standard of crime reporting found in local, provincial newspapers. I'm presuming you feel what you have to tell me is of some importance, or you wouldn't have gone to the trouble of going through George to get to see me so quickly."

"Nice to meet you too, Inspector Ross. George has told me good things about you, too, and thanks for the compliment. I'm not here to discuss my credentials, but suffice it to say, I used to work for a couple of London dailies in the past. I moved up to Liverpool for my wife's sake, when her father had a long illness and well, I liked it so much we stayed. Anyway, to business."

Ross immediately liked this man, with his businesslike approach and lack of the usual self-importance so often seen in members of the press corps.

"Yes, please, go on, Mr. Wallace."

"Okay. Well, as you know, we ran George's press release a few days ago and to be honest, I doubted you'd get much from it. Thirty three years is a long time, and most people's memories tend to dim after thirty-three days, never mind years. So, anyway, when a woman was put through to my desk this morning, I wondered first of all why she hadn't done as the press release asked and contacted Merseyside Police directly."

As he spoke, Wallace removed a small, miniature tape recorder from the inside pocket of his jacket, explaining as he did so,

"I often use this little gadget to tape interviews, to make sure I'm reporting facts accurately, and sadly, I was already about a minute into my conversation with this woman before I realized the potential significance of what she was telling me. At that point, I grabbed my recorder, turned it on and held it as close to the phone as I could. I had the phone resting on my shoulder, under my chin, and was holding the recorder as close to it as I could, while trying to make notes with my other hand on a notepad, so the quality is pretty awful, but we can still make out what the woman was saying. I'm sorry it couldn't be any better, but as I said, I was hardly expecting a call like this, and I hope you don't think I'm wasting your time in bringing it to you."

"We'd better hear it then, hadn't we?" said Ross, as Terry Wallace laid the recorder on Ross's desk and switched it to 'play'.

As Wallace had said, the quality of the recording was poor, with plenty of additional background noise from the various activities taking place in the newsroom, and lots of scratching sounds as Wallace had attempted to keep the recorder close to the phone, but he'd been able to hear the woman's words by listening carefully, his head cocked to the side as he tried to blot out the surrounding white noise of his office. Now, as Ross listened, he could almost feel the events of thirty three years ago taking place in his mind. As Wallace had warned him, the conversation was already under way before the recording commenced, but he could hear enough as the woman's voice, slightly distorted by the surrounding noises, spoke from the recorder's tiny speaker in the middle of his desk.

* * *

"…and I saw it all. I was lucky they couldn't see me, or I'd probably have suffered the same fate as Brendan Kane."

Next, Wallace's voice was heard, clearer, asking the mystery caller, "But tell me, why have you waited until now to come forward with this information? Please, just tell me your name, and if you want, I'll meet you somewhere, a place of your choice, and I'll even go to the police station with you, if you're afraid to go on your own. This is too important to just pass on to me, you do know that, don't you? And the police will ask for corroborating evidence, as well."

"Look, I'm telling you what happened. Never mind my name, at least for now. Why have I waited so long? Fear, Mr. Wallace. Fear and a mind that found it hard to reconcile what I saw take place that night in Liverpool all those years ago with supposed civilized human behaviour. Tell the police and I'm sure they'll be able to corroborate what I'm telling you by adding together what they've probably already discovered for themselves."

Obviously not wanting to lose the woman, just in case she was a valid witness, Wallace was heard encouraging her to continue her story, and her voice was heard again.

"I saw them walking towards the old warehouse, and heard the two of them bullying Brendan Kane as they pushed him towards the far side of the building, where it was darker than it had been at the front. The smaller man looked to be in charge of what was happening, but the taller one, with the Irish accent, he was the one who was pushing and shoving and swearing at Brendan. They obviously had no idea anyone was watching them, and they didn't even make any effort to keep their voices down, so they must have known the place was deserted and didn't expect anyone to show up and see what was happening. The Irishman hit Brendan a couple of times, once across the face and another blow to the back of his head. I heard him tell Brendan he was scum and not fit to be near honest and pure Christian women. He kicked Brendan at the back of his legs and he fell to the ground. As he lifted himself up, on to his knees, the Irishman pulled a gun from the waistband of his trousers. The other man, the older one, suddenly took a step back, with a look of horror on his face. "What are you doing?" he said to the Irishman. "I didn't say anything about guns. We're just supposed to scare the shit out of the little bastard." The Irishman didn't reply, and the .... (here, her voice broke up too much to hear clearly), I heard the sound of two shots from the gun. They were so loud, it was like a cannon going off, and then poor Brendan fell forward, screaming. I thought the Irishman had killed him when he fell silent, but then I heard him sobbing and realized he must be in shock. He just lay there, on the ground, bleeding, in the darkness. I could see enough from the light of the moon to make out what had happened, before you ask. Next thing I knew the Irishman was making the other, older man help him to drag Brendan towards the edge of the wharf. I wanted to call out, to stop them from what they were doing, but I was paralysed with fear. Even if I had called out to them, I was sure I'd end up being shot too. Before I knew what was happening, the Irishman pulled something from a pocket in his trousers. It was a hammer, Mr. Wallace, and without even hesitating he started to hit Brendan over the head with it. The sound of that hammer hitting Brendan's head has stayed with me a long time, and when the two men then pushed him off the edge of the wharf into the water, I heard a splash and then everything seemed to fall silent. It only lasted a few seconds, that awful silence and then the older man turned on the Irishman, calling him a crazy, mad fucker, those were his words. I was rooted to the spot on the corner of that warehouse, hidden from them by the darkness that shielded me from their view. I couldn't move, and my legs felt like they were going to collapse from under me, but I knew if they did, those two men would find me and kill me too. They carried on arguing for a minute or two, and then there was another splash. I think one of them had thrown the hammer in the water. The older man said, "What about the gun?" and the Irishman replied, "That goes with me, Jimmy boy. You never know when I'll be needing it again."

The one called Jimmy looked as though he was on the verge of panicking, he couldn't keep still, his feet all a-fidget, and then I heard him say, "What about Marie? What the hell do I tell my little girl when she wants to know where her fella is?"

The Irishman said, "You say nothing, you idiot. You know nothing. You were never here. How can you know where her filthy proddie boyfriend has run off to? As far as anyone knows, he's probably gone off somewhere with some proddie bitch who'll open her legs for him whenever he wants a good shag."

There's not much more to tell. I waited until they'd gone, and then stayed put for at least another twenty minutes in case they came back and found me, and then I ran. I just ran and ran and never looked back. I'd never thought to see such horror. I thought maybe I was dreaming, that it was all a nightmare, but of course, it wasn't. I knew who they were, you see. Both men. I knew who they were."

At that point, the woman's voice seemed to choke up, as though overwhelmed by the strain of reliving her nightmare. Wallace's voice was heard again,

"Please, tell me your name. Are you Marie Doyle? And the name of the men you say you saw carrying out the killing. Who were they?"

After a pause, with just a hissing sound on the line, the woman's voice finally returned, as she said, very quietly, "Marie Doyle died a long time ago, Mr. Wallace. As for the men who did it, the police will find out their names soon enough, though I believe they know one of them already."

"What do you mean about Marie Doyle dying? Who are you?" Wallace persisted.

"You can call me Jones, and I saw Marie die, too," the woman said, eventually.

"And Marie died too? When? Where? Did you know her?"

"I knew her," the woman said as her voice changed in tone, almost as though she was in a dreamlike state.

"And why were you there that night?"

"I was just walking, just walking, and I saw them and followed them."

"Listen, Miss Jones, you should go to the police. Tell them what you've told me," they heard Wallace say, but then came the sound of the phone being hung up. She'd gone, and all that now played on Wallace's recorder was the sound of static.

* * *

"I'm sorry I couldn't get any more, Inspector," said Wallace.

"Don't apologise, Mr. Wallace. You did well to keep her on the line that long and get that much from her," Ross said in reply, his face showing deep thought and worry.

"You look concerned, Andy," George Thompson ventured, seeing the frown on Ross's face.

"I'm very concerned, George. If this woman saw all that, why didn't she report it to the police right away? Where did she go and why suddenly crawl out of the woodwork and tell you this story, Mr. Wallace? If she was afraid for her life thirty three years ago, she must feel confident that nothing's going to harm her now, or, she's got no reason to be afraid any longer. Thanks for bringing the tape in. I hope we can count on your help in not letting this information out to the public until we've had an opportunity to check the truth of her story, Mr. Wallace?"

"Don't worry, Inspector. We won't print a word until you give the go-ahead. We don't want to jeopardise an ongoing investigation. In fact, you can keep the tape, in case you need to copy it, as long as we get it back at the Echo when you've done with it."

Ross thanked Wallace for his public-spiritedness and the loan of the tape, and quickly called Izzie Drake to his office and played the tape for her.

"Bloody hell, sir, who the hell is this woman?"

"Who indeed, Izzie, and what about this assertion of hers that Marie Doyle died a long time ago? What do you make of that?"

"Maybe she was a friend of Marie's? She may have seen the killing and may even know where Marie went afterwards. In fact sir, she might have been hiding Marie for years, maybe until her death, and now the case has made the papers again, she's decided to tell us what really happened."

"Sounds feasible, Sergeant, but, it still doesn't quite add up. She mentions Jimmy, and an Irishman, so that puts both Jimmy Doyle and Patrick Bryce in the frame, as far as I'm concerned. But why was this mystery woman out there, on the docks, at night, as she describes it, just conveniently around the time Doyle and Bryce show up with a captive Brendan Kane?"

"I don't know sir, but surely, everything she said on that tape fits with what we either know or have surmised so far?"

"Yes, it does, with a few gaps here and there." Ross fell into deep thought for a minute or so, then, making up his mind on his next step, spoke once more. "I want Jimmy Doyle brought in, as soon as possible. And we need to try and find this woman. She could be a genuine eye-witness."

"Could she be lying, sir? Could it be Marie, resurfacing after all these years?"

"But why, Izzie? If it is, why now? What can she hope to achieve?"

Before they could continue their conversation there came a knock on the door, quickly followed by the entry of Detective Constable Ferris, who almost fell into the room in his haste to reach Ross. The young detective's face was flushed. Something had obviously brought him to Ross's office in a hurry.

"Blimey, Ferris," said Ross, observing the state of his detective, "Where's the fire, lad? Slow down, take a breath, and then tell us what's got you so fired up."

Hardly able to contain himself, Paul Ferris thrust a sheet of paper into Ross's hand, and stood back from the desk. Ross looked at the paper, and his face assumed a look of shock.

"What is it?" asked Izzie Drake, and when no one replied immediately, again asked, "Paul, *what* is it?"

"Tell her, Ferris," Ross instructed him.

"Right sir. Well, you asked me to look deeper into Patrick Bryce, and I put in a further request to the R.U.C. for any additional background information they might possess on the man, and, well, this just arrived. He picked up the sheet of paper that Ross had now placed on his desk. Patrick Bryce is dead, murdered, Sarge."

"My God, when? How recently?" Drake asked, as both she and Ross felt their senses suddenly switch to red alert status.

"Just a week ago. His body was discovered floating in a restored canal lock near Lisburn, near Belfast, and get this..." Ferris paused for effect, and then announced, "he was shot in both kneecaps and then bludgeoned over the head with a heavy object, more than once, and his body dumped in the canal lock."

"Revenge," said Ross. "Someone has decided the time has come to avenge what happened to Brendan Kane and Marie Doyle."

"The mysterious Miss Jones?" Izzie Drake postulated.

"What have I missed?" asked Ferris, "and who the hell is Miss Jones?"

"You could be right, Izzie," said Ross, and then he passed the tape Wallace had loaned him to Ferris. "Take this, listen to it, then get me the best quality copy you can. It'll tell you all we know about Miss Jones. Get back to your friend at the R.U.C, Paul and get me all you can on Bryce's death, circumstances, witnesses, bloody hell man, anything and everything they have. We need to get the team together for a meeting, and fast. Arrange it will you, Izzie?"

"Yes, sir. What about the surveillance on James Doyle?"

"Tell McLennan and Dodds to pick up our friend, Jimmy Doyle, and bring him in. I want a nice long chat in an uncomfortable interview room with Mr. James Doyle."

* * *

Two hours later, old Jimmy Doyle was sitting at a table in interview room two at police headquarters, waiting to be interviewed by Andy Ross and Izzie Drake. Ross had deliberately kept Doyle waiting in an attempt to ratchet up the man's tension levels. He hoped Doyle would finally crack when faced with some of the information on the tape. Once he became aware that the police knew so many intimate details about the murder of Brendan Kane, Ross felt they just might manage to squeeze the full story and secure a confession from Doyle, always supposing of course, that the story told by 'Miss Jones' was as truthful as Ross hoped it was. For now, that was a gamble he was prepared to take in order to elicit Doyle's confession.

Before commencing the interview, he'd first had to spend an uncomfortable few minutes attempting to mollify Mickey and Ronnie Doyle, who Connie had called as soon as Doyle had been taken from their home under police caution. The brothers had both made their way to their parents' home, and at her insistence, had then taken Connie to headquarters, where they currently stood facing Andy Ross.

"We came to see you in an effort to help, because we mistakenly thought the remains were those of our sister, Inspector and in the end, you turn round and arrest our Dad," said Mickey Doyle. "Are you sure he had something to do with Brendan's murder?"

"Look Mickey, I'm afraid I can't go into details with you. The investigation has gone too far now, and as an ongoing murder investigation, even though you and Ronnie have been very helpful, there are protocols I must follow, one of which is not discussing those details with anyone not authorized to be privy to them."

"It's alright boys, really," said their mother, at long last saying something after maintaining a dignified silence since she'd arrived at headquarters and been placed in a waiting room with her sons. "The inspector has a job to do and I just wanted to be here, and have a word with him before he interrogates your father."

"What can I do for you, Mrs. Doyle, bearing in mind what I just told Mickey?" Ross asked Connie Doyle, who seemed to have shrunk since the last time he'd seen her, ageing at least ten years in the process.

"It's more a case of what I can do for you, Inspector," she replied. "I wanted you boys to be here, too," she said to both sons, "because you deserve to know what I'm going to tell the Inspector."

"Bloody hell, Ma, that sounds ominously serious," said Ronnie, and Mickey said, "Christ, Mam, what is it?"

"No need to take our Lord's name in vain, Mickey," Connie reprimanded her eldest son, who mumbled an apology, and then she turned to Ross once more and said to him, her voice small but filled with dignity, "After you called the other day, Inspector, you can guess, I think, that things between my husband and me deteriorated rather quickly after the things you accused him of. When you'd gone, I demanded that Jimmy come clean, at least with me. I told him that if he'd had anything at all, no matter how small a contribution, to Marie's disappearance, and poor Brendan's murder, he owed it to me, his wife, to be truthful with me. I knew he'd been evasive with you. I've been married to the man long enough to know when he's not being truthful. He continued to deny everything, even though I now knew he was lying with every word that came from his mouth. Your father is not a good man, boys, and I hope you can get him to confess his sins, Inspector.

Brian L. Porter

This is about his own daughter, in the name of God, and he still can't be man enough to tell me, his wife, what happened to her, or how he helped to murder Brendan."

Both Mickey and Ronnie blanched visibly at her last words, and she ended by saying, "Tell him he needs to look for God's forgiveness, Inspector, for I'm sure I don't know if I can find it in my heart to grant him mine. Please, take me home now, boys, and let the inspector do his job. We'll hear soon enough what he decides to do about your father."

With that, Connie Doyle and her sons left the room, Connie's arms linked with her sons, and Andy Ross prepared to begin his interview with Jimmy Doyle.

* * *

"Before we go in, there's one thing we need to remember," Ross said quietly to Izzie Drake as they stood outside the door to interview room two.

"What's that, sir?" she asked.

"We've all worked hard to try and solve this case, Izzie, and now it looks as if we've finally got our hands on one of the two perpetrators. The other, Patrick Bryce, is sadly beyond the reach of earthly justice, as we've recently learned. You and I know that the man we're about to interview is guilty as hell, but, and this is the sticky point about this bloody case, we have no hard and fast evidence to confront him with. With what we have at present, a good solicitor would have him out of here in a couple of hours."

"So, what exactly are you saying, sir?"

"I'm saying we go in there and do all we can to wring some form of admission of guilt from him. We use the accusations 'Miss Jones' made on the tape and see if he caves in when faced with the fact he was seen on that wharf when Brendan was killed. If he does, we might be able to hit him with a conspiracy charge, and even then, the C.P.S. might say we have little realistic chance of a conviction."

239

Drake's face revealed her understanding of her boss's words, and she certainly didn't like the implications of what he'd just said. She knew only too well that if the Crown Prosecution Service felt a case had little chance of obtaining a conviction, they wouldn't go ahead with the prosecution. The police needed to produce hard evidence, proof of a person's guilt before they'd go ahead.

"You're telling me that no matter what we do in there, that old bastard is likely to walk, aren't you?" she said.

"That's exactly what I'm saying, Izzie, unless we can unearth some physical evidence, or unless the mysterious 'Miss Jones' comes forward and agrees to be a witness, which might at least see Doyle having to answer in court for his crimes. Just be warned, don't be surprised by anything I say in there, and back me up as though we have a cast iron case against Doyle, okay?"

With a tinge of apprehension mingled with disappointment in her voice, Drake simply replied, "Okay, sir, let's do it."

Jimmy Doyle looked up as the two detectives walked confidently into the room and seated themselves in the two chairs on the opposite side of the table to where he sat. At first, Ross had been surprised when the man hadn't insisted on a lawyer being present while he was being questioned, but soon realized that the old man, despite his crimes, had previously had no close contact with the legal system and probably wouldn't demand a solicitor until he was faced with the severity of the potential charges against him, though, as Ross had just pointed out to Drake, the likelihood of such charges ever being laid against Doyle was pretty slim. Ross himself had been less than pleased when D.C.I. Porteous had pointed all this out to him in a brief but ultimately frustrating telephone conversation he'd had with his boss after learning the information on the tape, part of which he'd played over the phone to Porteous in an effort to save time.

Arrogant as ever, Doyle smiled a crooked smile, though without much feeling in it, as they stared at him silently for a few seconds, the atmosphere in the room one of expectancy, perhaps on both sides.

Doyle's first words clearly showed what his expectancy of this interview was.

"You ready to let me go home now, Inspector?" the arrogance in his voice tempered a little by a hint of nervousness. Leaving him alone for a while in the windowless, drab and sparsely furnished interview room had at least served Ross's purpose in making Doyle a little edgy and unsure of himself.

"What on earth makes you think that, Mr. Doyle?" Ross asked. "We've only just begun here. We have received some serious allegations against you and we're duty-bound to investigate them. Ross now turned on the dual tape recorders on the other table in the room, used to tape all such interviews, and quickly identified himself, Drake and the suspect, giving the time and date of the interview. Undeterred by Ross's actions, Doyle simply carried on as before, replying to the inspector's previous words."

"Allegations? What bloody allegations?"

"Oh, quite simple ones really, the same ones I discussed with you at your house the other day. It is our contention, Mr. Doyle, that you were a willing party to the murder of Brendan Doyle on a date as yet unknown during the summer of nineteen sixty-six, and that you acted in partnership with your cousin Patrick Bryce, a known member of the Provisional I.R.A. who you invited to Liverpool in order to carry out the act of murder. Also, we need to discuss the subsequent disappearance of your daughter, Marie Doyle, who, according to all known information, was last seen around the time of Brendan Kane's death, and who has never been seen or heard from since then."

As with the interview they'd carried out at his home, mere mention of his daughter's name served to galvanise Jimmy Doyle, who immediately raised his voice in indignation at Ross's insinuation.

"I've already told you, I know nothing about Marie's disappearance. Do you seriously believe I'd ever do anything to hurt my own daughter? What kind of man d'you take me for, Inspector Ross?"

Privately, Ross now believed that as a result of Doyle's vociferous and agitated denials of involvement in Marie's disappearance, he might possibly be telling the truth about that side of the case, but he wasn't going to let Doyle know that, at least, not yet. Instead, he replied to Doyle's outburst.

"A very bad man, is the simple answer to that, Mr. Doyle. I take you for a narrow-minded religious bigot who would stoop to murder before letting his daughter become romantically involved with a member of the protestant faith, even though, from what we've learned, neither Marie, nor Brendan Kane gave a fiddler's kiss for any form of religion. They were just two young people in love with each other, with music and the sheer joy that living in those early years of the nineteen sixties seemed to generate in the younger generation of that era. You masked your feelings well, making a pretence of not caring that your sons and daughter were having the time of their lives as part of a pop group that included a protestant. How soon after they began hanging around together did you develop your hatred of Brendan? Was it when they formed the group, or maybe earlier, going all the way back to infant or junior school? You're a man who has probably spent your entire married life imposing your will and your outdated religious intolerance on your wife and family, all of whom, I must say, appear to have inured themselves against your attitudes and even your wife has now decided to stand up and be counted, because, Jimmy Doyle, she's quite simply had enough of you."

"And I've had enough of you and your questions," said Doyle, still a hint of arrogance in his voice. "I've told you before that Patrick came here to look for work. Why don't you find him and ask him?"

"As it happens, we have found Patrick Bryce, or rather, the Royal Ulster Constabulary have, but we won't be able to ask him anything. Your cousin's body was found in a renovated lock on a canal near Belfast, with his head bashed in and two bullet wounds in his kneecaps. Does that sound familiar to you, Mr. Doyle?"

Ross's words stunned Doyle into silence. Deep down, he could feel his by now tenuous grip on reality, and on his freedom, beginning to slip away. Not knowing what to say or how to react to Ross's news without incriminating himself any further, Jimmy Doyle simply sat shaking his head, the beginnings of tears appearing to form at the corners of his eyes. He could be heard mumbling under his breath, over and again, the one word, "No, no, no."

Becoming irritated by the verbal sparring that appeared to be leading nowhere, and wanting to press home the advantage he felt the shock news about Bryce may have gained him, Ross now nodded at Drake, and on the prearranged signal, the sergeant opened the brown manila folder which she'd placed on the desk and made a pretense of reading something within the file, before looking Doyle in the eye, clearing her throat and at length, continuing the interrogation.

"What would you say, Mr. Doyle, if I told you a witness has come forward to tell us you were seen on the night of Brendan Kane's murder, acting in unison with your cousin, Patrick Bryce in the killing of that young man?"

"What? You're lying, that's what you're doing, lying to try to get a confession out of me, to something I didn't do. I know about these things. You read about the police trying to trick innocent people into false confessions all the time."

"Is that so, Mr. Doyle?" Izzie asked as she proceeded to repeat to him the words as spoken by 'Miss Jones' on the tape, with Doyle arguing with his cousin about the severity of what Bryce had done. Ferris had made a quick copy of the tape and Drake had made notes of the most important sections, those she felt could best be used in the interview with Jimmy Doyle. She fell silent and waited as both she and Ross watched and waited for Doyle's reaction.

Jimmy Doyle's face immediately paled and the man swallowed hard, both visually and audibly. After giving him time to answer, and receiving no response, Ross stepped in to the conversation again.

"Well, Jimmy, don't you have anything to say to us?"

A further pause followed, and then, speaking very slowly and deliberately, as if the gravity of his situation had finally hit home, Doyle said just four words;

"I want a lawyer."

With that, Ross had no choice but to bring the interview to an end. Under normal circumstances, he would send his suspect to the cells while a solicitor could be found to represent the man, but, knowing he was on pretty thin ice, and that a half-decent solicitor would take one look at the police case as it stood and have Doyle released in no time, he took the unusual step of releasing Jimmy Doyle on police bail, with instructions to return to the police station in forty eight hours in company with his solicitor. He offered to contact the duty solicitor to represent Jimmy, but Doyle insisted he could find a solicitor himself.

Before Doyle could leave headquarters, however, as the paperwork for his release was being completed, D.C. Ferris came looking for Ross.

"Sir, I'm glad you've finished the interview. While you were in there with Doyle we received a phone call from Ronnie Doyle. It seems that, while the whole family was here just after Doyle was brought in for questioning, someone broke into Jimmy and Connie's house."

"Bloody hell, what's next in this twisted case of ours Ferris? Did Ronnie say what, if anything, had been stolen, presuming it was a case of theft?"

"Not exactly, sir. He said someone had broken the small window next to the back door and reached in to open it using the key that was left in the lock. I said we'd get someone round there as soon as possible, and asked him to get his mother to make a list of anything she thought had been taken. I thought that was the best thing to do, sir. I hope I did right?"

"Yes, of course you did, Ferris. Well, as we have to visit the Doyle's home again, we might as well give Jimmy a ride home. You can ride along with him in the back, and help Sergeant Drake and me at the house, presuming that both sons will still be there as well as Connie. The more of us to take statements, the better. You'd better go and inform Sergeant Drake and then go and find Jimmy, before they finish processing his bail release and make sure he waits for us. I don't want him going home on his own."

Twenty minutes later, Ross, Drake and Ferris, accompanied by a surly and silent James Doyle were in a police car, heading once again to the Doyle's house. Ross may not have realized it at the time, but this strange case, and the mysterious and baffling disappearance of Marie Doyle, was about to take another and on this occasion, final twist.

Chapter 33

ANGEL!

"Looks like someone waited for you to leave and then took advantage of the situation to effect a quick break-in," said Izzie Drake as she surveyed the broken pane of glass beside the front door. She'd checked for blood, in case the thief had cut themselves on the broken glass, perhaps conveniently leaving them a potential DNA sample, but nothing was evident around or beneath the shards of glass that littered the kitchen floor.

Ross and Ferris had taken a quick look around the kitchen and the neat, tidy living room, and could see little evidence of anything looking out of place, never mind any visible signs of anything having been taken from the rooms.

The family members obviously hadn't expected Jimmy Doyle to be home so soon, and certainly not in the company of three police officers. Ross had explained to Ronnie the circumstances surrounding his father's release on bail, but Ronnie totally ignored the old man, who, seeming to be in a trance and without attempting to help with the inquiry into the break in, took himself out to the garden, where he began his usual pottering about among his small assortment of flowers.

Ronnie explained that Mickey had taken his mother upstairs to lie down. The poor woman had suffered enough shocks and upheaval for one day, Ross thought to himself as he mounted the narrow staircase, knowing he had to speak to Connie. She would be the one to tell him what, if anything, had gone from her home.

Knocking on the door to what he guessed was the master bedroom of the immaculately clean terraced home, Ross gently pushed the door inwards to reveal Mickey sitting on the side of his parents' bed, his mother lying flat on her back, covered by a blanket that Mickey had probably taken from the floral patterned ottoman that stood at the bottom of the bed.

"I'm sorry to disturb you, Mrs. Doyle," Ross said quietly, stepping tentatively into the bedroom.

"It's alright, Mickey," said Connie, placing a hand on his arm as she sensed her son was about to protest at Ross's intrusion. "The inspector has to ask his questions, or he'll not know who's done this to us. Please, come in, Inspector. I'm okay, really, just a little tired, that's all. Things have been rather hectic today, as you know, and I'm afraid I'm not getting any younger, you know."

The smile that Connie directed at Andy Ross could have melted any man's heart, and in that short second or two before it faded, he could see the once beautiful woman she must have been in her younger days, much as her daughter Marie must have been when she disappeared thirty three years ago. Smiling back at her, Ross also saw for the first time since he'd met him, just how kind and gentle Mickey Doyle could be. Any pretence at being a big, tough guy simply faded away as he sat at his mother's side, care and concern the two emotions prevalent on his face. If only his father had been blessed with such a personality, Ross thought to himself, instead of his mean and bigoted, cruel way of living. Shaking himself from such thoughts, Ross replied to Connie in a soft and kindly voice, knowing the poor woman had suffered enough in her life, and not wanting to add to her troubles.

"Mrs. Doyle, Connie, I'm sorry, I know it's an awful time, but none of us expected this. It may have something to do with Jimmy's arrest, or it may have just been kids, or an opportunist burglar who did this. That's why we need to know what was taken. Have you had an opportunity to look around and perhaps make us a list of missing items?"

"I'm sorry, Inspector. I was about to look around and see if anything was missing, when I came over all 'funny' and dizzy, like, and Mickey insisted I come up here for a lie down."

"That's alright, Connie, and I'm sure Mickey was justly concerned for you and did the right thing in making you come up here for a lie down and a rest. Mickey, would you know what was missing if you came and took a look round with Ronnie?"

"What about him, the old man?" Mickey asked. "I saw you pull up in the car with him. It's his house, Inspector, not mine. I wouldn't really know if anything important was gone, but I can say that nothing obvious was missing when we walked in, you know, the telly, video player, stereo system are all still here. They're the usual things thieves go for, aren't they?"

"Yes, they are," Ross agreed. "If you don't mind, if you feel well enough, Connie, I really would appreciate it if you'd come down and have a look around for me."

Connie Doyle pushed herself up into a sitting position.

"Mickey, help me up, will you? There's a good boy. I'll come and have a look Inspector, if you think it'll help."

"I'm sure it will, Connie, and thank you."

Ross led the way down the narrow staircase, Mickey supporting his mother at the rear. Halfway down, the sound of a small explosion reverberated in the narrow passage that formed the stairway. Mickey thought the sound was that of a firework being let off by neighbourhood kids. They seemed to let them off all year round nowadays, not just to celebrate Guy Fawkes night. Andy Ross, however, immediately recognized the sound of a gunshot, fired from a small calibre weapon.

"What the hell...?" Ross exclaimed and took the last few stairs in two leaps, running through to the kitchen, the sound having come from the rear of the property.

The kitchen stood deserted, the back door hanging open, and as he carefully walked towards the door, Ross realised that Mickey and his mother had entered the kitchen and were attempting to follow him. He quickly held up two hands in a 'stop' gesture, and said to the pair,

"Please, stay here, until I'm sure it's safe out there. Look after your mother Mickey. I won't be long."

Ross stepped to the back door, and before stepping outside, called to his sergeant.

"Sergeant Drake, D.C. Ferris, are you both okay?"

"Sir, we're okay, but you need to come out here, now," came the reply from Izzie Drake.

Ross stepped out into the garden, where he quickly took in the scene that awaited him. Drake and Ferris were standing over the body of Jimmy Doyle, who lay across one of his prized flower beds, blood seeping through his shirt from a gunshot wound to the chest. His youngest son, Ronnie knelt beside his father, cradling his head in his hands.

"What the hell happened here?" Ross shouted at his detectives, just as Connie and Mickey Doyle appeared in the doorway and saw the scene being played out in the garden. Connie gasped audibly and as Ross turned at the sound, the old lady's legs gave way as she fainted, thankfully being caught and supported by Mickey.

"Mickey, take your mother indoors and stay with her," Ross ordered and Mickey, stunned, meekly obeyed, lifting his mother tenderly in his arms and carrying her into the house, as Ross moved closer to the scene of the shooting.

"Now, will someone tell me what happened?" he asked again.

Izzie Drake provided him with the answer.

"You were upstairs with Connie and Mickey, sir, and Ronnie was checking around in the kitchen with me and Ferris, to see if he could identify anything that might be missing, and Doyle was out here, tending his flowers. We heard a noise, obviously the gunshot, and by the time we got out here, Doyle was on his knees, almost as though he was praying, and as we got to him, he keeled over, and Ronnie's been with him until now."

"Is he dead?" Ross asked.

"No, sir, at least, not yet. I radioed in for back up and an ambulance just before you came through the back door."

Ross moved to where Ronnie knelt beside his father, and placed a hand on his shoulder.

"Ronnie, has your father said anything at all about what happened?"

Ronnie looked up at Ross. Despite his loathing for what his father had possibly done in the past, he was, after all, still his Dad, and he couldn't help being upset and confused by the events of the last couple of minutes.

"He...he...tried to say...something," Ronnie almost choked on his words. "It, well, it sounded like, "An angel, an angel came for me." It doesn't make sense. Why would he think an angel had come for him when whoever it was bloody shot him? Dad, hang on, you hear me? The ambulance will be here in a minute."

Bending down, D.C. Ferris placed two fingers to Doyle's neck, then looked up and shook his head.

Izzie touched Ronnie gently on his right arm, and said, sadly, "I'm sorry, Ronnie. He's gone."

"Ronnie, please, you should go inside and be with your Mum and Mickey," Ross said, and he gently but firmly helped Ronnie to his feet, and motioned to Ferris, who slowly walked Ronnie towards the house, leaving Ross and Drake together with the body.

Ross turned to his sergeant.

"And nobody saw or heard anything, right?"

"Not a thing, sir. One minute all was peaceful, then we heard the shot, we came out, I ran to the back gate and looked both ways along the back alley, but saw nobody."

"So whoever shot Jimmy Doyle, came and went quietly, and moved pretty fast too. Pity we never had someone out front at the time, in case the killer had a car waiting on the street."

"We never expected someone would take a pop at him in his own back yard though, did we, sir?"

"No, Izzie, we didn't, but maybe we should have, after what happened to Patrick Bryce."

"But that was in Northern Ireland, sir."

"Which is only a ferry ride across the Irish Sea away, and so easy for a killer bent on revenge to slip over here to finish what they started with Bryce."

The sound of sirens interrupted their conversation, and seconds later, Paul Ferris was escorting a pair of paramedics, their skills now redundant to the situation, through the back door, where they quickly confirmed the fact that Jimmy Doyle had indeed gone to meet his maker. They were closely followed by Detective Constables Dodds, Gable and McLennan, who gazed almost unbelievingly at the death scene in the otherwise peaceful street. Jimmy Doyle's body was quickly and professionally removed from the flower bed, the blooms around him crushed and broken from his fall, and placed on a wheeled stretcher, and, to save the family unnecessary grief, taken through the back gate, and along the rear alley and round to the waiting ambulance on the street. As the ambulance pulled away, en route for the hospital mortuary, Ross gathered his team around him.

"Right, we have to move fast. As I was just saying to Sergeant Drake, this is all about revenge. Someone, and I believe it to be the mysterious 'Miss Jones', has carried out the murders of Patrick Bryce and Jimmy Doyle in revenge for the killing of Brendan Kane. We need to find her quickly, before she disappears back into the obscurity she's been hiding in for a long time."

"But, why revenge now, sir?" asked Derek McLennan. "It's over thirty years since Kane was killed. Why didn't she, if it is this Jones woman, take action against Bryce and Doyle years ago? Why wait until now?"

"I don't know, Constable. We can ask her that if and when we catch her," Ross replied.

"Sir?" said Drake. "What about what Doyle tried to say to Ronnie as he lay dying? What did he mean by 'an angel' coming to him? Was he just delirious or was he trying to tell Ronnie something about the killer?"

"I really don't know the answer to that one, either Izzie, not yet. Listen, we still haven't determined if anything was taken during the earlier break-in. We need to know whether that was the work of our killer, or a separate, unrelated crime of opportunity by someone taking advantage of the Doyle's absence."

A thought struck Ross, and he said to his sergeant, "You spent quite a while here a few days ago, Izzie. Please, it's a long shot, I know, but go inside, take a look around the downstairs rooms and see if anything looks different or out of place compared with your last visit. Ferris, go and talk to the family. They've had a few minutes grace to pull themselves together. I know it's a bad time for them, but we need to know if Connie, especially, has seen or heard anything lately that she might have viewed as suspicious. Be gentle with them, they've had a shock, but we need a statement from Ronnie too, he was one of the first on the scene. Find out if his father said anything else as he lay there. The family may not have liked Jimmy Doyle much at the end, but I doubt they would want his killer to escape justice."

Drake and Ferris were soon indoors carrying out Ross's instructions. Now, he directed Dodds and Gable to begin house to house inquiries in the street, in case any of the Doyle's neighbours saw or heard the killer, either before or after the shooting. Unfortunately, being the middle of the day, most of the residents would probably be out at work, and the chances of finding any useful witnesses were slim. Even the sound of the gunshot would probably have been mistaken for the sound of a firework being let off. The youth of today seemed able to obtain them all year round and Bonfire Night, the 5th November held little exclusivity any more when it came to the firework trade. He ordered Derek McLennan to assist him in examining the garden and the rear alley, for any signs the killer may have left behind, and was about to begin his search when, first of all the Scenes of Crime people arrived to carry out their own investigation of the crime scene, and they were closely followed by a slightly breathless Izzie Drake.

"Sir, I may have something significant to report," she said.

"Go ahead, Sergeant," Ross urged, "I could do with some good news amidst this god-awful mess."

Drake took a deep breath and said, "Well, sir, I just ran up and down stairs to check something with Connie, hence my breathless state, because when we were here the other day, she showed me a couple of things she keeps as reminders of Marie. One of them was Marie's little yellow transistor radio. She keeps it behind a photograph of Marie on the sideboard in the kitchen. When I looked around as you asked me to a few minutes ago, I looked at the photo and was about to move on when something made me look behind it. The radio's gone, sir, missing. I ran upstairs to where Mickey had made his Mother go and lie down. She was still in shock but I just had to know if she'd moved the radio, maybe while cleaning, or to put batteries in it, as she'd told me she still kept fresh batteries in it at all times. Anyway, she said she hadn't touched the radio since I was here the other day, sir. What kind of thief breaks in to a home with modern appliances in all the rooms, but only takes a thirty something year old transistor radio?"

Ross thought about it for a moment, before replying.

"The kind of thief who was here for one thing and one thing alone, Izzie. Listen, when Doyle was gasping out his final breaths, did you hear his exact words to Ronnie?"

"Well mostly, sir, yes, but he wasn't speaking clearly, coughing up blood and everything."

"Right, so, when he spoke about the 'angel', did he actually say, 'an angel, or could it have been, 'my angel'?"

"I'm not entirely sure, sir. I heard angel quite clearly but the rest was pretty garbled."

Overhearing their conversation, Derek McLennan made a comment that suddenly made Ross's hackles rise.

"Doyle talked about an angel at the end did he? Maybe he was visited by that nun me and Nick saw hanging around the other day."

"Nun? Did you say you saw a nun, McLennan?"

"Yes, sir. When we were watching Doyle the other day, and when him and Mrs. Doyle set off in the car to go shopping, as we followed them and turned at the end of the street we saw a nun standing outside the betting shop on the corner. She looked as if she was standing there, waiting for someone. We joked about it not being good for the bookie's business, having a nun loitering about outside their front door."

"That's it, Izzie," Ross shouted excitedly. "Remember, we, or rather you saw a nun hanging around on the street when we first came round to interview James Doyle?"

"Yes, sir, I remember," Drake replied. "What exactly are you thinking about her?"

"Don't you get it, Izzie? The nun, for God's sake. The nun, Miss bloody Jones, they're one and the same person, and under that habit, if I'm not mistaken is the answer to the other half of our mystery. Marie Doyle isn't dead, and for reasons known only to herself, she's resurfaced after all this time, to exact revenge for her dead boyfriend. It all makes sense now, apart from the question of where she's been for thirty three bloody years."

"My god, sir. Marie Doyle!"

"Yes, Sergeant, Marie Doyle. You, young Derek, are a bloody genius, well done lad."

D.C. Derek McLennan beamed with pride as Ross clapped him on the shoulder.

"I am, sir? Thank you, sir."

"Yes, Derek, you are. If you hadn't mentioned the nun just now, I'd not have worked it out as quickly. That's what Jimmy Doyle was trying to tell Ronnie at the end. He'd been visited by *his* angel, his missing daughter, back after all those years, except she wasn't his loving little girl, his angel any more, was she? Marie Doyle has become an avenging angel and we have to find her and end this now. The question is, where would she go? Did she have a special place locally, maybe somewhere she and Brendan treated as their own secret meeting place or something? Izzie, go and ask Connie, quickly, but for God's sake, don't tell her we think Marie's alive and is the killer of two people."

Izzie quickly disappeared back into the house, returning a few minutes later.

"Sir, Connie just remembered that something else went missing a few days ago. It may be significant. Marie keep a five-year diary, you know, one of those thick ones with a lock and key that people used to keep years ago. It was kept in a drawer in the sideboard, and the day we first called, Connie found it missing in the afternoon. If that nun was Marie, she might have slipped in to the house through the back door, which the Doyle's always left open by habit when someone was at home, though they'd locked it today when they all set off for police headquarters, and rifled through the sideboard, found it and taken it. She wouldn't have known her mother took it out regularly, just to hold it, feel it and feel a closeness with her missing daughter. But the thing is, she must have taken a hell of a risk, walking in like that, if the couple were at home at the time."

"Unless she knew they were both out, like the day they went shopping. There must have been other opportunities for her to sneak in and have a good look around," said Ross. "What about a special place?"

"Connie couldn't help us with that sir. She said, if anyone would know any of Marie and Brendan's special or secret meeting places it would be Clemmy De Souza, Clemmy Oxley as we now know her, of course."

"Right, Izzie, get on the phone right now. Try the Oxley's home number. If she's not there, but Phillip is, get her work number. Tell him it's important, but don't mention the murder, okay?"

"Right, sir, but just why the urgency? What do you see happening here?" Izzie asked her boss, who seemed galvanized by the need to move with all speed.

"Okay, Izzie, hear me out for a minute, okay? For the sake of argument, and based on the bits of information we've picked up from her friends and family, let's say that Marie left home one evening to meet up with her boyfriend. She didn't take her beloved transistor radio, which we're led to believe went everywhere with her, either because she forgot it, or, I suspect, she didn't expect to be out very long, or maybe the batteries were dead. Anyway, off she goes, but before she can meet up with her boyfriend, he's intercepted by her father and Patrick Bryce. Somehow, she sees them together, and follows them, unsure what's going on. When she sees Bryce and her father murder

Brendan, well, here my theory is admittedly a little fuzzy, but maybe her brain switches off, or she is just too terrified to say or do anything, so she runs. God knows where or with whom she ended up, but somehow she managed to stay out of sight for over thirty years, until word surfaced in the newspapers about the discovery of Kane's remains. Maybe that acted as a trigger and set her on this course of revenge for what took place thirty three years ago. If we catch her, we can ask her."

"Sir, it's a good theory, but when you say if...?"

"Look, Izzie, she's obviously unstable in some way, and she's accomplished what she set out to do, and she still has a gun. Do I have to spell it out for you?"

Instant enlightenment flashed across Drake's face. She knew what Ross was intimating, and could understand his reasoning. "I'll make that phone call right away, sir."

Ross could only stand and wait for what seemed an interminable few minutes as Drake made her call from inside the Doyle's home. Meanwhile he tried to take an interest in watching the crime scene technicians at work, but without much success. It wasn't as if they would find much that would add to his case, after all.

Eventually, Drake returned, and free from the burden of waiting, Ross's nerves relaxed a little as he listened to what she'd learned.

"Thankfully, Clemmy was at home, sir. She was obviously very curious about the urgency of my request, but I told her we'd fill her in later. She thought about the question for a minute and then remembered that Marie and Brendan loved to visit New Brighton. Brendan sneaked her over there for a long weekend on a couple of occasions. She'd lied to her parents and told them she was going to stay with friends. They had of course, no reason to suspect her of lying at that time, so, off they went. Marie told Clemmy she actually lost her virginity to Brendan one afternoon in a caravan he'd rented for the weekend."

She handed a piece of paper to McLennan. "Contact headquarters, Derek. See if this place still exists."

McLennan nodded and moved closer to the back gate to check the address via headquarters, as Drake continued speaking to Ross.

"I also took the liberty of asking if the name, 'Miss Jones' meant anything to her, just in case there is a second woman out there, maybe working with Marie. She laughed and told me that 'Miss Jones' was her own mother, sir. Apparently, when her father, the Portuguese sailor met her mother, her maiden name was Victoria Jones. Her father, Luis, was a big fan of Ava Gardner in those days, and took Clemmy's Mum, who he always said resembled Gardner, to the cinema to see the film, *Bhowani Junction*, which featured Ava Gardner and Stewart Granger. Luis was tickled pink that Ava Gardner's character was called Victoria Jones and would often refer to his wife as 'Miss Jones' as a term of endearment. Marie knew all about it, sir, it was just the kind of romantic story best friends would share, so I think you're right on all counts."

"That was good thinking, Izzie, well done. Any word, Derek?" he called to McLennan, who quickly finished speaking into his police radio and ran across the garden to where Ross and Drake stood.

"It's still there, sir, the holiday park. Modernised and upgraded, with chalets and things for those with a richer pocket, and it still has the same beach front and the wooded area for walks and so on, apparently. One of the guys at headquarters overheard me talking to Mackie on the phone and came across to give me that extra info. Told me he often spends weekends in a chalet with his wife and kids there, in the school holidays."

"Great work, Derek. Okay, here's the plan. We'll leave D.C. Gable here, and let Dodds carry on with the house to house. Derek, I want you and D.C. Ferris in a separate car. You can follow me and Sergeant Drake. Come on, let's hurry it up. We're going to the seaside!"

* * *

The road to New Brighton was relatively clear. Using the modern Kingsway Tunnel a mere one a half mile trip under the River Mersey made the trip easier and faster than having to catch a ferry in the 'good old days', and the two police vehicles made good time to the town of

Wallasey, and thence to its seaside partner, the once grand, but now slightly faded, New Brighton.

Following directions provided by D.C. Mackie at headquarters, they arrived at the aptly named Seaview Holiday Park a mere five minutes after arriving on the south side of the river. Pulling up at a gated entrance, Ross jumped from the car, allowing Drake to ease the car through, followed by Ferris and McLennan in the second car. Ross followed the polite instruction to drivers to 'Please close the gate, help keep our children safe' and ran across to the reception building ten yards from the gate, also adorned with a message, 'All visitors please report to reception'.

Ross virtually burst through the door to the reception office, built to resemble a log cabin such as might be found in the wilderness parks of Canada or the USA, taking the young woman behind the reception counter by total surprise, closely followed by Drake who had pulled up outside the door, leaving the police car's engine running.

Acting quickly to allay her fears, Ross shouted one word, "Police" to her, producing his warrant card in an instant as though by sleight of hand.

"H…How can I help you?" the trembling young woman, who looked no more than eighteen or nineteen asked, still unsure what was happening. Ross read the name badge pinned above her left breast.

"Kylie," he said, "I can't take time to explain right now, but we need directions to your woodland walk and the beach area, and we don't have time to waste."

Quickly attempting to pull herself together after the initial shock of Ross's unorthodox entry, Kylie picked up a copy of one of the holiday park's glossy introductory leaflets for those holidaying at the park. Opening it out fully on the counter she pointed to a map of the park, conveniently spread across the two centre pages of the leaflet.

"Just follow the main road through the park," she said, "then follow the green signs for the woodland walk and beach where the road forks off to the various chalets and static caravans. It's a much narrower road, more a wide path really, and it comes to a dead end about half a mile from the actual beach, and I'm afraid you have to walk from there. Cars aren't allowed. Please, can't you tell me what's going on? My manager will want to know."

"We don't have time to explain, Kylie. We'll tell your manager all about it later. Thanks for your help"

With that he made for the door, Izzie Drake in his wake. It took no more than a minute for the two police cars, easily exceeding the park's five m.p.h speed limit, to arrive at the blocked-off entrance to the path that would lead them through the small wooded area to the beach.

The four officers gathered together and Ross quickly issued his instructions.

"Listen carefully," he began. "I want you all to stay close to me until we come out of the woodland walk, which, according to the map opens out about a hundred yards from the beach. These fuzzy little tufts on the park's map seem to indicate an area of long grass between the trees and the beach, so we'll stop there and assess the situation before deciding how to carry out the search for the woman."

"Are you certain she'll be here, sir?" Ferris asked.

"No, Paul, I'm not a hundred percent sure, but all my instincts tell me this is where she'd want to be after completing what she sees as her work. When we do split up to search, I want absolute silence maintained. I don't want anyone doing anything to spook her into doing something stupid. Got that?"

Receiving nods of acknowledgement from his three officers, Ross took a deep breath, said "Let's go," and slowly led his small team through the narrow entrance to the woodland walk path.

* * *

Standing in the long, waving strands of sea grass that formed a natural border between the woodland and the beach, Sister Mary Dominique looked out at the gently undulating waves as they seemed to lazily approach the shore, small white caps forming as they broke upon the beach. She smiled as her mind began to drift, and in seconds, she'd ceased to be Sister Mary Dominique, the nun, dressed in her drab grey and white habit. Now, she saw herself as she'd once been, a young woman, just twenty years old again, and as she looked down, she admired the pretty yellow sundress with its gaily decorated floral print pattern. She giggled as the sand tickled her bare feet, and she peered out across the beach, watching the tide roll in. In her mind, she reached in to her long-handled beach bag; in reality, she was reaching into the large pouch-like pocket in the front of her habit, from which she extricated her treasured transistor radio and her diary. She looked across the beach, out to sea, as though expecting to see someone. Somehow, she knew he wouldn't be coming. Marie Doyle turned on the little radio, turning the tuning dial until she found a station playing the latest chart sounds. Listening hard to the music that seemed to have to fight its way past the tiny and well-worn speaker in her radio, she realised that this music was all wrong. This wasn't the sound that she and Brendan had grown up with, and she sighed as she turned the dial again, finally finding a station that played a constant stream of 'golden oldies,' the sounds of the sixties, hers and Brendan's sounds. She began to tap her bare foot and smiled as the sound of The Searchers' *When You Walk in the Room* played through the tiny speaker, just as it had done so many times, so many years earlier.

The sound of The Searchers was just fading out as Ross and his small team of detectives emerged from the tree line and stepped on to the path leading to the beach. The radio began to produce another golden oldie, The Cascades singing, *Rhythm of the Rain*, and as the sound drifted across the open space between the police officers and Marie, she turned to look at them as if she'd sensed their presence from the second they'd appeared on the path.

Marie smiled in Ross's direction, and then turned once more, staring out towards the incoming tide, her face a mask of concentration. She tensed for a second, and a slight breeze blew up, carrying the sound of the music from her radio clearly towards Ross and his officers. Ross stared at the woman, the nun, standing mere yards away from him, though he felt somehow as if he was watching a surreal tableau, something real and yet not real, as Marie reached a hand into the pocket in the front of her dress/habit and slowly pulled what could only be her old five year diary from within. She turned towards Ross once more, holding the diary out towards him as if in invitation, and then she slowly and deliberately placed the diary on the ground, beside her treasured transistor radio.

She turned around once more, facing the incoming tide, and reached once more into the pocket of her dress. Ross suddenly went cold, knowing exactly what she was about to remove from the voluminous folds of her habit. Time appeared to stand still, the whole surreal tableau playing out before the detectives in slow motion as Marie slowly retrieved from her pocket the menacing shape of a small handgun. Knowing it was the weapon used to kill both Patrick Bryce and Marie's father, Ross now had no doubts as to what Marie intended to do next, yet he inexplicably felt rooted to the spot, frozen in that moment in time as Marie half-turned towards him one last time.

She smiled once more and looked out across the waves again, before turning to face Ross and saying, quite clearly, her voice carried by the breeze, "He's waiting for me."

In the next few, confused and terrifying seconds, as the detectives appeared to regain control of their faculties, Marie raised the weapon, placing it against her right temple as Ross shouted "Marie, no, don't do it," and the sound of the gunshot resonated across the sands, Marie falling to her left as the gun fell from her lifeless fingers to fall with a soft thud on the sands of New Brighton.

Beside the now lifeless body of Marie Doyle, no longer a missing person, her small, insignificant yellow transistor radio played Herman's Hermits' *No Milk Today.*

Ross bent down, picked up the radio, turned it off and placed it in his pocket.

Epilogue

In the days following the death of Marie Doyle, Ross and Drake were able to piece together much of the mystery surrounding her disappearance and subsequent years in obscurity.

Before ending her life on the beach at New Brighton, Marie had, as Ross suspected, left a few detailed notes in the back of her old five year diary that contributed greatly towards filling in the blanks.

It transpired that Marie Doyle was a genuine nun. Sister Mary Dominique had come into being soon after the death of Brendan Kane. On her way to meet him on that fateful night thirty three years previously, Marie had missed her bus and was subsequently delayed. When she finally arrived in town, she hurried to meet Brendan near the docks, where they usually called in to a small cafe there, that provided privacy and ice cold Coca Cola. As she was about to turn into the street where the café stood, she heard raised voices, immediately recognizing those of Brendan, and to her surprise, her father, Jimmy Doyle. Marie had sensed something was not right and she pulled back into a shop doorway where she heard her father telling Brendan he'd been seen, by a friend of Doyle's, with her, coming out of the caravan park in New Brighton on their last visit there. Doyle had quickly put two and two together and rightly surmised the reason for the couple hiring a caravan in the holiday park. She saw Patrick Bryce, her so-called Uncle Patrick step from the shadows and push Brendan in the back.

Her diary went on to describe the events on the wharf, exonerating her father from directly committing violence against Brendan, but not from instigating what happened next. It was all there in those last, sad pages, the beating, the kneecapping, her father's protestations and Brendan being hit with the hammer and tossed unceremoniously into the Mersey at Cole & Sons wharf.

Horrified by what she'd seen, frozen by fear, Marie heard Bryce telling her father to go and get rid of Brendan's car, and her father had rushed off to where Brendan had parked his car, and she never knew what he did with the car, though she wrote that she suspected her father had hidden it for a day or two and then sold it for scrap to one of the city's many shady scrap metal dealers who would ask no questions and pay a decent price.

She couldn't go home, not after what she'd witnessed, and she'd walked for miles until she'd arrived at the gates of a convent where she'd been taken in unquestioningly by the sisters who dwelt within its safe and solid walls.

Ross had visited the convent, where the Mother Superior, Sister Mary Angela, had filled in more of the blanks for him. They'd never known Marie's real name. She'd simply called herself Clemency when she arrived, borrowing the name of her best friend, Clemmy De Souza. The previous Mother Superior who'd been in charge at the time of Marie's arrival, respected her need for privacy, realizing that the girl had been the subject of some terrible tragedy, and Marie was never asked about what had brought her to the doors of the convent, and Marie certainly never volunteered any information about whatever had befallen her, and eventually she had taken holy orders and become a valued member of their convent, though shunning the many opportunities she was given to become involved in work in local schools and on various projects in the community, preferring instead to stay within the sanctuary of the convent, tending the gardens where the nuns grew vegetables and also some very impressive flower beds. Ross thought her father might have been proud of his daughter for that.

The years that followed had proved uneventful, though Mary Dominique, as Marie became known after her ordination, always seemed to be weighed down with some great sadness, and her eyes would sometimes betray a hint of fear, as though, even in the safe haven provided by the convent, she felt threatened or unsure of herself. She'd possessed a beautiful voice and had been a valued member of the convent's choir.

Things had taken a turn for the worst around six months before the murder of Patrick Bryce, when, after a short illness, Sister Mary Dominique had been diagnosed as suffering from an inoperable brain tumour. Her personality changed, and she suddenly decided to become involved with an outreach project that helped former convicts in their rehabilitation into the community. Ross guessed she obtained the gun, which had proved impossible to identify, from one of her new-found friends in the criminal fraternity. She certainly wouldn't have known how to file off the serial number of the weapon, or where to obtain the correct ammunition for it. Most recently, she'd taken a short holiday from the convent, which Ross presumed would coincide with her visit to Northern Ireland where she'd meted out her own version of poetic justice to Patrick Doyle.

As her condition deteriorated, she'd spent more and more time away from the convent, and most of her fellow nuns merely thought she was perhaps visiting places and people she'd once known before the tumour led to the inevitable conclusion. Little did they suspect what was really happening to her mind, as her illness finally led her to seek a terrible revenge for the wrongs done to her and Brendan so many years earlier.

There wasn't much more to tell, and the police were satisfied no-one else had been involved in Marie's plot to kill Bryce and her father. Someone, probably a friend of James Doyle who worked at BICC had probably typed the fake letter for him to send to Brendan's landlord, but nothing would be gained by pursuing a new inquiry into that one detail of the case. Ross had stamped 'Case Closed' across the file he'd opened on Brendan Kane and latterly, the long-time missing Marie Doyle.

* * *

Dr. William, (Fat Willy), Nugent had carried out the obligatory post mortem examination of Marie Doyle's body, confirming the presence of the brain tumour that he estimated would have killed her in less than three months. Apart from arthritis, present in her hands and feet, nothing else of significance showed up in his examination.

A hastily convened coroner's inquest recorded Marie's cause of death as 'suicide while the balance of her mind was disturbed' and the body was released for burial.

A leading psychiatrist had confirmed to Ross that the human mind, complex and at times unfathomable, had the capacity to 'switch-off' when faced with events or sights that were simply too terrible to bear, and this was in all probability what had happened in Marie's case. Unable to cope with what she'd seen that night when Brendan had been murdered, she'd blocked it out, withdrawing into herself, and remaining in a new, safe world of her own until the news of the recovery of Brendan's remains had reached her and set in motion the tragic recall of those events that had led to such a tragic conclusion.

With the cooperation of the police and the coroner's office, the Doyle family decided to hold a joint funeral for Marie and Brendan Kane, whose mortal remains would be finally laid to rest alongside those of the woman he'd loved, his beautiful Marie.

By contrast with the previously held funeral of Jimmy Doyle, attended only by Connie and his sons, and even then only because they felt an obligation to be present, the funeral of Marie and Brendan became something of a media circus. Despite the fact that Marie had murdered Patrick Bryce and Jimmy Doyle, her story, and that of her doomed love affair with Brendan Kane and the part played in the young man's murder by Bryce and her father had become national news, and with a little help from the media, Marie had become something of a celebrity in death.

All of a sudden, Brendan Kane and the Planets achieved a level of fame they had perhaps only dreamed of back in the early nineteen sixties, when, as young men, they'd tried and failed to make it in the ruthless world of the pop music industry. A record company even went to the trouble of contacting Mickey, Ronnie and Phil Oxley in an attempt to persuade them to accept a recording contract to produce an album based on some of the songs penned by Brendan Kane back in their early days. To a man, all three declined the offer. They'd grown up, life was different now, and they would never have withstood the glare of the modern media, even if the songs had been successful in the current charts, something they all privately doubted would happen.

The joint funeral was massively well attended, with even a few of today's crop of chart toppers present to pay their own tributes to one of the forerunners of the modern pop industry, a description that Brendan Kane would have loved. Connie Doyle and her sons paid glowing tributes to the beautiful but ultimately damaged daughter and sister, who time and circumstances had taken from them, not as a result of her recent death, but due to the evil that lurked in the hearts of men who should have known better over thirty years previously. They each paid additional tributes to Brendan, to the love he shared with Marie, and to the fact that what they were robbed of in life, they would now share forever in death.

Ross and his team were there, only Paul Ferris being absent, as he and his wife attended the Children's Hospital with their young son Aaron after being notified that a kidney had been become available following the death of an eight year old boy in a road traffic accident.

Dr. William Nugent and Hannah Lewin, who had worked so hard to identify Brendan's remains, attended to pay their respects, as did Ethan Tiffen, who'd made the journey from London, having been touched by the story of the two lovers whose impossible dream had been to live and work in his country,

Phil Oxley was there of course and he spoke succinctly of his old friend Brendan, and of Marie, always happy, always smiling, and always accompanied by the music from her radio. Perhaps the final word went to Marie's former best friend, Clemmy, now Mrs. Phil Oxley, who wept as she recalled their days together, as they grew up in what she called, "A different world, a cleaner, happier world, and one those of us who grew up in will never forget. Wherever you are now, girl," she said, "One thing's for sure. You'll make sure the music never dies."

As Marie's coffin slowly disappeared into the ground, the sound of Neil Diamond's 'America' played from a nearby sound system, installed specially for the day. It was, Connie Doyle said, after asking that Marie's transistor radio be buried with her, suitably fitting for the occasion.

Connie, of course made sure the little yellow radio was fitted with new batteries before it joined Marie in her final resting place.

About the Author

Brian L Porter is an award-winning author, whose books have also regularly topped the Amazon Best Selling charts. Writing as Brian, he has won a Best Author Award, and his thrillers have picked up Best Thriller and Best Mystery Awards.

His true-life dog rescue book, Sasha, a biography of his epileptic Staffordshire Bull Terrier, has become an International best seller and award winning nonfiction book, winning the Preditors & Editors Best Nonfiction Book Award for 2016 as well as being voted into 7th place in the Best Indie Books, 2016, awards. Sasha was followed by UK bestseller, Sheba: From Hell to Happiness, about another of his remarkable rescuedogs.

Writing as Harry Porter his children's books have achieved three bestselling rankings on Amazon in the USA and UK.

In addition, his third incarnation as romantic poet Juan Pablo Jalisco has brought international recognition with his collected works, *Of Aztecs and Conquistadors* topping the bestselling charts in the USA, UK and Canada.

Brian lives with his wife, children and a wonderful pack of ten rescued dogs.

He is also the in-house screenwriter for ThunderBall Films, (L.A.), for whom he is also a co-producer on a number of their current movie projects.

A Mersey Killing has already been optioned for movie adaptation, in addition to his other novels, all of which have been signed by ThunderBall Films in a movie franchise deal.

45434317R00156

Made in the USA
Middletown, DE
16 May 2019